# TWISTED THREADS

## A Cape Trouble Novel

### By Janice Kay Johnson

ISBN-10: 0-9890418-9-1
ISBN-13: 978-0-9890418-9-8

This book is a work of fiction.  All names, characters, locations and incidents are products of the author's imagination, or have been used fictitiously.  Any resemblance to actual persons living or dead, locales, or events is entirely coincidental.

# CHAPTER ONE

Shit like this made Detective Sean Holbeck wonder why anyone ever risked having kids. From that first unfocused, vulnerable look after birth, they were heartbreak waiting to happen.

The powerful beam of his flashlight illuminated a slice of the dense, wet woods ahead. He swept it methodically from side to side, aware of other searchers in a line stretching to his right and left doing the same. One of them regularly shouted some variation of "Arianna! Please come out. Your parents are scared."

Yep, forget having kids.

A thick clump of sword ferns demanded a closer look. In lieu of a walking stick or staff, he carried a golf club given to him by one of the search and rescue volunteers. It had a whole new life as a walking stick and tool for probing. He waded into the ferns and tapped with the butt end of the club until he was confident no body lay hidden beneath the dripping wet fronds.

Fifteen year old Arianna Keezer had apparently been threatening suicide for days. Not one of her empty-headed friends had thought to confide in a parent, teacher, counselor. The grocery store clerk, the librarian. Any adult.

When she'd been discovered missing from her bed this morning – something like sixteen hours ago – the friends were shocked. Maybe she'd just run away, they said hopefully. Until someone thought to check her Facebook page, which had what was, in essence, a suicide note. If she'd posted it in hopes of grabbing attention, she'd succeeded beyond her wildest dreams.

He took a swipe with his forearm to clear his face and only made it wetter. Damn, if only this miserable drizzle would let up. Too bad that was unlikely, given how usual this weather was for western Oregon in early March.

Cursing the darkness, he started forward again and swept the beam of the flashlight from side to side. He watched for obstacles, hiding places, a color or texture that didn't belong. He diverted to check the backside of a rotting log. Nada. Two steps later, he set his foot down only to find no ground beneath it. Next thing he knew, he'd crashed to the forest floor.

He lay with his cheek on sodden earth slick with rotting leaves. Never having a kid. No way, no how.

"You okay, Sean?" the volunteer to his right called.

"Yeah. Stepped in a hole." He rose to his knees, pulling his foot from the deep depression, and got up. Despite a rain slicker, he was soaked to the skin. He'd be cold, too, if he stopped moving for long enough.

His whole day had been spent trying to figure out where Arianna might have gone. They'd scoured beaches, contacted everyone she'd ever known. Searched her bedroom for a clue. The parents sat side by side in the living room, clutching each other's hand, their faces tight with dread and, in the father's case, guilt, because he'd discovered a Colt Revolver he hadn't kept locked up was missing. That guilt would tear this man apart if his daughter was found dead. Sean understood guilt.

Not until nightfall neared had one of the girl's friends remembered this super romantic spot in the woods where Arianna and her boyfriend went to be together. "You know." She almost sounded shy. The shell-shocked father had only nodded.

This was the boyfriend who'd ditched her two weeks ago, precipitating the crisis. When asked for directions to "their" spot, he'd wrinkled his brow and mumbled, "Well, uh, we just hiked. I mean, we didn't go one place. You know."

Favorite words.

He had showed them where he usually parked, out of sight of any passing traffic on Highway 101 running up and down the Pacific Coast. By the time family members, neighbors, volunteers and cops had gathered, it was pitch dark and Arianna had been missing for a minimum of twelve hours, and likely a lot more depending on when she'd slipped out. Now, when Sean briefly illuminated his watch, he saw that it was almost 11:30.

He wiped water from his eyes just as his flashlight beam found the trunk of a huge fir or hemlock rising from a tangle of vegetation that might disguise the well sometimes found around the old trees.

More ferns, salal, whips of currant or huckleberries. The guy to his left and he converged on it.

Sean thumped the golf club, praying for all he was worth not to find the girl. Let somebody else get there first for a change. The dead rarely gave him pause anymore. Dead kids...they were different.

Because secretly, he did want to have kids of his own despite seeing his own parents' unending grief. Or, at least, he had once upon a time. Before he'd scraped too many off the pavement of major highways, cuffed abusive parents while the morgue techs carried out small, battered bodies, found lost children too late. A few months ago, he'd been part of a surf rescue. Eight year old boy. They never could get him breathing again.

*Tap, tap, tap.*

A shout came from his left. "Found her!" He sagged forward, his forehead resting on rough bark, before he resigned himself and pushed away.

By the time he reached the source of the shout, several dark shapes were already clustered around the girl and had her illuminated in the converging beams of their flashlights. Ill-dressed for a cold, rainy night, she huddled in a shivering ball, but she was alive, staring dazedly at her rescuers. One had already wrapped her in a space blanket.

Sean unzipped his slicker and lifted his shirt to pull out his Glock. He aimed it high and well-ahead, pulling the trigger twice in the pre-arranged signal.

Then, after holstering his own weapon, he stooped and picked up the Colt that lay on the ground beside the girl. Which, thank God, she hadn't used.

Sean raised a shout, "She's okay! Just wet and cold!"

Like an echo, it continued on in each direction, down the ragged line of search and rescue people. "Okay! Wet and cold."

As pissed as he was at Arianna Keezer for putting the people who loved her through this, Sean still felt knee-buckling relief.

Her father had another chance. He wouldn't have to spend a lifetime damning himself.

*****

Sean's body jolted hard enough to give him whiplash. What the hell—? That could not possibly be his phone.

It was. He'd had it on vibrate as well as ring, so it gave an emphatic little bounce on the bedside stand. He blinked a couple times to bring the lighted numbers on the clock into focus. 4:13. Unlucky?

He groped for the phone, stabbed it with his thumb, and cleared his throat. "Holbeck."

"Sorry, Detective, I know you were up late last night."

More like this night, he thought grumpily, recognizing the dispatcher's voice.

"Deputy Walker asked me to call. She has a body. She says the throat was cut. And, um, you're up next."

Wonderful. "Location?" Sean asked.

The address was in one of the many small ocean-front communities that contracted with the sheriff's department for law enforcement. This one, unfortunately, was as far away from Cape Trouble as it could get without being in the next county north.

"All right," he said, still groggy enough to sound drunk. "Tell Walker I'm on my way. It'll probably be half an hour."

Call over, he swung his feet to the floor, groaned and scraped a hand over his face. When he went out the door five minutes later, he was unshaven but dressed and carrying instant coffee in a travel mug. Unlike earlier, a crescent moon added some silver to the landscape before a scudding cloud covered it while he watched. He let the salty night air wake him up as he walked to his Subaru, parked in the driveway since he had yet to figure out what to do with all the crap piled in the garage.

He pushed the remote to unlock, but paused before opening the car door. Except for the constant, background murmur of the surf, the night was quiet enough for him to hear an intermittent, mechanical hum he knew came from his next-door neighbor's house. One window glowed softly, through and around drawn blinds. Did that damn woman never sleep?

She gave him something to ponder as he drove, wending his way through town to the highway. He liked mysteries once he had enough clues to become confident he'd arrive at an answer. Too bad all he knew about Emily Drake was that she was beautiful, she kept really strange hours even by his standards, and she rarely emerged from her house, which, like his, was one of the aging cottages in old town Cape Trouble. To all appearances, she lived alone, although just the other day he'd heard the old guy who lived across the street call, "Feels like spring, Mrs. Drake," when she ventured as far as her mailbox.

She'd smiled and waved at Gus Rumbaugh, which was more than she did when she set eyes on Sean. For him, any nod she gave in answer to a greeting was distinctly chilly.

What had become a familiar frustration every time he thought about Mrs. Emily Drake finally kicked his brain into gear, and finally back to business. A slit throat? Burris County, situated on the Oregon coast, had a population of not much over 25,000 people. Murder was unusual and, when it happened, typically was either a domestic or the result of a drunken confrontation in a tavern. Like anywhere, they had exceptions; one doozie was the discovery last summer that Cape Trouble held the burying ground of a serial killer who'd been active for twenty-something years.

Odds were this would turn out to be a domestic. Except cutting someone's throat… That'd be a hard thing to do if you were intimate with the victim. A stabbing, sure, usually with a knife grabbed from the kitchen counter. A gunshot, fists, those were weapons used when a husband or wife lost it. Cutting a throat would have to be more calculated.

He frowned. No point in reasoning ahead of the facts. Sean checked the names attached to that address – Francis and Rita Lowe – and otherwise concentrated on the narrow, winding Pacific Coast highway which on this stretch clung to a cliff-edge. Every once in a while, that sliver of moon reappeared and let him see a shimmer of seafoam breaking on rocks a stomach-plummeting drop below. Once he'd had to repel down the cliff along this stretch to reach a car that had plunged through the guard rail.

From long practice, he blocked the memory of what he'd found at the bottom.

He didn't quite make it in a half hour, but close. Sean found the house, no problem, a fancy place in a development he'd driven through before of nice homes on half acre or more lots. In daylight, all would have spectacular views and some were oceanfront. He didn't need to see the house number, not when light blazed from the front windows and a marked sheriff's department car sat in the driveway.

As he walked up to the porch, the sound of a woman sobbing rose over the ever-present roar of the surf. It was like a metronome: inhale air, exhale wail.

Ringing the doorbell, Sean wondered if anyone else was here besides the deputy. Please no kids, he thought with unusual fervency.

The minute the door opened and he saw Rebecca's face, he winced. "She have a relative or friend who can come?" he asked in a low voice.

One of only two women deputies with the sheriff's department, Rebecca was about his age, he thought. She looked like the runner he knew she was. Along with working patrol, she had been trained as the department negotiator. He'd seen her in action, and knew her to be good. Rebecca had a natural warmth. Everyone liked her.

He'd never seen her look haggard or so grim. "I wanted you to see the scene before I let anyone else in the house," she said.

"All right. You started a log?"

"I did."

Sean took the notebook she handed him, scribbled his own name and the time, and stepped inside. The woman sitting on the sofa with her hands over her face appeared small in the midst of a vast living room that swept into dining room and kitchen. Sean was made instinctively uneasy by the vaulted ceiling and huge open space with walls of windows, most without blinds or drapes. The wife seemed oblivious to his arrival.

"Bath in the master bedroom," Rebecca murmured. "Mrs. Lowe woke up, her husband wasn't in bed with her. Bathroom was dark, which puzzled her as he usually turned on the light when he went in to take a leak. Uh, not her words."

Sean nodded his understanding.

"She called his name, didn't get an answer, but decided to use the bathroom herself before she went looking for him. It wasn't her habit to turn on the light. She tripped over something."

Sean grimaced.

"Remembering that made her start to cry. I haven't gotten anything else coherent out of her." That even Rebecca hadn't been able to calm her was bad news.

"Okay. It's a good start."

"She'd turned the light on," the deputy said to his back.

Sean felt sure she wouldn't have touched anything but the doorbell and the comforter she'd found to wrap around Mrs. Lowe, but Sean would have to ask eventually. Right now, he just wanted to get a look. The sobs were like fingernails on a blackboard, creating a desperate need to silence them.

He snapped on gloves before he reached the hall. Place appeared to have three bedrooms, a linen closet and a second bathroom. He edged open each door, turning on lights and taking a cursory look. He couldn't imagine anyone lurked, but better safe than really sorry. He was relieved to see that one bedroom was probably set up for guests, and the other was a home office. So one blessing: no terrified kids.

The master bedroom was vast, too, with the kind of deep carpet that made him feel as if sand was sucking at his feet. King size bed, covers rumpled on both sides. A dresser and an armoire. Two additional doors, both partially open. Behind one was a walk-in closet as big as his kitchen.

The bathroom…well, even with his experience, it was hard to look past the naked body slumped over the tiled rim of the Jacuzzi tub. The angle of the hairy lower legs looked wrong – probably because the wife had knocked them askew. The arms and head hung down, allowing the blood to run into the tub. And, man, the knife had bitten deep enough to damn near decapitate this guy. He'd been forced to kneel and bend forward, Sean thought. Mess minimized. The killer might even have gotten away without being sprayed.

Or maybe not. Sean watched a drop fall from the faucet. A few seconds later, another. It might be a chronic drip, the kind a homeowner put off having fixed. But it might also be that a stranger didn't know how tight that handle had to be turned.

He wouldn't have let more than a gentle stream run for fear of awakening the wife, but that would be adequate to wash off his hands, rinse some blood off his forearm. Who knew?

He had taken the time to dip a probably-gloved finger into the blood and write three large letters on the tiled wall: BCD. Maybe it was only that they were written in blood, or the way it smeared and dripped, but Sean thought the breadth of the letters, the slashing strokes that made them, projected more rage than the skillful slice of the knife across the victim's throat. Was the killer signing his work, or were those three letters supposed to mean something?

Sean took another look at the picture as a whole and shook his head. He'd never seen anything like this before. An assassination.

Squatting, he leaned forward far enough to allow him to see the face in profile, at which point he swore. Oh, damn. He knew this guy.

*****

In unison, everyone gathered in the living room gusted sighs of relief when the EMTs ushered Mrs. Lowe out the door. For a minute, nobody said anything. Sean's ears still rang, and he could only imagine how Rebecca felt after her prolonged exposure.

They'd tried to call a friend of Mrs. Lowe's and gotten no answer. She had no family locally. Sean assumed she would be sedated and admitted to the hospital for the night.

At least he hadn't had to do a notification. The dead had done it for him.

The ME was currently in with the body, and Major Crimes Lieutenant Wilcynski had summoned state crime scene investigators who had immediately gone about their business. Another detective, Jason Payne, had showed up not long after the lieutenant, who'd barked, "What the hell are you doing here?" Sean hadn't heard the answer.

Out of the corner of his eye, he saw a flash where a photographer worked, and a minute ago he'd watched a tech fingerprinting the French door that led from the master bedroom out to a small deck to the side of the house. A square of glass had been neatly cut out to allow the killer to reach in, unlock and open the door. Unbroken, the glass that had been removed sat on the decking to one side. They suspected it had been done earlier. Mrs. Lowe had said dully that she'd never opened the drapes that day and therefore wouldn't have noticed.

"Okay." The lieutenant turned his very dark eyes on Sean. "What did you get out of her?"

Wilcynski was new to the department, replacing the fat-ass who had finally retired. The sign on his desk said B.J. Wilcynski, inspiring ribald speculation as to what the B and the J stood for. He had informed everyone he was fine with being called BJ or Will. Or – he'd paused - lieutenant. So far, Sean stuck with lieutenant.

Wilcynski was maybe five years older than Sean's thirty-two. He'd admitted to having been a sergeant working homicide for the Los Angeles County Sheriff's Department, most recently in Compton, known for high crime. Rumor had it that something bad had happened, or that he'd burned out, or he'd been fired, or was madly in love with a woman who lived up here. Take your pick. He wasn't saying. Sean suspected he'd been referred here by Adam Rostov, a detective also from the L.A. area who had been in Cape Trouble a few months ago, trying to keep a woman alive. Otherwise, what were the odds?

All Sean knew for sure was that Wilcynski was sharp, professional and experienced enough Sean didn't mind serving under him.

Sean didn't know Jason Payne well, either. He'd joined the department something like four or five months ago. Detectives didn't partner here; there weren't enough of them. He was fresh out of uniform, that Sean did remember, but he seemed to be catching on fine.

Now Sean repeated what Rebecca had gotten out of Rita Lowe as a sequence of events, then the results of his own, difficult conversation with her.

"She said her husband had an upset stomach after dinner. He took some antacids before bed. She was vaguely aware he'd gotten up a couple of times. Once she heard him crunching on some more antacids. Sounded like she's a pretty heavy sleeper, though. Certainly didn't hear anyone coming in the back door. Thinks she might have heard someone talking quietly, but she didn't pay any attention. Apparently Frank took calls sometimes at night and it wouldn't have been unusual for him to go in the bathroom so as not to wake her. Anything louder - a shout or thud – she's sure she'd have heard."

"What's your take on her?"

"She didn't do this," he said right away. "I didn't get any undertones. I think she was really worried about him when she realized he must have gotten up. Her shock looks genuine to me."

"Not to mention her hysteria," Rebecca muttered.

Wilcynski's mouth twitched. "Thank God for sedatives."

Amen. "This looks like a professional hit. I can't imagine we'll find fingerprints."

The lieutenant grunted. "Come daybreak we'll search for the knife in case he tossed it, but that doesn't seem real likely either."

They all turned when the ME appeared. Sean knew Dennis Yates, balding but fit. He'd almost have to be, with the hours he had to stand during his workday, Sean figured. As small as Burris County was, they were lucky to have their own medical examiner, and one who was actually a doctor. The hospital in North Fork, the county seat, was a decent size, and he was their pathologist. Sean had had longer conversations with him than he'd ever had with two of the other three cops from his own department who were present. The only one he'd spent any time with was Rebecca Walker in her role as negotiator.

Yates tended to be direct. "I'm going to say time of death was between one and two. 911 call was 3:37, right?"

Rebecca nodded. "I was fairly close by, got here at 4:00."

The ME nodded. "Bruises on his cheeks pre-mortem. A hand closed hard over his lower face, presumably to keep him quiet. The blade was sharp, non-serrated."

"Butcher knife?" Sean had seen the wooden block of knives on the kitchen counter. Personally, he kept his knives out of sight. Why advertise an assortment of weapons to an intruder?

Yates frowned. "Possible, but I'm thinking hunting or military surplus. Something with a four, five inch blade. Sharper than most people keep their kitchen knives. I can tell you more once I have him cleaned up on the table." He shook his head. "I know this guy."

"We all know this guy," Sean muttered.

His lieutenant's eyebrows rose. "I don't. I take it he wasn't well liked?"

"What can I say? He was a defense attorney." The name hadn't rung a bell because he knew the victim as Frank, not Francis. Sean had been cross-examined by him in court half a dozen times or more. "He was no worse than most. It's just...the possibilities for who could hate him are almost limitless. Somebody he failed to get off? Or who he refused to defend? A witness he shamed? A victim who didn't get justice thanks to him succeeding in getting the scumbag off? Someone who didn't like the bill he sent? A family member of any of the above?"

"The wife should know if he's received any recent threats," Payne contributed.

"He has a partner in his practice, too. A woman." Sean didn't like her any better. The last time he'd met her in court, he wondered how any woman could defend a rapist. And the odds of her answering questions openly, even given that her partner had been murdered and you'd think she might be scared? Zero. He predicted she'd fight to the death any attempt they made to get a look at client files.

The ME excused himself, but paused when Sean raised a hand.

"I don't want the fact that he wrote letters in blood to get out. Let's keep the message to ourselves."

"Agreed," the lieutenant said.

"Nobody talks to me anyway," Yates said, and departed.

Wilcynski let Rebecca go, too. Then he turned to Sean.

"BCD. What does it mean?"

"First thing I thought of is Burris County Sheriff's Department. But he left out the S, and what sense does that make anyway?"

"Birth Control Device," the photographer called from the kitchen.

Wilcynski grunted. "I guess death is one form of birth control.."

"Battlefield Command Detachment," Jason threw out. When the others looked at him, he shrugged. "I was Army."

"I'll look it up online," Sean said. "God knows, in the age of acronyms, it probably has a hundred meanings."

"You were involved in looking for that missing girl, weren't you?" the lieutenant asked.

He nodded. Scratches on his hands and face stung.

"Then go home and catch a few hours of sleep. I want you to stay primary on this, which means you need to be sharp. I'll stay here until the CAU people are done and then I'll check on Mrs. Lowe at the hospital. If she's awake, I'll talk to her, then the partner. We can't rule out this being entirely personal, but I'll get started on a warrant for his office."

"That'll be a tough sell to any judge."

"Have to try." He glanced at Payne. "Since you're here and look bright-eyed, I'll have you knock on doors as soon as neighbors start stirring. One of them might have seen a vehicle parked or slowly driving the neighborhood in the past few days. Even someone walking up to the house. This guy would have had to case it. Tonight wasn't his first visit."

Payne nodded.

Sean said, "The rain didn't let up until after midnight." He probably didn't have to say this, but he didn't know Wilcynski well enough yet to leave something this important unspoken. "There almost has to be footprints."

"I'll make sure they look."

"Then thanks. Some sleep will help."

"Good. I'll see you when you can get in." Looking energized, the lieutenant headed for the bedroom. Hey, without a recent homicide in Burris County, he'd been going cold turkey.

"I'll walk you out," the other detective said, grinning when Sean let loose of a jaw-cracking yawn.

They'd almost reached his vehicle when Jason said, "I just wanted to apologize because I'm kind of sticking my nose in here."

Sean looked at him in surprise.

"I happened to be talking to Carol about something else, and she mentioned Walker's call." Carol being the dispatcher. He shrugged. "This sounded more interesting than the couple of homicide investigations I've been involved in. Thought I could learn something."

That made sense, and Sean understood his eagerness even though he knew most people wouldn't. Women especially were either fascinated by what he did for a living in a way he found ghoulish, or they were creeped out and he could see them wondering when he'd last touched a dead body.

He opened his door but stopped before getting in. "It's good you jumped in. Unless this turns out to be something easy—" and what were the chances of that? "—you'd likely have been pulled in anyway. This way you're already up to speed."

Jason backed away. "I'm glad you don't think I'm being too pushy."

"Nope."

Jason was already loping up to the porch when Sean got in and started the engine. He rolled down the window, needing the cold air to keep him awake during the half hour drive home.

*****

Emily peeked through the blinds but saw nobody. She appreciated the kindness of her neighbors – really, she did – but sometimes all she wanted was to go out and get her newspaper or mail without having to make conversation. She could have anonymity if she were willing to sell the house and move to a city, where people ignored their neighbors. But this was Cape Trouble, and...she couldn't leave this house.

This early, not many people were up yet. She was blessedly alone when she walked the short distance out the gate in her picket fence to her mail and newspaper boxes. Clutching the paper, she heard a car engine and glanced to see the Subaru Outback turning into the driveway of the house next to hers. She'd heard her neighbor come home sometime after one in the morning, then leave again only a few hours later.

A man got out, his gaze locked on her even before he slammed his door. He always looked at her with the same open intensity, part of what made her so uneasy about him. The other part was...she didn't quite know. His size, maybe? He was a big guy, probably six foot two, if she had to guess, broad-shouldered and solidly built, his easy power visible in the smallest movement. His brown hair always looked unruly, as if he never combed it or had cowlicks winning the war. He was good looking, not that she had any intention of looking ever again.

Mostly, she thought it was his eyes that disturbed her. They were bright blue, well-suited for his laser sharp stares.

Usually, she would dip her head the minimum amount to be polite and retreat as quickly as possible without appearing to flee. But today, a gasp slipped out before she could cover her mouth with her hand. He looked terrible. Lines carved deep aged him a decade from the last time she'd seen him. Scratches decorated his face. What had to be two-day stubble shadowed his jaw. Exhaustion and something indefinable in his stance and eyes had her moving toward him before she'd had time to think.

She stopped perhaps ten feet from him, the closest she'd been since the day he came to her door to introduce himself. "Are you all right?" she asked.

He blinked, mitigating the force of his stare, and rubbed his palm self-consciously over his jaw. "That bad, huh?"

"Well…yes." That was probably rude, but she couldn't help herself. "I heard about the missing girl. Did…was she found?" She hadn't been able to think about anything else all day. Usually she managed a few hours of sleep during the afternoon, but not yesterday.

Detective Sean Holbeck's hard face softened. "We found her. She's okay. She threatened suicide, you know. Took her dad's old Colt Revolver, but I guess she chickened out."

Emily closed her eyes momentarily. "Oh, thank God. I was so afraid—" Then she focused again on his face. "That's how you got scratched."

"Yeah. We had to search the woods."

"Is that where you've been all night?"

He shook his head. "Got in at one-thirty or so, then was called out again."

"In the middle of the night?" She couldn't believe she'd said that. Of course terrible things happened in the middle of the night. They happened any hour of the day or night. Any minute. She of all people knew.

She'd given something away. His eyes narrowed slightly. After the briefest of pauses, he said, "I work major crimes. This was a murder."

"Oh, no."

His mouth twisted. "You'll be reading about it in the paper." His eyes dropped to the one in her hand. "Not this morning's. But by tomorrow."

"Was it…bad?" The idiocy of her question almost made her moan. Was there such a thing as a good murder? A so-so one?

Her next-door neighbor gave no indication he thought the question to be dumb. "Yeah." It came out rough. He didn't seem to notice. "It was."

She wanted to run away, but didn't let herself. "I'm sorry."

"Thanks. As nights go, this one sucked."

"Except you found the girl alive."

"You're right. Her parents were really scared."

She felt herself blanch. What had she been thinking, to talk about something like this?

Sean took a step toward her. "Are you all right?"

"Yes." She edged backward. "Yes, of course. I shouldn't have kept you standing out here. You must be exhausted."

She could tell he was thinking about her reaction, but he didn't comment on it.

"I'm going to grab a bite and then get some sleep," he admitted.

"Okay. Um…I hope you sleep well." Her heel caught a crack in the sidewalk and she had to do a quick two-step to stay on her feet. Now her cheeks were undoubtedly flushed.

Sean Holbeck hadn't moved. He kept standing right where he'd been, still watching her.

*But I don't have to keep watching him.* She nodded, which was what she should have done in the first place, and turned away to march the last few steps to her gate.

"Emily." His voice just reached her.

She paused with her hand on the latch. "Yes?"

"I can't help wondering. I hear what sounds like a machine running in your house, often through the night."

"Oh. I'm sorry. Does it bother you?"

He shook his head. "Only because I can't figure out what I'm hearing."

"I'm a quilter. It's my sewing machine."

"Ah." One corner of his mouth lifted in an almost-smile. "Thank you for solving the mystery."

"You're welcome." She opened her gate and entered her yard, protected by shrubs that would soon be in bloom. Even so, she saw him cross his own yard in a few strides and let himself into his house.

She felt…raw as she climbed the porch steps and slipped into her own house. She tried so hard not to feel any more than she could help. Worrying about that poor, troubled teenage girl had lowered her guard. Perhaps because of what he did for a living, her neighbor's gaze seemed to penetrate it effortlessly. He made her feel vulnerable, something she couldn't allow.

No more neighborly sympathy, she told herself. Or neighborly anything else. Not where Sean Holbeck was concerned.

Agitated more than she wanted to admit, she went to the room where she stored fabrics, already envisioning a wall-hanging quilt. Browns and deep greens to suggest dense forest, but touched by shafts of golden sunlight. Or were they flashlight beams in the night?

# CHAPTER TWO

Sean's prediction had proved to be absolutely correct. Frank Lowe's partner in the legal practice had dug in her heels at any request for cooperation. Two days later, Sean's original distaste had progressed to active dislike.

He was back today at the firm of Lowe & Graafstra for yet another try. When he'd been ushered into Sandra Graafstra's office by a subdued receptionist, she had led him past a couple closed doors. One had to be Frank's office.

"He surely had clients who made him more uneasy than others," he suggested, once they settled down with her desk between them.

"Of course he did. *I* do." Sandra Graafstra looked at him as if he was an idiot. "We recognize that some of our clients actually committed crimes."

He refrained from saying, *No, really?*

"As you have pointed out, however, the killer could just as well be an individual Frank declined to represent, or a family member of a victim he had never even met, or, who knows, a neighbor he offended when he used a weed killer too close to the property line. Your desire to browse at will through records we are legally obligated to keep confidential smacks of a witch hunt."

He knew she was right, but he also thought she didn't entirely get it. Likely in her early forties, medium height, Ms. Graafstra was a painfully thin woman with a razor-sharp haircut that followed her jawline. Her composure was absolute. She didn't bother to hide the fact that she didn't like cops any better than he liked defense attorneys, and especially her. Sean was more tempted than he should be to slap a photo of her partner's body on the desk in front of her and see whether that would even shake her.

Probably not, considering her expertise at verbally brutalizing rape victims in the courtroom.

"The likely presumption is that your partner was killed by someone angry at him because of an action he took or didn't take in his legal practice. I'd think that might make you a little nervous," he said.

"Detective, are you not familiar with the concept of attorney/client confidentiality?"

Her condescension grated. She knew damn well he understood her legal obligations.

"I wonder how big Frank was on it while he was kneeling naked in his own bathroom feeling that knife start to slice his throat," he said.

Anger flashed in her eyes, but that was all. "It would be one thing if you wanted to look at records pertaining to a single suspect individual, but to allow you open access? Impossible. I cannot help you."

"Can you at least tell me if any clients have the initials BCD?"

She looked curious, no wonder since the letters written in blood were a detail they hadn't released. Finally she nodded. "I'll check and let you know."

The initials – or was it an acronym? – were frustrating Sean. Online, he'd discovered BCD could be short for anything from Binary-Coded Decimal to Behind Completion Date. Not surprisingly, there were at least a couple military applications besides the one Jason has mentioned, including Brigade, Corps, Division and Sean's personal favorite, Bad Conduct Discharge. He'd checked, though, and Frank had never served. He'd also never been a mathematician and hadn't worked in construction, another field where BCD had several meanings.

Shaking off that question, he moved onto another. "May I ask how many active cases he had?"

"I've…barely begun reviewing those." She actually sounded hesitant. That might be grief on her face, but, if so, it was gone before Sean could be sure. "Twenty or thirty," she said. "Many of his clients, of course, had been accused of relatively minor offenses. We don't have a lot of spectacular trials here in Burris County."

"We don't," he conceded. "But I'm assuming the two of you represented clients in courts in other counties."

"Certainly, but only neighboring ones. Given that there are no cities of significant size in this part of western Oregon, I'm sure you understand that people accused of a DWI, drug offense or burglary make up the largest part of our practice."

He knew for a fact that Frank had in the last year also represented clients who'd committed child sexual abuse, rape, and assault.

"Anyone whose life was seriously impacted by a conviction could be moved to violence," he said. "This guy could have lost his job because of a DWI. His family might have cut him off if he was convicted of child sexual molestation. We can't assume he had previously been accused of a violent crime."

Nothing he said moved her, which wasn't unexpected. Realistically, she couldn't say, sure, take a look. He'd hoped she might drop a hint. But maybe she and Frank hadn't discussed anyone in the recent past that made him nervous. People could appear completely normal until they cracked. And this particular murder struck Sean as so cold-blooded, the man who committed it might have given off no aberrant signals in advance.

He was taking a leap even to assume the killer was male, but Sean couldn't see a woman overpowering Frank so easily, even if he was stumbling sleepily into a dark bathroom.

Fortunately, they had backdoor ways of looking into the cases he'd handled. The district attorney had set some people to combing records for any obvious red flags – or the initials BCD. Cases Frank had handled that actually went to trial or were plea-bargained were matters of public record. Sean wasn't optimistic, though. Unless someone remembered an unusual outburst or threat, they were running out of avenues to pursue. If this had been a rape/murder, they could expect the offender to repeat what had been a successful experience for him. Domestics were usually a one-time deal. But this kind of killing? All Sean knew for sure was that this guy had killed before. He was too good at it to be a newbie.

In the intervening two days, none of their inquiries had borne fruit. Not a single neighbor had noticed a person or vehicle that didn't belong. It turned out that neither of the nearest neighbors were home. Both wintered in Arizona. He'd wondered why lights hadn't come on in other houses that night. Police activity was usually guaranteed to draw a crowd.

Mrs. Lowe insisted her husband hadn't seemed unusually concerned about anything or anyone. She was quite certain he'd have told her if he had been threatened.

The ME hadn't had been able to offer anything useful. How Frank was killed hadn't exactly been a mystery. What was more frustrating was that the CAU folks hadn't found anything, either. The no fingerprints, Sean had expected. But every hair and flake of skin in the bathroom and bedroom came from the victim or his wife. Sean had learned they didn't employ even a weekly housecleaner, and Rita made a habit of shutting their bedroom door when they entertained to discourage guests from using that bathroom. Outside, the investigators had found depressions left by footprints, but the ground was too wet for any detail to remain. Man's shoe size ten or eleven had been their best guess.

What it meant was, the killer had come and gone as if he had no substance whatsoever. Which put weight behind Sean's belief that he'd had practice.

Somewhere else, presumably. This kind of murder was virtually unknown anywhere closer than Portland. If the guy was a hired hitman who'd already gone home to Chicago or Miami or wherever he came from, they were shit out of luck. In the back of Sean's mind, though, was the knowledge that a significant percentage of Americans had been trained to kill by their own government. The average artillery grunt probably wouldn't have had a lot of opportunity to slit throats over in Iraq or Afghanistan, but Special Ops guys were another story. He didn't even want to think about how many residents of Burris County had served in the military.

Yeah, but then why Frank, who hadn't served?

Damn, Sean thought, still sitting outside the law firm. He was spinning his wheels. It was time to call it a day. Maybe going to the gym or for a run would help. Shake something loose.

It seemed fortuitous when, about a mile before he reached the Cape Trouble city limits, he spotted a man dressed in camouflage plodding along the shoulder, humping a huge pack. Larry was a Vietnam War veteran who'd never reintegrated into society. His braided gray hair hung to his belt. A certain smell clung to him, but he wasn't filthy. Worried about him, Sean had asked around awhile back and found a woman who let him take showers at the old motel and campground she managed in exchange for the aluminum cans Larry picked up beside the road.

"Saves him his dignity," she had explained. "I tell him if the weather's bad, he can stay the night, too, but he hardly ever does. I don't know if he's found a cave or has built a shelter or what, but he must be able to get out of the rain somehow."

Sean suspected there were people in town who found a way to feed Larry, too. Whenever he happened to see the old guy, he'd slip him some bucks, and he probably wasn't the only one who did.

He put on his blinker and pulled to the side of the road, waiting until Larry had reached his open window.

"Hey. Haven't seen you in a while. How are you keeping?"

Larry's faded blue eyes looked clear. Whatever his problems, he wasn't much of a drinker. He scowled. "Enemy's sent a scout ahead. He thinks I'm a problem, and he's trying to run me out."

Paranoia being Larry's middle name, his conversation was frequently studded with vague warnings of enemy incursions. Given Sean's earlier speculations, though, he asked, "A scout? What can you tell me about him?"

"Young guy." Larry mulled that over. "Well, younger'n me. Wearing clothes like me, trying to blend in. Could be one of Saddam's boys, or even that new crowd."

"ISIS?"

"Scary thought. Them guys chop the heads off anyone they don't like, you know."

Sean stiffened then made himself relax. The killer he was hunting hadn't beheaded Frank Lowe, although he'd come close. He sure as hell wasn't some Islamic terrorist. What would any of them want with Frank, a small time lawyer in smaller-time Burris County?

"This scout look Arabic?" he asked, out of mild curiosity.

Larry leaned in, his breath wafting under Sean's nose. "Haven't gotten a good enough look yet to say for sure. Got black hair, though."

"How's he trying to run you out?"

"I got a couple places," Larry said vaguely. "He's moved right into one of them. He pointed his rifle at me and warned me away. Don't know why he didn't take me out right then."

"I appreciate the warning." Sean poked a twenty dollar bill into one of the multiple chest pockets on Larry's camo jacket. "Can I give you a ride anywhere?"

Larry pondered. Every once in a while, he accepted, but today he shook his head and stepped back. "Don't have that far to go."

"You take care, then," Sean told him, putting the Subaru into gear and pulling away. He cast a couple glances at the rearview mirror, seeing that Larry had resumed his plod toward whatever destination he had in mind. Sean worried about him, but also believed he was happier with his peculiar lifestyle than he would be if social services got their hands on him. What's more, he was a hell of a lot better off than his counterparts in downtown Portland and Seattle, and probably every other major city. Winters here were wet and miserable, but not bitterly cold. Enough people watched out for him. He did all right.

The enemy scout might be entirely in his mind, although Sean guessed it was also possible that another homeless man was passing through or even settling down here. Could even be another vet; there were enough guys back from Iraq or Afghanistan suffering from PTSD, no different from the Vietnam veterans.

Frowning, he decided to keep a better eye out for Larry. He might struggle if he'd been pushed out of whatever shelter he had found.

At home, Sean changed quickly, hearing Emily Drake's car pulling out of her driveway just as he reached for his own keys. Damn. He'd have liked an excuse to try to start a conversation.

Because that usually worked so well, he mocked himself. Apparently, looking pathetic was his best shot at catching her attention, but shock and pity weren't exactly what he was going for from her.

He frowned as he backed out of his own driveway. He couldn't say what he did want with her, but a friendly conversation would be a good start. Honesty compelled him to admit that sex would be even better. It had been awhile since any other woman had caught his eye. He didn't like to admit that he hadn't so much as looked since his first glimpse of the woman who lived next door to the house on which he'd just made an offer.

And why was he brooding about her again? He was supposed to be clearing his mind.

He decided to cross Mist River to the old resort, soon to be in the hands of a nature conservancy, and run on the sandy beach that stretched for miles. He'd only done that a few times, because he'd been living in North Fork, the county seat, until he decided to put down roots and bought the house here in Cape Trouble just a couple months ago. It had been a wet late winter and early spring; he'd stuck to the gym more often than not since his move. But he liked the extra burn he got from running on sand.

He liked the idea even better when he bumped along the deteriorating track past the tumbledown cabins, and saw a car he recognized beside the head of the trail that cut between dunes to the beach. Emily's Prius. No sign of her, but he parked right behind it, locked and jogged along the trail until it opened onto the beach. And there she was, dressed in form-fitting running clothes, doing stretches.

And, God, she looked good. He stopped for a minute so he could study her hungrily before she realized she wasn't alone anymore.

*This* was why he was obsessed with his reclusive neighbor and worried that she might be married, despite the non-appearance of a husband.

Tall for a woman, maybe five foot ten, she had generous breasts and well-rounded hips, plus long, long legs with enough muscle to let him know she either ran or worked out on a regular basis.

Hair so dark it was almost black was captured in a braid that hung nearly to the ground as she bent and grabbed the back of her legs, pulling on those hamstrings. Unlike most dark-haired people, she had the kind of ivory skin that likely refused to tan. And her eyes were as green as any he'd ever seen, even though her driver's license probably called them hazel.

"Emily," he said, walking toward her.

She straightened, alarm flashing on her face. "Detective."

"Make it Sean. We are neighbors." He nodded toward the beach, empty as far as he could see. "Didn't know you ran over here."

"Yes, quite often." She sounded grudging; she didn't want to admit to any part of her routine, he guessed. "I prefer it to a treadmill when it isn't absolutely pouring, and I appreciate the solitude."

He gave a crooked smile at that. Way to tell him.

"If you'd rather run alone, that's okay. Although I won't promise not to pass you if I'm faster."

"I doubt we're well matched." She eyed him as he started to stretch. "You'd probably leave me in your dust."

"Except for the lack of dust."

A tiny smile rewarded him. "Except." Her forehead puckered as the silence extended. "You're welcome to start with me if you'd like."

He knew half-hearted when he heard it, but wasn't going to let her off the hook. Nor would he warn her that any speed she ran was sure to be fine by him.

She walked in circles while he stretched, and then they broke into a trot together, away from the river that separated this old resort from town. He couldn't forget the graves they'd discovered last summer in the gritty soil behind the lodge, where the resort owner's nephew had buried his prey, all pretty blonde women. They had barely been in time to save Sophie Thomsen, the fiancé of Cape Trouble's current police chief, a guy Sean liked and had worked with on half a dozen investigations now. In fact, Sean had stopped by the police station just a couple days ago to let him in on everything they knew about Frank Lowe's murder. The investigation might well lead them to Cape Trouble.

Emily started at a leisurely pace, but once they reached the hard-packed sand at the sea's edge, she began to stretch those long legs and soon reached a speed that was only a little slower than he'd have gone on his own. Their initial silence felt surprisingly comfortable.

She was the one to break it. "Have you heard any more about how that girl is doing? Did she really plan to kill herself?"

"I kind of doubt it," he said. "I think it was all big drama, except that she got herself lost in the woods and could have died of exposure."

She flicked a sidelong glance at him. "You sound…contemptuous."

"I'm not. Just…a little angry, I guess." He had to think about that. "I get that teenagers are self-centered. I probably was, too."

Without breaking stride, Emily managed a lifted eyebrow with a tilt of her head that spoke volumes.

Sean grinned at her expression more than the topic. "Okay. No probably. I was." Until he hadn't fulfilled a promise, with such devastating consequences. "But I'd never have knowingly put my parents through anything like that, either. And do you have any idea the resources it took to haul her little ass home? We had upwards of a hundred volunteers searching for her by the end. She sucked up a day and a half of my time alone. And now all her friends are probably cooing over her, poor heartbroken Arianna."

Maybe he should have softened what he said, since Emily was obviously more sympathetic than he was, but he wouldn't lie. That kid had wasted the time of a hell of a lot of people. With all the crap you saw in law enforcement, it hardened you in some ways. How could he do his job if he agonized over every victim, sympathized with every sad story? Nor could he afford to let his worst memories be awakened by every bereaved father, brother, child.

"You don't know what her family is like, though," Emily suggested. "No one ever does from the outside. You can't assume it's like yours."

"You're right, of course."

"You are, too, though," Emily said. She wasn't even breathing hard yet, although her cheeks were pink. "No matter what her motivation, she probably never thought about all those people who would have to look for her." A few strides along, she added, "I'll bet she was really scared, though, by the time she was found."

"Yeah." His mouth twisted. "I hear her parents put her right in counseling, which is good."

"Yes."

They ran right through a flock of sandpipers that darted out of their way before returning to their preoccupation – a seemingly never-ending search for food bared by the retreating waves. Emily turned and jogged backwards briefly to watch them, laughing.

Sean did the same so he could see her face, lit with momentary happiness that made him realize how sad she had looked every other time he'd seen her.

Turning to go forward again, she said, "They're ridiculously cute."

"My favorite part of running on the beach."

"Mine, too."

They must have covered another quarter mile before she said, "If I'm holding you up…"

"You're not."

After another period of silence during which the pace grew faster, he said, "Your quilting. Do you make bed quilts?"

"Mm? Oh, sometimes, but also crib quilts, throw-sized quilts, wall hangings, runners and placemats."

"You sell them?"

She sounded a little breathless now. "Yes. Gift and quilt shops as well as galleries up and down the coast. Mostly in my own shop." Her mouth curved. "The Sandpiper. Trite but true."

"I've seen it, but never gone in." It was on Schooner Street, which paralleled the beach and was where tourists shopped and the best restaurants in town were. He remembered noticing some beautiful ceramic pieces in the window along with artfully arranged jewelry as well as lace that made him think of fishing nets. Now that he had his own place, he'd been thinking about buying some art, but when he wandered into one gallery, he had winced at the prices. Oils by the best known local artist, Elias Burton, went for $5,000 plus, which wasn't happening on a cop's salary. "You seem like you're home more than you are at the store," he commented.

"I have a manager now." She was quiet for a long time, but Sean sensed she might go on if he kept his mouth shut. "I used to run it myself," she said slowly, something in her voice he couldn't quite decipher. "But I'm happier concentrating on my quilting now. I have stayed involved in the decisions about what we carry. We don't sell tacky souvenir stuff. Everything we do offer, from jewelry and ceramics to weaving, other textiles and paintings, is created by craftspeople up and down the coast."

"Do you sell Elias Burton's art?" he asked.

"Occasionally a small watercolor. His oils are higher priced than we go. You've seen his work?"

"Yeah, in the window of that gallery next door to the Sea Watch Café."

"And you coveted."

"I'd have bought one of his paintings if it had been a couple of hundred dollars."

She really laughed at that, making him feel as if his feet were hardly touching the beach. He sensed she didn't laugh often anymore, if she ever had.

When she said she needed to turn back, he circled with her. They talked less on the way back; even he'd worked up a good sweat despite the chilly ocean breeze, and he was content with the progress he'd made.

He wanted to ask where Mr. Drake was, but didn't. She'd been reluctant to get personal at all. If he pushed too hard, too fast, she'd pull back into her shell like a clam. There was time, he told himself. Proximity of a sort, with them right next door to each other.

He speeded up, and she matched him. Only when he judged they were maybe half a mile from their starting point did he slow to a jog. She got ahead before she noticed and followed suit. When they finally stopped, she bent over, hands on her thighs, and gasped for breath. Tiny tendrils of hair stuck to her temples and forehead, and she was bright red. He could have run a little harder, a little farther, but had had a decent workout and the satisfaction of company.

Plus, he'd inserted a small wedge in the door she'd carelessly left open.

"Ugh," she said finally, straightening and pushing hair back from her forehead. "That was farther than I usually go."

He smiled crookedly at her. "Competitive, are you?"

"I'd have called it pride."

"That's a positive spin," he teased.

As they started toward the dunes, she stole a look at him. "The murder you told me about. Do you think you're getting anywhere?"

Sean opened his mouth to issue his usual line. *We're pursuing leads.* Only they didn't have any. And he found he didn't want to be evasive with her.

"Don't repeat this," he said, "but no. Nobody saw anything. The guy came and went unseen, and didn't leave much of anything behind." More like nothing. "The victim was an attorney, which means he probably made a lot of people mad along the way. We don't have access to his files, but even if we did..." He hesitated.

"Knowing who was mad at him might not help, because lots of people get mad at an attorney but don't kill him."

"And if they did, it would likely be an enraged outburst, not a carefully planned, cold-blooded murder."

When the path narrowed, he let Emily go ahead of him. They had momentarily lost sight of the ocean, although he could still see and smell it. He felt as if he was in a maze, twining between sand dunes that were tufted with beach grass and a surprising variety of other plants, too. He recognized the shrubby growth of beach knotweed and a clump of lupine. Mostly, he looked at the woman in front of him. He liked the view from the front, but this was as good, especially with skin-tight pants that let him see every flex of muscle. She had an amazing ass and amazing legs. He itched to wrap that thick, dark braid around his hand, too.

Damn, he was getting aroused, and even the jockstrap he wore under thin sweatpants wouldn't hide an erection.

*Murder*, he told himself desperately. Think about murder. Because he had a bad feeling that Emily would take offense if she saw him with a hard-on now. He wouldn't get near her again. And Sean wanted very much to get close to her. Often.

Unless it turned out she had, say, an invalid husband secreted away in her house. Or what if she'd stayed behind when her husband took a temporary job of some kind overseas? Hell, what if he was National Guard, currently deployed?

Damn it, he needed to just ask.

She turned her head to give him a shy glance over her shoulder. "I'm sorry."

She was sorry? Because she really was married? It took him a couple of beats to get it. Murder. That's what they'd been talking about. She was sorry because his investigation was going nowhere.

"I don't like the idea of anyone getting away with a crime like that."

They popped out at their cars. "But sometimes people do," she said.

He couldn't deny it.

She took her car key from a pocket that had been invisible and unlocked her car. "Thank you for the company."

"Even if you didn't want it?"

She had the oddest expression on her face as she stared at him for a moment too long. "I...enjoyed myself more than I expected to," she said at last.

"If I'm home the next time you want to go for a run, knock on my door. I try to go at least four days a week. I liked the company, too." He hesitated, not wanting to ruin the beach for her, but needing to say this. "Plus, it's pretty isolated over here for a woman alone."

"I've never had trouble before."

"And you probably won't."

"Oh, for heaven's sake!" She yanked her door open. "Way to kill a mood."

Contrite, he said, "I'm sorry. Cops tend to have a dark view of the world."

Her shoulders eased and she sighed. "I understand." She slid behind the wheel before giving him a last, grave look. "Me, I'm fatalistic. It's one reason I don't worry. I wouldn't kill myself, but if it happened...I don't think I'd mind." And then she closed the door, started her engine, and drove away without so much as glancing his way again.

Stunned, Sean stayed where he was for a long time.

# CHAPTER THREE

Emily knotted the thread and pulled the needle through the quilt top, tugging until the tiny knot disappeared beneath the surface. Then she cut off the thread, pushed the needle into her pin cushion, and let herself sit for a minute without moving, her eyes closed. She didn't need to study the quilt in the frame; the image was on the back side of her eyelids. It was queen-size, a Wedding Ring quilt she'd hand-pieced. Tiredness blurred her thoughts. Yes, she might be able to fall asleep now.

She turned out lights as she went, then stripped and pulled on her usual flannel pajama pants and too-large T-shirt. She had always worn pajamas on the rare occasions when Tom was away, not in bed to warm her. She'd had them on the night the police came to the door, and worn them every night since.

*Don't*, she told herself sharply. If she thought about Tom, or even worse, about Cody, she'd never sleep. She knew better than to do this to herself.

But, of course, it was too late. A fine tension in her body told her she'd already lost the hard-won sense of peace she'd won by placing hundreds – no thousands – of stitches.

Nonetheless, she slid between the sheets on her side of the bed. In the first year, she had quite often found in the morning that she'd gravitated to Tom's side, seeking his heat and solidity but never finding it. She had done that less and less often, until she sometimes felt an invisible barrier down the middle of the bed. It made her think of early sitcoms, when Mom and Dad slept in twin beds and the watcher was never encouraged to so much as imagine the pair entwined on one. Half of her bed was now lost to her, along with the man who had occupied it. Was her half even as wide as a twin bed?

She lay on her back and stared at the ceiling. She tried to make herself think about fabric, or an abstract quilt she was presently piecing, or the dark woodland quilt taking shape in her mind. But that didn't work, so she watched herself feeding fabric beneath the foot on her sewing machine as the needle rose and fell, rose and fell, rose and fell. Or perhaps gathering layers onto her needle. The minute detail of the work was sometimes sleep-inducing.

But instead she saw herself running on the beach with a man at her side, effortlessly pacing her. Of course he could have gone faster and farther, and she knew why he hadn't. She'd seen the way he looked at her from the first time their eyes met, his slightly narrowed and possessing that intensity. He wanted her.

She'd done so well keeping her distance until the day she saw him weary and disturbed. And today, she'd been too polite to say, "I'm sorry, but I do prefer to run alone."

*You can start with me if you want.* Really? What had she thought he'd do? Jog half a mile with her and then wave casually and turn on the after-burners? What she'd convinced herself was bare civility had really been something else, and being polite had nothing to do with it. She had surrendered to temptation.

Because he did tempt her. Lying here in the dark, this was the first time she'd let herself acknowledge a dangerous truth. She was attracted to the man next door. A man who wore a badge and gun, who daily made decisions that could destroy people's lives. He could be hard, she knew, lacking in compassion. All she had to do was remember how angry he'd been at a girl who'd been only slightly more foolish than other girls her age.

Yes, but she'd seen other, powerful emotions surging beneath his surface disgust. He hadn't signed off at the end of his shift - did detectives have shifts? - and left the searching to others. He'd been determined to find her, save her. Would have done anything to do just that, Emily suspected, and he'd have been devastated if the poor girl had been found dead.

Emily hadn't so much as set eyes on him in two days now. She hadn't been consciously trying to tell him she was unavailable, but apparently her subconscious had taken over the job. Unfortunately, the memory of what she'd said still made her cringe. She was surprised he hadn't placed her under some kind of suicide watch.

*I did say I wouldn't kill myself.*

For Pete's sake, she'd been out there to do aerobic exercise to keep her body strong.

Did it matter what he thought? Evidently what she told him had worked to scare him off, and that's what mattered. He might...draw her, but she didn't have anything left to give another person. It was all she could do to make it through a day. A full night's sleep still, after four years, eluded her.

Something crashed.

Emily bolted upright, fear pulsing through her. That had been in the house – the living room or kitchen. Without conscious thought, she leapt from bed and rushed to close her bedroom door, for what good that did when there was no lock. Her head turned wildly. The dresser. She rushed to the far side of it and shoved it in front of the door, even knowing its bulk would barely slow someone down. An antique, it wasn't very large; in fact, because it lacked the mirror that had once been attached, the top fit neatly beneath the doorknob. There was nothing larger or heavier in the room except the bed.

*I'm being ridiculous.*

Had she left the iron too close to the edge of the board? This was an old house. The aging timbers could have...shifted. Sighed. Made the iron topple.

The effort to calm herself failed. No shifting of timbers would send something as heavy as the iron thudding to the floor. Anyway, the sound hadn't been only a thud. It was if someone had fallen over…what? The rocking chair? The quilt frame that filled the middle of the room? The ironing board itself? If a burglar had broken in, without turning on a flashlight he wouldn't have known her living room was really a workroom.

Even as her mind raced, she stood, completely rigid, staring at the door. She still wanted to believe she'd overreacted. Could the crash even have been outside?

But her body, stiff with fear, knew what her mind wouldn't accept. Her breath backed up in her lungs. The light in here was scant, but her eyes had adjusted enough for her to focus on the doorknob.

No, no. Whoever had broken in was undoubtedly long gone. He would assume she'd dialed 911 by now. Oh, God, she should have.

She almost whimpered but wouldn't let herself make a sound. She'd set her phone on the kitchen counter earlier and never given it another thought. If it had been here at her bedside, would she have called anyway? What if the police came, found something silly –

raccoons had gotten into her garbage can? – and she caught them rolling their eyes?

It might make sense to call in the morning once she saw what had really happened.

The doorknob turned and the door hit the dresser, which shook and moved an inch or two.

Emily screamed, shoved the dresser hard against the door again and bolted to the room's single window. The ancient wood frame groaned as she shoved it up. The whole time she was looking over her shoulder. Something – no, someone – slammed into the door, scraping the dresser across the wood floor. In a frantic rush, she pushed the screen off, slung her leg over the sill and threw herself forward, over the azalea that grew beneath her window and onto the cold, damp grass. She scrambled to her feet and ran for the single gate in the six foot fence, still screaming.

It opened before she reached it.

Her scream seemed to bubble in her throat and she stumbled back.

*****

"Emily! It's me." Sean grabbed her arm to keep her upright. "Sean."

"Oh, my God," she whimpered.

"What is it?"

"Someone...in my house."

He shoved his phone at her. "Hide behind a bush. Call 911. Tell them I'm in there."

Then, gun in his hand, he ran toward her window, leaping to hook his elbows over the sill. With a single heave, he rolled to her floor and to his feet, Glock extended before him. Her bedroom door gaped open, a dresser standing askew in the middle of the room. Her small closet had no space for a man to hide.

He didn't turn on a light. Instead, he slipped into the hall and moved silently down it with his body turned sideways to minimize the target he made. He didn't hear so much as a whisper of sound.

Another bedroom door, closed. Small bathroom, empty. A cool breeze moved over him as he stepped into what he assumed was the living room. He moved slowly, carefully, seeing odd shapes looming everywhere.

The window that looked toward his house was wide open. The blinds had been raised, and when he leaned out slightly, he saw the screen propped against the siding.

No movement.

Of course the intruder was gone. After the ear-splitting screams, he'd have heard Sean's voice. Even so, Sean cleared the house, remaining cautious. Through a door off the kitchen, he found a washer and dryer and, incongruously, a treadmill with a laundry basket left sitting on it. Finally, he turned on the porch light and let himself out the front door at the same time as he heard an approaching siren. He hadn't heard another vehicle. He turned his head, scanning the street and every deeper shadow. Rounding the house to the gate, he raised his voice just enough to be heard in her back yard. "Emily! It's okay. He's gone."

She crept from a mass of shrubs along the fence. "You're sure?"

"I'm sure." He met her mid-lawn, and yanked her into his arms, as much for his sake as hers.

For a moment she stayed stiff, even straining away from him. He was about to accept her resistance and let her go when she suddenly sagged, grabbed onto him, and laid her head in the crook between his neck and shoulder. Then she shook, her fingers biting into the bare flesh on his back. Through her thin T-shirt, he felt the thunder of her heartbeat, matched by his own. He didn't remember ever being as scared as he was when that first scream tore him from his sleep. He'd known instantly it had to be her.

The patrol car pulled up in front and the siren abruptly cut out.

Sean rubbed his cheek against her dark hair, inhaling a scent he knew he'd forever associate with her. It was herbal, he thought: thyme or rosemary and possibly lavender. "Emily," he murmured. "The police are here. We need to go talk to them. Take a look and see if we can tell exactly what happened."

She went utterly still. He felt her gathering herself before she straightened. "Oh, God, I'm sorry," she said in a shaken voice that told him how embarrassed she was. "I don't know why I was...clutching you."

"You were taking momentary comfort from another human being," he answered, sharper than he should have.

"I...yes. Of course. I'm sor—" This time she cut herself off.

Knowing some of his anger was a rebound from fear, he kept his mouth shut, only laying his hand on her back to guide her through the gate.

"I'm Detective Holbeck," he called. "BCSD, here with the homeowner."

A uniformed officer with his hand on the butt of his still holstered weapon crossed the front lawn to meet them. Sean suppressed a sigh. It was one of the painfully young ones. Tall, rawboned. Sean couldn't make out the freckles in this lighting, but the stirring of a faint memory told him they were there. He must have met or at least seen this guy.

"I'm Officer Slawinski." He looked and sounded suspicious. "What's a county detective doing here?"

"I live next door." Sean nodded toward his house. "I heard Ms. Drake scream." Damned if he'd call her missus. "I already cleared the house. The guy's gone."

"You're sure there actually was an intruder?" the officer asked. "I mean...excuse me for asking, ma'am, but--"

She stiffened beneath Sean's hand.

He rubbed his hand in a soothing circle. "I'm sure."

No surprise, lights had come on up and down the block, and neighbors were already cautiously venturing out to the sidewalk, clutching robes tight around themselves. Mr. Rumbaugh hovered on his porch, but Louella Shoop was on her way across the street.

After Sean bought his place, the Cape Trouble police chief, Daniel Colburn, had told him wryly that he had reason to believe Louella Shoop owned military grade binoculars with night vision capability. Sean hadn't been surprised when she showed up on his doorstep within an hour of his moving truck arriving, a casserole dish in hand. He'd appreciated the gesture even though he had a suspicion she just wanted to get a look inside. Since then, he'd learned she was scarily well-informed about everyone in town.

Sean had left Emily's front door open, and, ignoring the audience, they all climbed the porch steps and went inside. Sean's eyes went first to the fireplace mantel. He hadn't done that earlier.

No photos were displayed there. Otherwise… A broad frame that held an unfinished quilt partially rolled filled the center of the room, a straight-backed wood chair pulled up to it. On a long open desk sat a sewing machine, a second chair in front of it. The wood surface of a large, sturdy table could barely be seen beneath bolts of fabric and a section of a quilt, partially pieced with tiny triangles. A handsome wood rocking chair in a corner was the only furniture typical to a living room.

Because it wasn't a living room, it was her studio, he thought, then focused on the ironing board that lay on its side and the iron that had tumbled almost as far as the hall, the cord snaking behind it.

"That must have been quite a noise," he said, wondering if the man who'd tripped over it had crashed to the floor, too.

"It was." If she hadn't had her arms tightly crossed in front of her and he hadn't felt the quivering tension beneath the hand he'd kept on her back, he might have been fooled.

Officer Slawinski stood gaping.

Sean took charge. "I found that window open. The screen is leaning against the wall of the house. The blinds were raised as you see them now."

"But..." Emily's voice was soft.

He raised his eyebrows and waited.

"I never raise the blinds," she blurted.

He'd noticed.

"And I know the screen was on."

The young officer had pulled himself together. "Was the window locked when you went to bed, ma'am?"

She looked stricken. "I...don't know. I had it open while I worked. I like the fresh air. It wasn't that cold." She closed her eyes. "I don't remember closing it. I don't always."

Sean saw Slawinski almost say something but then change his mind. Even he could see that she'd never go to bed again without locking and checking every window and door compulsively.

"I'm guessing our intruder expected a usual layout for a living room," Sean said. "Which means he didn't turn on a flashlight."

Unlike heavy drapes, blinds wouldn't entirely block a beam of light moving through the house. A neighbor who happened to be up and saw it would wonder, and conceivably call the police.

The fact that the guy had taken a chance of crossing a cluttered room without benefit of any light meant he wasn't looking for electronics to steal. But Sean already knew that.

"So he fell over my ironing board." She stared down at it..

"That would definitely wake you," Slawinski said kindly.

"I wasn't asleep yet. Just...trying."

Again, neither of the men remarked. A glance at a wall clock told Sean it was now almost four in the morning. He nudged her into motion, and they all proceeded down the hall to her bedroom.

"What else did you hear?" he asked gently.

"Nothing, until..." She stopped, started again. "If it had been a smaller crash, I'd probably have convinced myself I left something on the edge of a table and...I don't know. But this—" Her long white throat worked as she swallowed. "I jumped out of bed and closed the door, but it doesn't have a lock. They don't in houses this age," she told them, as if that was something important to know. "Not even those push-button ones, so I shoved my dresser over in front of the door."

The door gaped enough they could all slide sideways into her bedroom, even Sean who wasn't a small man. That chilled his marrow, just as it had earlier. If she hadn't reacted as fast as she had, the intruder would have gotten his hands on her.

It took an effort to sound calm. "That was smart."

He didn't know if she heard him or not. She continued, "Then...then I sort of froze, trying to convince myself I was imagining things, or overreacting. It was so quiet, I thought whoever it was had taken off. I mean, he must have known even someone sleeping would have heard and probably called 911."

"As you did," Officer Slawinski observed.

"But I didn't. Not then." Her sidelong glance held shame. "I'd left my phone in the kitchen."

Something else she'd probably never do again at night, Sean guessed. She already carried so much sadness, he hated knowing that a new fear would now add a weight, that sleep would become even more elusive as she lay straining to hear the smallest of sounds.

"Then the doorknob turned and the door whacked into my dresser. I think I screamed and that's when I ran to my window, opened it and practically fell out. I could hear the dresser scraping on the floor." She shivered.

They all looked at the long scratches in the polished oak.

Sean rubbed her back, stroking up and down. Despite her height, her bones felt so fragile. "Smart again," he murmured.

"And...and I was barely outside when Sean was there. I called 911 with his phone while he went in the house."

"Let's go back to the living room," Sean suggested. "Do you have a sweater, Emily?" He could tell she was feeling some shock, plus the night was cold for her to be wearing only a thin knit shirt with a drooping neckline that bared a good deal of her shoulder. Both Slawinski and he had been trying not to look, although a vision of her delicate collarbone and creamy skin stayed with him anyway.

"Oh. Yes." She looked around vaguely before opening a dresser drawer and taking out a sweatshirt. She put on some slippers, too, before returning to the living room with the two men. They had her look for her purse, which she said was exactly where she'd left it. The wallet was inside, cash and credit cards where they should be. Setting the purse down again, she asked if they might be able to find fingerprints.

"Yes, ma'am, although we'll have to borrow a tech from the sheriff's department."

"I'll arrange that," Sean said. "It probably won't do any good, but you never know." He hesitated. "Have you had anything like this happen in town recently?"

"Oh, we get a break-in now and again, but it's usually teenagers. This seems more..." Slawinski's gaze touched on Emily then shied away, meeting Sean's instead.

Purposeful, was what he wanted to say. Potentially violent. Yes, Sean could think of a lot of ways to end that sentence, and he didn't like any of them.

Taking advantage of an open window and sneaking in to see what could easily be grabbed... That made sense. But breaking through Emily's bedroom door to go after her once she'd already screamed and probably awakened neighbors made no sense at all. If rape had been this guy's goal, once he'd screwed up and made a racket, he should have fled.

"Ma'am, is there someplace you can spend the rest of the night?" Officer Slawinski asked.

She had somehow summoned a polite smile. "Don't worry about it. I won't sleep anyway."

"I have a spare bedroom," Sean said abruptly. "Ms. Drake is coming home with me."

She kept her mouth shut until the uniform was gone, then faced Sean, her expression cool and closed. "Thank you for your offer, but I'll be fine."

"Then I'll stay here." Did she really think he'd leave her alone? Unprotected? Not happening. He sat down on the rocking chair, planting his feet solidly on the floor. "Go to bed, Emily. Nobody will break in on my watch."

Recognizing that she was cornered, she glowered.

Finally, she let out a huff. "You know perfectly well there's no way I can go to bed and leave you sitting out here on a hard chair. You win. I'll go home with you. It's only for a couple of hours anyway."

He smiled. "You need anything?"

She shot him a glare. "My phone. My purse." While she fetched them from the kitchen, he closed and locked her bedroom window and turned out lights. He returned to the living room to see her crossing to the still open window. "I'll do that if you bring me a dishtowel. We don't want to add fingerprints."

She gave a jerky nod and produced a plain muslin cloth. He wrenched down the stubborn window sash and locked, leaving the blind up in the unlikely hope the intruder had touched the plastic doohickey at the end of the pull cord with a bare hand.

She locked her front door, and Sean once again placed a reassuring hand on her back, disturbed to remember all the fantasies he'd had about bringing Emily Drake home with him. In none of them had she come only because it wasn't safe for her to stay in her own house.

*****

Emily opened her eyes, confused because the room was too bright. And...the window was off to her right, not her left. Alarm quickened her pulse before she remembered.

She had gone to bed in Sean Holbeck's spare bedroom after repeatedly insisting she wouldn't sleep anyway. She'd thought if he went back to bed she could curl up on his sofa and watch TV with the volume low. But he had somehow escorted her all the way into this bedroom and persuaded her that it wouldn't hurt to lie down and try to rest.

"You can't survive with no sleep at all, Emily," he'd said in a low, husky voice that was also somehow...tender.

She frowned. She didn't remember ever using that word in reference to a man before, not even the husband whom she'd loved with everything she was and who had loved her as deeply. And how strange to associate it with a man who was also so obviously capable of violence. She closed her eyes and had a flash of him flinging himself in her bedroom window. Somehow then she had hardly noticed he was barefoot and shirtless, but in retrospect, it was different. The play of muscles on his broad back had been beautiful. Now she was faintly appalled that the big, black handgun had seemed a natural extension of his hand, but then...her relief had been huge. After she scrambled behind a rhododendron, her knees had given out and she'd made herself small, waiting.

But once he'd coerced her into coming home with him... *I slept, because he made me feel safe*, she realized. But...for how long? There was no clock and no bedside table in the bare bones room.

She eased out of bed, pulled the sweatshirt over her head and stuck her feet in her slippers. She felt surprisingly good, she realized, disconcerted. Suddenly shy, she opened the bedroom door and went down the hall to the kitchen.

Fully dressed but wearing neither badge nor weapon, Sean sat at the small kitchen table with a laptop open in front of him. He looked up with a smile. "Morning, sunshine."

Her mouth fell open at the sight of the clock on the microwave. "It can't be after eleven."

"Accurate to the minute." He sounded obnoxiously cheerful and pleased with himself. "You needed the sleep."

She sank onto the only other chair. "But..."

"But what?"

"I slept for six hours."

"Closer to six and a half."

"I haven't done that in years." And why was she telling him anything that personal? She didn't know.

He stared. "Seriously?"

"I usually sleep a couple hours at a time." If she was lucky.

Even without looking at him, she saw him shaking his head. He pushed back from the table. "Breakfast or lunch?"

"You don't have to—"

"Indulge me," he said, with no give.

"I thought I'd go home and shower."

"I took the liberty of grabbing a change of clothes for you while I was over there meeting the fingerprint tech."

Which presumably meant he'd helped himself to her keys. Her mind took a sideways jump. "You went through my drawers?"

"Sorry," he said, not sounding sorry at all.

She felt her lower lip poke out as if she were a sulky child. "Why can't I just go home?"

Suddenly, he was all cop, his expression implacable. "Because we need to talk first."

Her heart skipped a beat. "You found something?"

"No, Emily. Nothing like that." There he went, gentle again, even though this morning she was very aware of his size and masculinity. "Why don't you just take that shower and then have a bite to eat?"

She had two choices: do as he wanted, or stomp defiantly out his door and go home. She couldn't forget he'd charged to her rescue last night without any hesitation. And...she'd slept so well in his house, she felt as if she had champagne in her veins. It was the oddest sensation.

"Fine," she said, still sulkily, her eye lighting on the neat pile of familiar clothes that sat on the counter. She stood, snatched them up, and went back down the hall without looking again at him.

Many of the houses in this part of town had been company-built for workers back in the logging days. The additions of second stories, attached garages, broader porches and architectural embellishments made it hard to tell now which houses had begun life as basic wooden boxes. Sean's had been altered little, in contrast to hers; somewhere along the way, a homeowner had added gingerbread trim to the eaves of her house and widened the porch enough to allow for a swing that hung from the rafters. Sitting in it, setting it to swinging, was her way to time travel. Memories were so bound to objects and places, and she didn't want to lose any.

The last update in the hall bathroom here in Sean's house had to have been done in the late sixties or early seventies by someone with no appreciation for the age of the house. Would he remodel? She turned on the shower in the bathtub and waited for hot water, then stayed under it longer than she'd intended. A fresh bar of soap and a full bottle of shampoo might have been set out just for her.

Sean had been busy that morning.

Tucked among her clothes, she'd found her hairbrush, toothpaste and toothbrush and an elastic band for her hair. His thoughtfulness gave her a funny, soft feeling in her midsection. As she braided her still wet hair, Emily studied herself in the mirror in perplexity. Something about her face seemed different today.

She'd slept, she finally decided, what else could it be? She was used to seeing the strain of exhaustion. Nothing else had changed, except that her home had been violated. She made a face at her own image. Oh, yes, one other thing: she'd learned that, while death was inevitable, she didn't want her own to be violent.

Sean had decided on breakfast, she found upon returning to the kitchen. Omelets smelled fantastic, and he was buttering thick slabs of whole grain toast to go with them. When he saw her, his smile crinkled the skin beside those very blue eyes. "Perfect timing." He nodded toward a carafe. "Pour yourself some coffee, or there's orange juice in the fridge."

She went with both, pouring him some juice, too, when he asked.

Her lingering shyness fled the moment she put the first bite in her mouth. The omelet was filled with chunks of bacon, a variety of vegetables and cheese. He offered homemade blackberry jam she recognized; she, too, bought her jam from Selena Pratt, who had a table at the farmers' market regularly held at the river pier where fishing boats tied up. Jed Fitzpatrick ran a whale and sealife cruise that left from the pier, too, from April through October. When she and Tom first moved to Cape Trouble, she'd sold small quilted pieces at those markets herself until she was able to open the store. She'd loved chatting with her fellow craftspeople and the tourists and local residents that browsed her offerings.

Emily didn't let herself think about what Sean wanted to discuss until she had cleared her entire plate. Then she took a sip of coffee, sighed and said, "Thank you. That was wonderful."

He smiled. "You're welcome." He'd eaten every bite, too, even though this might have been his second breakfast. He'd likely been up for hours. And…that big body must burn a whole lot more calories than hers did.

He watched her as she took another swallow of coffee, then set down her mug.

Bracing herself, she said, "Okay. I've been obedient. So what is it I need to hear?"

The intensity in the eyes that drilled into her had a different cause than she'd seen before, but made her just as uneasy.

"What happened last night doesn't make sense," he said bluntly. "Most burglaries happen when the homes are empty. People are at work or on vacation. That said, if someone was casing our neighborhood, your open window might have been a temptation." He held up a hand as if he read her mind. "This is a safe town, relatively speaking. You should be able to leave windows open at night. In fact, my bedroom window was open, too. I like my room cold when I sleep."

She nodded, grateful that he didn't seem to think she'd been asking for someone to break in.

"But let's assume the intruder thought sleeping residents wouldn't notice if he hopped in that window."

She didn't want to understand where he was going with this, but did. Her fear last night had been a kind of horror. When she saw that doorknob turn, she felt the presence on the other side of the door as malevolent. Evil. Melodramatic, but she couldn't think of another word as fitting.

Relentless in the way of a freight train bearing down on her, Sean continued. "A burglar would have turned on a flashlight, started looking for goodies. No high-end DVD player? He'd have looked for an iPod, the latest smart phone. Gone through your purse. It was in plain sight on the counter. If he knew a woman lived there alone, he might have gotten ballsy and opened the door to a spare bedroom to check for a laptop, a rare coin collection, who knows." He leaned forward. "But all of that is irrelevant, because the minute he picked himself up after tripping over the ironing board, he'd have been back out that window and running for all he was worth." Muscles clenched in his jaw. "There's no way in hell, *knowing you had to be awake*, he'd have gone down your hall, straight to your bedroom. Unless his real goal was *you*."

# CHAPTER FOUR

She couldn't look away from Sean now that he'd laid bare the frightening truth.

There had been nothing even remotely rational about the behavior of the man who'd broken into her house last night.

No, that wasn't what Sean was trying to tell her; the truth is, the intruder did have a rationale, only it was far more frightening than she'd wanted to believe.

Evil, whispered that voice in her head.

Nausea swept over her. She hadn't wanted to believe she was the target even if, deep down inside, she knew. "I suppose I thought..." Her throat was so tight, this was hard to say. "That he might have seen me and..."

Rage mixed with the sympathy in Sean's eyes. "Had rape on his mind?"

Her head bobbed.

"When I searched your house, the doors were closed to the two spare bedrooms. Had you left them that way?"

She nodded again.

"Do you think you'd have heard him opening those doors?"

Emily closed her eyes. "Yes," she whispered. She had been listening so hard, she hadn't even breathed. She would have heard a pin drop.

"That means he knew which bedroom was yours."

"How?" If she sounded pitiful, she couldn't help it.

"He was watching," Sean said flatly. "He'd have seen which light you turned off last when you went to bed."

So easy. Oh, God. On top of everything else, it made her skin crawl to think that, while she had hand-quilted long enough to buy herself an hour of precious peace, he had been out there watching. And...what if it hadn't been for just the one night? He could have been waiting for her to leave a window open.

The worry on Sean's face ratcheted up her fear. "Emily, a would-be rapist should have taken off, too. You might have called the cops. A lot of women living alone keep a gun handy. Even if he got as far as trying to open the bedroom door, his nerve should have broken when you screamed. He'd lost any chance to subdue you, keep you quiet."

She didn't say anything, just sat staring at him. The champagne in her veins had gone flat. Fear had flattened her sense of well-being.

"Emily." His stare compelled her. "Do you possess anything at all that is either rare enough or valuable enough to make someone so reckless?"

"Nothing," she cried. "I swear. I have some diamond earrings, but they aren't worth over a thousand dollars. And my engagement ring...I mean, it's nice, and I'd hate to lose it, but it wasn't that expensive, either."

His face changed. "Are you a widow?"

She turned her face away. "Yes."

"Your husband wasn't a spy, or doing some kind of research others would do anything to get their hands on, or..." He apparently ran out of ideas.

"No. No, of course not! Tom was a pediatrician. A completely nice man. He didn't even make the kind of money he would have as a doctor practicing in a metropolitan area. But he'd grown up here, wanted to come home. I didn't care about money, either."

Sean nodded, although she assumed he was only acknowledging the information.

They both sat unmoving for a long time. Not wanting to meet his eyes, Emily kept her gaze on his muscular chest, covered by a gray T-shirt. The silence grew until it made the air thick, hard to breathe. Goosebumps prickled. She slid each hand up the opposite sleeve of her sweatshirt and rubbed her arms.

Finally she had to say it. "You think he intended to kill me."

The creases on his forehead reminded her of his expression the morning after that awful murder. "I think," he said slowly, "that if you hadn't made it out the window, and I hadn't showed up when I did, he'd have either killed or abducted you. What I can't figure out is why."

She shook her head, and rubbed even harder. "There's no reason," she said desperately. "I'm nobody special."

Something shifted in his eyes. "You're beautiful."

"I'm not—" At his expression, Emily gave up her argument. She no longer thought of herself in those terms. Really, even as a woman. When pain didn't tear at her, she was otherwise empty inside. Her only satisfaction – she couldn't call it pleasure, far less joy – came from her creativity, from completing quilts that would endure, perhaps giving other people the happiness she'd lost.

She tried again. "If he wasn't going to rape me, what difference does it make what I look like?"

"If he planned an abduction, rape might still have been his goal," Sean said grimly.

Her fingernails bit into her forearms. "Thank you for the thought."

With shocking suddenness, Sean leaned forward, anger crackling on his face, his teeth bared. "Do you think I like saying any of this?"

Breathing shallowly, she gave her head a tiny shake.

"You need to take this seriously. You need to be scared until we can figure out what this was all about and catch the son of a bitch. Do you understand me?"

"What do you suggest I do?"

"Have a home security system installed."

After last night, she didn't even hesitate. "I'll do that."

"Until it's installed, I want you to stay here at night."

Her first instinct was to rebel. Once an extrovert, she had crawled so deep inside herself after Tom and Cody were killed, she had trouble forcing herself to interact with other people at all. But the terror was fresh in her mind, and she knew she wouldn't sleep at all alone in her house.

"I have…" She hesitated to say *friends*. Once upon a time she'd had friends. Now she had…acquaintances. Associates. "There are other people I can stay with." She made herself look directly at him. "You hardly know me."

How odd, it occurred to her, that she hadn't said, I hardly know you. But she hadn't because…she did know him enough to trust him.

"Are any of these other people armed?"

Oh, God. "No. Probably not."

"He could follow you."

She felt herself hunch, and she began again to rub her forearms. What was this, like ritual handwashing?

Sean swore. "I'm sorry, Emily. I may be overreacting, but…"

She shook her head. "No, you're just not letting me hide my head in the sand." She tried to smile. "And, unlike dust, we do have sand."

His chuckle was probably as forced as her smile, but he was trying.

"Do we have a plan?"

She took a deep breath, let it out, then nodded. "Yes."

\*\*\*\*\*

After meeting with Daniel, in his role as the Cape Trouble police chief, to discuss the night's events, Sean spent his afternoon trying to hunt down a recently released convict named Barry Rollins. Sean had found a message left on his phone by Sandra Graafstra, Frank's law partner, saying that a client of Frank's had been released from the state correctional institute in Salem something like a month ago. She remembered Frank seeming alarmed.

"Frank considered the result of the trial to be a win because this Rollins was convicted only of second degree murder instead of first, but he was enraged that he didn't get off entirely. This was a long time ago, of course, but I thought you ought to know."

Glad this wasn't a Saturday or Sunday when he might have been frustrated in his inquiries, Sean checked to find that indeed Rollins had been paroled to live with his sister in Beaverton, a suburb of Portland. He reached the sister who, sounding very constrained, said her brother now had his own place. She didn't have the address. Pretty clearly, she didn't want to know where he was living. Apparently, taking in her ex-con brother hadn't gone well.

The parole officer did have an address, but when Sean asked the Portland P.D. to send someone out to contact him, he wasn't there and none of the neighbors in the complex even knew who lived in that particular apartment. To be paroled, Rollins had needed proof

he had a job lined up, but the roofer who had hired him told Sean
that with so much rain these last couple weeks, he'd had to idle some
of his crews. He felt bad because he hadn't had much work for
Rollins, but that's the way it was.

Sean had just hung up when Wilcynski stopped by his desk to
ask for an update.

"Nothing useful." Sean told him what he'd learned. "I haven't
found any evidence this guy is actually here on the coast, but…" He
spread his hands.

The lieutenant half sat on the next desk, currently unoccupied,
his dark eyes keen on his face. "You took the morning off."

Sean told him why. He didn't admit that since coming in he'd
had trouble keeping his focus on the job he was being paid to do. He
kept reliving Emily's piercing scream and his frantic race to get to
her in time. Kept seeing her face when they talked this morning as
he forced her to accept how much danger she had been in.

"It's freakin' nuts," he said in frustration. "This guy didn't take
off until she'd gotten out of the house and he heard my voice. Then,
I think he had to have waited until I went in her bedroom window to
go out the living room window." Every time he pictured it, he
shuddered. Certain the intruder had already fled, he had left Emily
alone in the backyard and vulnerable to being grabbed. If he hadn't
told her to hide… If she'd been too paralyzed to do as he asked…

Sean imagined how he'd have felt if he had returned to find her
gone. Bile rose in his throat. After failing Matt, he'd been able to
go on only by dedicating his life to protecting other people. And this
was Emily.

"You didn't hear a car," his lieutenant said thoughtfully.

"I was inside her place, but I was listening. Cape Trouble is
pretty quiet at night. If it was parked close by, I should have
noticed."

"He could have been on foot."

"Maybe a bike." Sean hadn't liked what he had been thinking.
"Easy to leave where it wouldn't be seen, and once on it he could
move fast."

Either possibility meant abduction had never been part of the
plan. And that understanding squeezed his heart in an icy grip.

He'd much rather believe the guy had had a vehicle in a driveway nearby, and had only hunkered down until no one would notice a car driving away. Also a good possibility.

Wilcynski grunted. "You're thinking he lives in town."

"Not necessarily. He could have had a vehicle up by the highway. There's some traffic up there at all hours." Because of Highway 101, there was an all-night restaurant and a couple of gas stations that kept their pumps open. "With a pickup or SUV, he could toss the bike in the back and be gone."

"But you think he'll be back."

He was so tense, pain was creeping up his neck. "I don't want to think so. But this asshole was determined beyond common sense, which means we have to take precautions."

A dark eyebrow rose. "It's not our jurisdiction."

"You know we've been working major cases with Chief Colburn." Sheriff Mackay's hope was for the cooperation to become routine and county-wide. He'd hit a stumbling block, however. North Fork, the county seat, was the only other city besides Cape Trouble with its own police department. Unfortunately, the North Fork police chief, an old-timer named Howard Lundy, wasn't about to tolerate any infringement on his authority. By God, his department didn't need any help.

After a minute, during which the lieutenant crossed his arms and said nothing, Sean said, "Ms. Drake is my next-door neighbor."

He did his damnedest to keep his expression impassive. If he got an ass-chewing and a lecture on priorities, he wasn't sure he could keep his mouth shut.

But the other man only nodded. "I understand. If you need support, let me know."

Blown away, Sean was left gaping after him. Had he just been given permission to split his time as he thought appropriate?

Yeah, he thought he had.

That being so, he was going home. Tomorrow, he'd set the eager-beaver Jason Payne to trying to locate Barry Rollins. Payne might as well learn the patience it took and how many tedious details had to be sifted to pursue an investigation when the killer's identity was a genuine mystery. Sean would be doing him a good turn while freeing himself up to chase down other leads…and to try to figure out who had targeted a woman who tried so hard not to draw anybody's attention at all.

*****

Guilt and gratitude had compelled Emily to do something she hadn't in four long years: cook dinner for someone else.

She had already been far more aware of her new neighbor's comings and goings than she'd wanted to be. Until this week, she'd convinced herself she had noticed only because he didn't have the same kind of routine everyone else on the block did. Naturally she'd pay attention when she heard his car at strange hours.

Since she had no idea when Sean would be home, she put on a goulash to cook in her crock pot. She suspected he wouldn't be late. Sean hadn't liked leaving her alone.

Earlier, she'd gone online to find companies that installed home security systems. It turned out there were none in Burris County. The closest was in Cannon Beach, with another in Nehalem. A representative from the Cannon Beach company had promised to come tomorrow morning to take a look at her house, make suggestions and sell her on a system. Emily hoped Sean could stay home long enough to talk to him. He would have a better idea what she needed than she did.

She found herself clock-watching, trying to deny her tension. Not long after Sean left, she had begun to wonder what would keep last night's intruder from returning in the daytime. Many of her neighbors would be at work. Would it be so impossible for someone to slip into her house unseen, even in daylight?

At least every half hour, she'd made the rounds to confirm to herself that every door and window really was locked. The house felt stuffy. She resented not being able to open a window. What would happen when summer came? Fear would turn her into a shut-in.

*Aren't you already one?* murmured her inner critic, but right now, she didn't want to listen.

She froze at hearing every noise on the street or in surrounding yards until she identified it. She accomplished almost nothing.

At barely five o'clock, she heard Sean's SUV turn into his driveway. Not two minutes later, her doorbell rang.

As she went to let him in, Emily's intense gratitude was mixed with more resentment, because she didn't want to need him. She felt apprehension, too, and a host of emotions she couldn't even identify. She so rarely felt anything for anybody. Pain did that. It had made her self-centered, in a way. Until now, she hadn't thought of it that way, and she wished she hadn't.

When she let him in, she said, "I didn't expect you so early."

His blue eyes took in her face, making her wonder if he could read her thoughts, see the unavoidable strain.

"I hit a roadblock and decided to hang it up for the day." He shrugged. "I was going to ask you out to dinner, but I smell something good."

"Hungarian goulash. I made plenty if you'd like to stay."

His grin surprised her. His face was craggy enough to seem harsh when he was in cop mode. Right now, she had a sudden picture of him as a little boy, probably dirty, adventurous, stubborn. The center of a gang of boys. Of course, his hair would always have been sticking up no matter how his mother tried to tame it.

"I was hinting at an invitation," he admitted. "I think my nose is quivering like a rabbit's."

Not liking how breathless that smile had made her, Emily couldn't help returning it. "Let me put on the noodles, then. I have asparagus," she added as she led the way to the kitchen. "Or we can just have a salad, or both."

"Both, if it's not too much trouble. I don't eat enough greens. My mother lectures me on a regular basis."

As she put water on to boil and took the vegetables from the refrigerator, she asked about his family, although the minute she did she knew she'd made a mistake. He'd want to know about hers.

Some flash of emotion in his eyes made her think the question might have been a mistake in another way, too, but the next second whatever she'd seen was gone.

"I grew up in Cannon Beach," he said. "My parents are still there. Hey, I can do the salad if you want."

He wouldn't be able to watch her with that thoughtful gaze if he had to concentrate on dicing carrots and bell peppers, so she put him to work. It felt so strange, having a man in the kitchen again. And this one filled the space in a way her lanky husband hadn't. The effect wasn't all physical, either, she realized; Sean's intensity charged the air, as if a lightning storm threatened.

"I had a brother who died," he said, making understandable his reluctance. "That's...tough to get past." He reached for the peeler. "Then there is my bossy older sister, who is married and lives in Portland. Thanks to her, I have two nieces and a brother-in-law who makes more in a year than I will in ten."

Emily set the box of rotini on the counter and looked at him. "You don't like him."

"I shouldn't have said that." He was obviously chagrined. "I don't know why I did. He's okay. Just..."

When he didn't finish the thought, Emily said, "Does he look down on you?" The idea fired a temper she'd almost forgotten she had. Would the smug brother-in-law have raced to the rescue of a neighbor he didn't even know well?

Sean laughed. "You can dial it back. The truth is, I don't know. We get along okay. I make myself play a round of golf with him once in a while. We'll never be best friends. It's possible the disdain is all in my head."

She found herself curious, in a way she hadn't been about anyone in a long time. "What do your parents do?"

"My dad is a physician, like your husband. Family doctor, not a specialist. Mom was a nurse, although she quit work when my sister was born. When I was a teenager, she went back part-time."

His casual mention of her husband surprised her. Out of misplaced sensitivity to her pain, or their own discomfort, people usually shied away from saying anything about Tom or Cody. Perhaps it was having lost his brother that made Sean different.

"Your sister?" she asked, as if he hadn't said anything surprising.

"Planned to go to law school but ditched it when she met Michael."

So far he'd talked with seeming willingness, so why not ask?

"How did you end up a cop?"

"I wasn't interested in medicine, I knew that. And I was never the student my sister was. When a subject interested me, I aced it.

When it didn't, my attention drifted," he said ruefully. "The cop part... I guess I can blame it on a couple of things that happened when I was growing up." He glanced at her. "You know about the bodies we found last summer at the old resort across the river."

"Yes." She shivered. "How horrible. You were involved in that investigation?"

"I was. The thing is, I remembered when those women disappeared. One had lived in Cannon Beach. I was just a kid, but my parents were freaked because my sister was a teenager. She was blonde and blue-eyed like those women, too. She sulked because they restricted her activities, but, me, I started devouring the news about it." He scraped diced cucumber into the salad bowl. "I was really bothered when the whole furor dwindled into nothingness. Those women were just *gone*, and nobody knew why. There were no arrests. Eventually, it seemed as if everyone forgot."

"And you ended up helping make that arrest."

"I was support, that's all. Daniel Colburn was instrumental in bringing that scum down. He and Sophie, his fiancé. Do you know her?"

"Yes, I donated some pieces to the auction to save Misty Beach. I like her."

Sean watched as she dumped noodles into the now boiling water. "Then there was my brother." His voice had changed. Become terse. "He was murdered."

She whirled to face him. "Oh, Sean."

"It wasn't a great mystery. He'd started going with a girl whose previous boyfriend didn't want to let her go." His throat worked. "He caught Matt alone—"

At the hitch in his voice, she whispered, "I'm so sorry. Were you close?"

"Yes, maybe because we were only eighteen months apart. He was older, a senior when he was killed. The guy was arrested." Sean's mouth twisted. "He was an adult, so he got some time, but he's long since out of the pen and moving on with his life. Unlike Matt."

No wonder Sean had gone into law enforcement.

This part of his past, however briefly told, had changed her perception of him. The grief he still felt so powerfully might be part of why she had been so drawn to him from the beginning.

"Anything else I can do?" he asked, and she realized he didn't want to talk about it anymore. The door he'd cracked open wasn't the kind to be left standing open.

"Salad dressings are on a shelf on the door in the refrigerator. I'd like the balsamic. Will you grab it and whatever you want?"

He carried the salad and dressings to the table in the nook looking out at her backyard.

Still thinking about his story, she slid the pan of asparagus under the broiler in the oven. She hesitated, but finally decided to ask her question. "Do you know what happened to your brother's girlfriend?"

Sean shook his head. "I've wondered. She was devastated. Completely blamed herself. But she didn't come back to school and didn't stay in touch."

Emily identified better with that girl than he would ever understand. Rationally, she knew nothing about the accident had been her fault, but Tom had wanted her to go with them that weekend and she'd refused. She was too busy with the store, she always felt as if his mother didn't like her, and then there was the question of whether they would take Braden or leave him, but with whom? Her mother-in-law wouldn't have approved of them having taken a teenager into the house with her precious grandson. "He'll be trouble," she would have announced, in her all-knowing way. Tom had intended to tell her about Braden that weekend, but Emily had no idea whether he actually had.

What she did know was that if she'd gone, everything would have been different. They might have left for home sooner, or later. They wouldn't have been where they were at the exact wrong time. And if they had been...she would have died, too. For a long time, she wished she had.

She still felt guilty about Braden, too, so she fell back on the only possible solution. She wouldn't think about him.

There was nothing she could do to change the past.

"You look sad," Sean said, and she saw that he was watching her again.

"It was a sad story."

His expression told her he knew there was more to it than that, but he didn't push her. In fact, for a very pushy man, he had a gift for knowing when to back off. Perhaps because he had his own closed doors.

"How about you?" he asked. "How did you learn to quilt?"

This was an easy answer. "My grandmother. This is my mother's parents. They have a farm near Corvallis, and a lifestyle that probably hasn't changed much from that of Nanna's parents, who had the farm before them. Most women of her generation didn't quilt even if their mothers had, you know. It was a dying art. Mom never had the least interest, but I was captivated watching Nanna piece and hand-quilt. I learned so young, it's as natural to me as breathing."

"Are they still alive?"

"Yes. I...visit." But not as often as she should, she was guiltily aware. They knew her too well, and worried so much about her. She had to pretend with them.

The kindness on Sean's face made her suspect that again he'd known what she was thinking. "Is that where you grew up? Corvallis?"

"No, Mom fled to the big city. Seattle, actually. I went to the University of Washington, and met my husband when he was in medical school there." There. The explanation was out of the way. Casual.

"What do your parents do?"

"Dad's a businessman, Mom an interior designer. We're not close." They had been more so until the tragedy. Mom couldn't understand why Emily wouldn't just get over it, remarry, start another family.

Forget the family she'd had.

The thought struck a chord in her as she remembered Sean talking about the women who had gone missing all those years ago. He had sounded outraged because people let themselves forget so easily. He might understand, she thought, but the next second wasn't sure why she thought his understanding mattered.

"Do you still see your husband's family?"

His question felt like a blow. "No. No."

He didn't ask, but the speculation in his eyes drove her finally to say, "His mother never liked me. She dismissed me as 'artsy.' She blamed me for Tom not being as ambitious as she wanted him to be. She'd hated Cape Trouble when they lived here, and couldn't understand why he'd choose to bury himself in a small town in the middle of nowhere. She liked to see Tom and—" Aghast, Emily couldn't believe she had let herself ramble like that.

But it was too late. His expression had changed, faint shock becoming the pity she had feared. "And?"

If he hadn't asked so very gently, she would have retreated with a shake of her head, but as it was she whispered, "Cody. We had a son."

"They died together."

She looked down at her half-finished dinner and knew she wouldn't be eating another bite. "Yes."

"How old was he?"

"Two." Her throat felt tight. All she could see was her son's face. Drowsy brown eyes, his thumb still often tucked in his mouth despite their best efforts. If she closed her own eyes, she would be able to hear his giggle. "Only two," she said, so quietly she wasn't sure the man across the table would hear.

"Will you tell me what happened, Emily?"

A flush of anger let the words come. "They were on their way home from Portland. There was a police pursuit. An officer tried to pull over a pickup. It sped away, and he went screaming after instead of letting it go. The state patrol joined in. I'm told…" She faltered. "The pickup was going over ninety miles an hour when it hit our Civic. Tom and Cody were killed instantly. The driver died on the way to the hospital." Hate filled her. Her eyes burned. "Unfortunately, the deputy who chose to endanger everyone on the road didn't die. He wasn't even fired." What she'd eaten felt like battery acid in her stomach. "The man they were chasing wasn't a suspected murderer or rapist. His license was suspended because of DUIs. He wasn't supposed to be driving. That's all. If they'd let him go…"

Sean half stood, as if he meant to come to her, then sank back down on his chair. "Oh, damn, Emily. I'm sorry. So sorry."

Her hostility nearly choked her as she stared an accusation at him. "I suppose *you* think the police weren't to blame."

# CHAPTER FIVE

With Emily glaring at him, all Sean was able to think was, *Oh, hell.* Her wounds went so much deeper than he'd guessed. Losing a husband was hard, but he knew what losing a child had done to his parents. In Emily's case, both had been ripped from her in a moment, leaving her utterly alone.

He'd known how resistant she was to getting involved with him on any level, but hadn't guessed that he bore a particular handicap. In her mind, a cop was responsible for her husband's and son's deaths. Sean was a cop, and therefore, on a cosmic level, also guilty. He doubted she wanted to hear the truth from him, but he also didn't want to be dishonest.

"I don't know the exact circumstances," he said carefully, and saw her lip curl. Okay, that sounded mealy-mouthed. "Here's my perspective, as a police officer. If the entire chase happened because an officer tried to pull him over, then no. The high speed pursuit wasn't justified." He paused, watching the shift of emotions on her face. "But is there any chance he caught that officer's eye in the first place because he was already exceeding the speed limit? Perhaps dangerously so? If that's the case, sticking with him, summoning other officers in to maneuver him to a stop, might have been the right call."

"They claimed he was speeding," she said furiously, "but they would, wouldn't they?"

Sean wished he could deny that law enforcement officers ever lied, but that would be a lie. Of course they did. They were human beings. Seeing your career about to go down the toilet, the temptation was great. "Why are you so sure it was a lie?" he asked, trying to come across as neutral.

Her glare didn't soften. "Why are you so sure it wasn't?"

"I'm not," he said bluntly. "Cops screw up, like anyone else. Situations escalate. You get caught up in the moment, quit thinking about consequences. I can't deny it happens. But you need to remember that a guy who'd been stripped of his license got behind the wheel anyway. *He* was the one who chose to flee instead of maybe getting thirty days in jail. *He* killed your family. Hate *him*, Emily."

Sean remembered hearing about that particular chase and it's horrific ending. He'd long since forgotten the names of the people who died. He did recall that a small child had been among them. What he didn't know was how the chase had begun. He couldn't answer the question Emily had been asking herself since police came to her door to tell her that her husband and son were dead. Even if he were to ask around and find her an answer, what would that change?

High-speed pursuits looked exciting in movies and on TV cop shows, but they were actually pretty controversial. Sticking to the tail of someone trying to get away was one thing, but when speeds climbed like that, the smart thing to do was back off. Let the driver think he'd gotten away. Radio cops down the road to watch for him. There was rarely a justification for risking the lives of other people on the road. The Boston bombers…maybe. A guy driving with a suspended license and a history of drunk driving? No way. The one thing his record had told them was that he wasn't safe behind the wheel of a car, far less handling that vehicle at high speeds.

Emily held that burning stare long enough to singe Sean's skin. Finally, she shoved back her chair and rose, picking up her dishes and silverware. He'd swear she looked betrayed along with furious. "I have plenty of hate to go around," she said with a coolness belied by the turbulence in her eyes. Then she carried the dishes to the sink.

Sitting in front of his unfinished dinner, Sean was both frustrated and ashamed. He'd let her down. Had he automatically leaped to the defense of a police officer he didn't even know, out of some kind of fellow feeling?

He couldn't be sure.

"Emily."

She shook her head hard. Her braid flopped from shoulder blade to shoulder blade. "I don't want to talk about it anymore. I don't know why I did."

"Thank you for telling me," he said quietly.

That was it for conversation. His own appetite gone MIA, he helped her clear the table and clean the kitchen. Her face remained stony. He didn't know how angry she was at him. She might also be covering up grief. Talking about the deaths of the two people she'd loved most probably felt like tearing open a gaping wound.

He was afraid she'd balk at going home with him, but once they were done in the kitchen, he asked if she'd rather they stayed at her house for the evening or go to his.

"Yours," she said shortly. "I can bring work with me."

He waited while she disappeared down the hall. He used the time to study the quilt she had in the huge frame in the living room, awed at the incredibly tiny stitches she somehow made through the thickness of batting and two layers of cotton fabric. Sometimes more, he realized, because the quilting frequently crossed a seam from the piecing that added another layer, yet the stitches remained even in length and spacing. He touched a part she'd already quilted, fascinated by a stiff texture despite the soft materials, then withdrew his hand guiltily when he heard her coming.

She pulled a small rolling suitcase and carried a huge tote bag from which fabric bulged. Seeing his gaze go to it, she said stiffly, "I use a hoop to quilt smaller pieces. That's what this is."

"My mother has a quilt passed down from…I think she said her grandmother, but it might be a great-grandmother," he heard himself tell her, sounding as awkward as he felt. "Mom calls it a flower garden. The stitches aren't quite as small and close together as yours, but almost."

"Grandmother's Flower Garden," Emily said unexpectedly. "That's what the pattern is called."

That's why he'd had 'grandmother' stuck in his mind. "It's worn some, but still pretty," he said, for no good reason.

Ignoring his meaningless conversation, she turned out lights and locked. With them more exposed outside than he liked, Sean kept his body between hers and the street as they covered the short distance to his house. His gaze roved nonstop, probing every shadow. The salty smell of the ocean was sharp in his nostrils, the muted rush of the ocean as familiar as his own heartbeat. He'd missed it when he was away at college and working those first few years inland.

They'd reached his porch when Emily said, "I'm sorry."

Startled, he looked at her. "What for?"

"You got stuck with me."

He thrust his key into his front door lock with unnecessary force. "Don't apologize. You're the one being inconvenienced. If I'd caught the bastard..."

"How could you?"

He only shook his head. He didn't want to increase her nightmares by telling her how vulnerable she'd been when he left her alone in her yard.

Inside his house, he locked. "I forgot to ask. Did you get in touch with anyone about a home security system?"

"Yes." She told him which company she'd selected, and he nodded. "He's coming tomorrow morning at ten." She nibbled on her lower lip, having an unintended effect on him. "I was sort of hoping..."

"I'd be there?"

Her nod was as timid as her apology, rubbing him the wrong way. She must have thought she'd lost everything that meant anything when her husband and son were killed, and now she was finding out that she had more yet to lose – her right to feel safe in her own home. Conceivably even her own life.

"Of course I want to be there," he said. His chest hurt, thinking about this woman having to be afraid on top of everything else.

Whoa, he thought. He needed to watch it. He was getting in deep, and with a woman whose sense of gratitude probably stung given his profession, not to mention her own, desperate need to keep a distance from everyone else.

Maybe not everyone. He couldn't be sure. She might have close friends.

But he knew better. He hadn't seen anyone coming and going from her house. The very fact that she chose to spend her days working alone, that she limited even her time in the store she owned, said it all. And he remembered what she'd said about running on the beach: *I appreciate the solitude.*

"Thank you," she murmured again, after which her eyes widened. He didn't like thinking what she'd seen on his face.

Whatever it was, she offered a hasty excuse and disappeared immediately into the guest bedroom.

He heard the door close, and made her evening even more perfect by knocking on it. When she opened it, her chin high but her eyes already red, he had to say, "I won't intrude, but please leave the door partly open. I won't shut my bedroom door, either. If someone happened to be watching, he'll have seen you coming home with me. My house doesn't have a security system, either. I want to be able to hear if there's any disturbance."

The disquieting memory of that pane of glass so neatly and quietly removed from the Lowe's French doors blurred with the intrusion at Emily's house to make him want to insist she sleep with him. Hell. He could wrap himself in a blanket on the floor. But he knew he was overreacting. If the guy intended to come after her again, he'd wait until he thought he could get her alone, not break into a cop's house. This wasn't Frank Lowe's assassin.

She swallowed, then nodded. Sean retreated.

In the living room, he turned on the TV, but five minutes later stabbed the remote to turn it off. There wasn't anything on he wanted to watch, but more to the point was his fear it would drown out some faint noise he should hear.

A watcher would know what bedroom she was in, because that light never came on in the evening. His attention had been on her house, but if he was observant at all, he'd have taken note of what time neighbors went to bed, whether their rooms faced her house or away from it.

Sean found the book he'd been reading. But as he tried to concentrate, he had to keep flipping back because he didn't remember what was on the previous page.

*****

Sean's eyes snapped open in the gray light of morning. He looked at the time. Barely after six, damn it. Well, he hadn't been sleeping well anyway, and might as well get up.

He brooded for a minute, thinking about his day. Frank Lowe had been murdered Sunday night, five days ago. Making an arrest became less likely with each passing day. Phone calls today, he decided; he'd work over the weekend, but some people would be harder to reach then

He wasn't going anywhere, though, until he'd met with the rep from the home security company at Emily's house.

Since he was decent in the flannel pajama bottoms and T-shirt he wore to bed in the winter, he'd check on her before he took a shower. The moment he stepped into the hall, he saw her hovering in her doorway, her eyes huge in a face even paler than usual.

"I heard something."

"Just me getting up."

"Do you have to go in this early?" She was trying to sound calm, but she had a white-knuckled grip on the doorframe.

He shook his head. "I'm sorry I woke you. I had a restless night."

She relaxed visibly. "Oh."

"You must be freezing. If you're not going to go back to bed, why don't you put on something warmer and join me in the kitchen?"

She nodded, and he gave the thermostat a nudge before taking a quick shower and getting dressed. On his way to the kitchen, he smelled coffee. She'd already started it, bless her.

Rather than a robe, she'd thrown a Portland Trailblazers sweatshirt on over the thin tee she'd worn with pajama pants. He recognized it as the same one she'd put on the other night, then realized something else. It hung below her hips and the sleeves were long enough she had them rolled up several times. He'd be willing to bet it had been her husband's. The knowledge felt like a kick to his gut.

*I'm jealous*, he realized with some incredulity. Stupid. It wasn't as if they had anything going. He might wish they did, but that didn't give him any rights.

He wondered if she wore that shirt frequently, or reached for it this time because she especially needed comfort.

From her dead husband.

Hoping she hadn't read his thoughts, he went to the refrigerator. "It's early, but I'm hungry."

"Me, too," she said. "No wonder, after I ruined dinner for both of us."

He gave himself a minute before turning around. "Emily, we talked about something upsetting to you. You didn't sabotage the meal."

A tiny smile rewarded him. "It was pretty spicy."

Damn, he wanted to touch her. But he only smiled in response. "It was fabulous. I'm hoping there's enough left for dinner tonight."

"Of course there is. And I promise, we can talk about, I don't know, the weather."

His smile faded. "No, Emily. Let's…not censor ourselves."

Her eyes searched his. "Okay," she said at last, softly.

The sting he still felt because she was wearing her husband's shirt faded. She'd heard him and understood. She'd agreed to…he didn't know yet, but something important. Honesty, maybe. A willingness to share, even anger or anguish or accusation.

It felt important.

He nodded. "How about waffles? I make good ones."

"That sounds wonderful if it isn't too much trouble."

She pulled up a bar stool and teased him about his domestic skill as he heated the waffle iron and mixed the batter from scratch. He knew she was faking it, but admired her for making the effort.

He could do as much. "Hey, what's wrong with a man learning to cook?"

This chuckle sounded more genuine. "Absolutely nothing. I just have the impression most don't."

"I'm better at breakfasts than any other meal," he admitted. "Cereal is boring, and during the day I have to grab meals on the fly often enough, I try not to with breakfast."

"That makes sense. I'm ashamed to admit I have cereal almost every morning."

"Then I'm enriching your life," he said with exaggerated gallantry, and loved the sight of this smile, too.

He wondered if she ever wore makeup. She didn't need it, not with those long, thick, dark eyelashes, lips just lush enough to kick-start a man's imagination, and that luminous skin.

He made himself concentrate on getting a couple of plates down from the cupboard. It was lucky she was wearing the damn sweatshirt that swallowed her curves.

They discussed her plans for the day. She had decided to spend most of it at The Sandpiper, which he approved. There were enough tourists in Cape Trouble even at this season, she was unlikely ever to be alone in her store. He offered to drive her. She refused, not wanting to be stuck there if he was held up. He couldn't deny that was always a possibility, but he didn't like the idea of her arriving home alone, either.

Conversation wandered over breakfast, with her talking about favorite local artisans. Her store carried a range of crafts including ceramics, jewelry, stone carving and woodwork, but specialized in textiles. It happened all were from women artists, although she said there were male quilters and weavers. When he raised his eyebrows, she laughed at him.

"Probably not many who are cops."

"If any are, they keep it a deep, dark secret."

When she asked, he told her a little about how he reasoned during a major investigation and crushed the expectations she'd learned from TV shows like NCIS.

"They make it look so damn easy," he grumbled.

Eventually she went off to shower, then sat down in his living room, stretched part of a lap-size quilt in a large wood hoop, threaded the tiniest damn needle he'd ever seen, and bent over her work. One hand disappeared underneath, while she wore a leather thimble on the finger that pushed the needle through. He watched in fascination as she gathered multiple stitches on that miniscule needle before pulling the thread through.

He could see that she hadn't used a traditional pattern to make this quilt top. It was too…not abstract, but definitely modern. Circles of varying sizes formed from half a dozen shades of teal green stood out against a blue backdrop. On the blue…she was quilting ripples.

"Waves," she said, without looking up. "I'll call this 'Japanese Floats'. See, I've quilted netting on some of the floats, and tiny bubbles on others. And a couple of fish, swirling around the floats."

Sean looked more closely. Being only quilted, the fish were mere shadows, as if he was seeing a flick of movement in deep water. "It's beautiful," he said honestly. "Will you sell it?"

"Yes, of course." She tied a knot, took a small stitch then cut the thread. A moment later, she'd re-threaded and started elsewhere.

Figuring his stare would make her uncomfortable, he booted his laptop and pretended to work while sneaking looks at Emily. The day might be overcast, but the warm light from the lamp illuminating her work made her hair shimmer when she moved the smallest amount. Her back stayed straight, but the bow of her neck and the way she held her arms made him think of the graceful pose of a ballerina.

He wanted to toss the quilt and hoop aside, sweep her up into his arms and carry her down the hall to his bedroom.

Not happening.

It was an enormous relief when he was able to say, "We should probably get over to your house."

\*\*\*\*\*

Daniel Colburn sat with his chair tipped back and his feet stacked on his desk. He'd printed off the resumes of the half dozen candidates for police officer he'd received in response to his listings on law enforcement websites, Craig's List - yes, he was desperate - and the Portland Oregonian newspaper. He was paging through the very short stack yet again when his receptionist slash dispatcher, Ellie Fitzpatrick, called from the front desk. "Chief, Mrs. Grove is on line one for you."

"Thanks," he called back, and swung his feet to the floor. He dropped the resumes to his desktop with a sense of relief. Repetition wasn't making any of them look any more promising.

On the down side, Linda Grove was the principal of the high school, so a phone call from her most often meant he or one of his officers were being summoned to arrest a juvenile delinquent masquerading as a student.

"Linda," he said. "Daniel here."

She didn't beat around the bush. "You're allowed to break into someone's house if you have reason to be concerned for their health, right?"

"Sure, we sometimes do that kind of check for a concerned family member. What's up?"

"Our biology teacher didn't show for class this morning. Darryl didn't call in sick, either, which isn't like him. I sent Terry Geller over to his house. She rang the doorbell and even walked around back to look in his sliding glass door, but got no response. He probably thought he'd requested a personal day for some reason and is off doing who knows what, but I'm concerned. He lives alone, so if he's really sick or injured himself too severely to call for help, there's no one to find him."

"Could she tell if his car was there?"

"A shade covered the only window into the garage."

His inner alarms jangled, but he kept his voice casual. "Okay, I'll run over there myself. What's his last name?"

"Roff."

"I don't know that I've met him. Is he of an age where a heart attack or stroke are at all likely?"

"I wouldn't have thought so." She sounded doubtful and also stressed. "He's...let me think. Early forties? I'd have to look up his personnel info to tell you for sure."

"No need yet." While talking to her, he'd looked up Roff's address. "I'll call you when I know more. Did you find a sub to fill in okay?"

"No," she groused, "or I might have let this go until tomorrow. I'm having to turn his classes into study periods today, and diverting other staff to supervise them."

"I'd be a little peeved if I were you, too," he admitted. In fact, he was already peeved after one of his pitifully few officers had quit without giving notice, leaving him so short-handed he was pulling double shifts himself when he could be in bed with Sophie.

After getting Linda off the phone, he told Ellie where he was going and went out to the patrol car he reserved for himself.

Roff's house turned out to be a small rambler that probably dated to the 1960s or 70s. Cape Trouble had had a modest economic boom around then and some developments had sprung up on the east side of the coast highway. As tourism became the principal industry, utilitarian businesses like the dry cleaner and the hardware store had relocated over here, too, leaving downtown to the art galleries and restaurants that catered to tourists. Even farther west was what

Daniel thought of as the industrial sector: a sheet metal business, auto repair and body shops, a sprawling storage facility.

He parked in the driveway and first rang the doorbell and then knocked, just to cover his ass if Roff was annoyed to come home and find a door splintered or some glass broken. Daniel anticipated being able to get in without breaking anything, though; people were rarely as careful as they thought they were about locking, or the locks were so damn flimsy, anyone could pop them.

He walked around the house, starting on the garage side, and saw that the school secretary was right; a roller shade was drawn, blocking any glimpse inside. But when he reached the back of the house, his eyes went right to a window that caught the light wrong. He had a bad feeling he knew what he'd find even before he got close enough to see that a small square of glass had been cut out of the larger sheet.

Glad he hadn't sent one of his baby officers to check on the missing teacher, Daniel hurried back to his patrol car to grab some gloves before he so much as touched a door knob.

*****

Sean stayed in the bathroom doorway so as not to inadvertently screw up the scene. He could see plenty from here. For some reason, Darryl Roff's naked body looked even more obscene than Frank's had. Maybe it was just the angle, with Sean directly behind him. Sometimes he could be entirely clinical, but every so often he had this all-too human urge to grab a blanket and cover the body. He cringed at the idea of a bunch of law enforcement people seeing him like that, nothing hidden.

Ignoring his discomfort, he assessed the scene. No bathtub, so the teacher had been forced to either kneel or get on all fours with his front half in the shower stall. He pictured the killer straddling Roff, a hard grip on his face that silenced him. Had he leaned over to whisper in his ear? Taunted his victim before yanking the head back hard and slicing almost from ear to ear?

And then vanishing, but not before using the blood to write BCD on the fiberglass wall of the shower.

Staring at the dripping letters, Sean had no more idea than ever what that meant. And, Jesus, he hated knowing his stalled investigation into Frank Lowe's murder had left a monster free to kill again.

*My fault.*

No, it wasn't, but he wished he could be sure in his own mind he'd done absolutely every single thing that could be done. If he'd missed a clue, shrugged off a possibility, not pursued a lead however nebulous…

He still couldn't think of anything. Didn't mean he was off the hook. The sense of responsibility he had cursed himself with after letting his brother down was too unrelenting. This was different. If they couldn't figure out what the freaking hell was going on, who knew how many more deaths there would be?

Daniel had officers out canvassing the neighborhood, but Sean knew damn well they wouldn't find a soul who'd seen anything even though here the houses were close together, the yards small. This killer was too smart. Plus, this was the kind of neighborhood where people all held jobs and their kids were in school. Most would be in bed by ten o'clock. A light sleeper might hear a car engine in the middle of the night, but why would he think anything of it?

Sean returned to the small living room to join Daniel Colburn, who was just finishing a call.

"Any significant differences?" he asked.

"Except for the fact the bathroom doesn't have a tub, no. This is act two, but I don't get the plot. Unless he was a client of Frank's at some point, what could a Cape Trouble high school biology teacher have in common with a criminal defense attorney who lived at the other end of the county and practiced in North Fork?"

"You make it sound like Burris County is bigger than it is," Daniel pointed out. "These were two men of a similar age. You never know what they could have in common. Maybe both belonged to some civic organization or, hell, a group of rock hounds."

"It's possible." Although if Frank had any hobbies besides doing the New York Times crossword puzzle and sipping expensive wine, Sean had yet to learn of it. "I'll interview the wife and partner again."

"Pray the victims weren't random choices," Daniel growled.

"Age and gender argues against that." Which wasn't to say the next victim wouldn't be a twenty year old woman.

"Yeah." Daniel's head turned. "Sounds like the crew from CAU are here."

Every local jurisdiction in Oregon could count their blessings at being able to draw on the support of specialists from the Oregon State Police Crime Analyst Unit. Daniel had worked homicide for San Francisco P.D. before taking this job, but if no one in the department had been capable, CAU could have taken over managing the entire investigation. The biggest benefit to small police agencies was the evidence assistance. They couldn't afford CSI units or labs of their own. No matter what, they didn't need them often enough to justify the expense.

*Hadn't needed them,* he thought grimly. Because as of right now, they knew a serial killer was once again working in Burris County and Cape Trouble.

And until they had a clue what linked the two victims, they couldn't even issue warnings. Everyone had to sleep sometime, get up to use the john in the night. People in these parts were used to feeling safe in their own, locked houses.

Emily hadn't been any more than Darryl Roff or Frank Lowe had.

*Focus.*

"Shit," Colburn muttered. "We'll have widespread hysteria if we don't find answers quick."

Sean grunted his agreement. The thought had already crossed his mind. "I need to let my lieutenant know," he said, and Daniel nodded.

"I have to call the school principal back." He grimaced. "She couldn't find a substitute today. I'm not looking forward to telling her she has to find permanent one."

"It would help if she knows who his friends are, whether there's a girlfriend in the picture."

"I have a lot of respect for Linda. I think she'll have a good idea where we can start."

Sean nodded. "If you don't need me, I think I'll see if Lowe's wife is available. We've been concentrating on his practice and clients.  Unless it turns out Roff was a client, we'll need to shift our focus."

"You think the partner will tell you?"

"She implied that if I had one name, she would.  I'll call her first."

Daniel nodded.  "Keep me informed, and I'll do the same."

"Count on it," Sean said, and walked out to his car, his phone already to his ear, tension all but choking him.

His job was to protect.  He hadn't protected Darryl Roff.

# CHAPTER SIX

"There's nothing." Sean's voice was rough with frustration. "I can't find a single connection. I'd swear those two men never met. And why would they have?" He prowled his living room while Emily watched uneasily.

Her 'Japanese Floats' quilt lay loose on her lap. She had been hemming the binding when she asked if he'd made any progress on his investigation. The second murder had happened two – almost three – days ago, and she knew he was worrying now about who else might be killed – and when. Given that there'd only been five days between the first and second murders, Sean must feel as if he could hear a stop watch ticking.

"This is a small county," she said tentatively.

"Have you ever met either of them?"

She'd had a chance to think about this today, and had made a decision. She hadn't ever met Mr. Roff. And…she couldn't tell Sean what little she knew without telling him how she'd learned it. She shouldn't care what he thought of her, but she'd discovered she did. It would be different if her minor connection would be of any use to him in finding out who'd killed the man, but how could it?

Having had time to prepare herself meant she could keep her voice steady, even if she wasn't able to look him in the eye as she lied. "I've heard the high school teacher's name, I think. This isn't a very big town. One of my clerks has a teenage daughter, so maybe she said something. The lawyer…I wouldn't have had any reason…" She frowned a little. "Actually, I did hire a lawyer." She faltered. "You know. For the will. After Tom died."

The darkness of Sean's expression changed. Emily didn't let herself look closely. "But I went to a woman named Bonnie Myers. I don't think she practices criminal law."

"If she does, I haven't encountered her." He thrust his hand into his hair, forcing it to stand up even more wildly than usual. "Your husband was a doctor. Didn't he socialize with other professionals?"

"Not especially. I mean, not because of their jobs. He wasn't like that. Anyway, I'd likely have met anyone he did. Unless it was a parent of one of his patients."

"Roff had no children. Frank Lowe and his wife have a daughter, but she's in college."

"You said Mr. Roff is a biology teacher. He might have been interested in the beach cleanups that are organized at least once a year. Could Mr. Lowe have done something like that?"

"I don't get the feeling he volunteered to do anything. He and his wife did entertain, but only people they thought were worthwhile. Probably not a lowly teacher."

Emily told herself he needed to vent. That wasn't why she'd prodded him into talking, though. She had wanted to distract them both, her from her acute awareness of him, him from watching her with the intensity that felt…predatory. Because the home security company didn't do installations over weekends, Emily's stay with Sean had been prolonged. This was her fifth night in his house, and the tension between them had grown until she didn't know if she could stand it.

Mornings weren't so bad. He cooked, and they talked about their plans for the day. The deepening crevasses on his face suggested he wasn't sleeping well, while despite everything she was. She hadn't achieved anything as normal as eight hours, but she'd come closer than she had in years. She felt safe knowing he was across the hall. Even four nights had been long enough for her to begun to feel almost at home. This morning, she'd awakened with no moment of disorientation while she wondered where she was. Instead, dread had curled in her belly, because she had only one more night. This was Sunday; the alarm system was to be installed tomorrow morning. She could go home.

She didn't want to go home. Except she did, because she had to get away from him before he touched her.

Before she let him.

"This is making me crazy," he growled suddenly, shooting her a look that was almost hostile as he circled the living room again.

"The investigation?" Emily congratulated herself for her calm.

He came to a stop, his blue eyes hot and intense. "And you."

"Me?" she whispered, her heart stuttering.

"I can sleep with you across the hall. I don't know if I'll be able to sleep when you're back in your house."

"You're the one who told me to have a security system installed. It's supposed to make enough noise to scare anyone off!" Her voice had been rising.

This time he yanked his hair and yelled, "I know all that! But I trust myself more than a bunch of plastic units that can be—" He slammed to a stop.

They stared at each other.

"Can be...what?" she asked, almost numbly.

He swung away, presenting her with his back. "Accidently turned off? Knocked over or broken? Shit, I don't know what I'm saying. A system like yours is pretty reliable."

Pretty reliable. How reassuring.

"People fail you, too," she said unsteadily. Even the people you love. They died.

*Or they abandon you. Like I did to—*

*No, no. I won't think about it.*

She heard him exhale and saw his shoulders sag before he turned to face her again. The intensity was suppressed, if not gone. His eyes were troubled. "I shouldn't have said that. There really isn't any reason to think you won't be completely safe given a warning system. I'm just...on edge."

"You heard me last time."

"Because you screamed."

She understood what he didn't want to say: If she hadn't had a chance to scream, nothing would have saved her.

The whole idea still felt unreal to her. Why her? She was virtually a recluse. How had she caught that man's eye in the first place? As women went, she was tall and strong, not an obvious victim. And there were plenty of pretty women in Cape Trouble, if that's what interested him.

But she lived alone, and her very reclusiveness may have made him consider her vulnerable, perhaps even believe no one would notice if she disappeared. And he would have been right if the house next door had still been empty with the For Sale sign in front. If Sean hadn't moved in.

Feeling peculiar, she looked around Sean's living room. The air seemed to shimmer, as if what she saw was a mirage. She'd hardly known Sean Holbeck – in fact, she'd been quite sure she didn't *want* to know him – and yet, of all people, he was the one to come to her rescue, to take her into his own home, to care so much it was making him crazy.

How had this happened? Emily had no idea, but felt her heart squeeze with an emotion so fierce, her eyes stung with the pain.

She had never wanted to love anyone again. She'd sworn she wouldn't. She couldn't survive another such loss. And yet, she was very much afraid she had begun...no, not to love him, but the possibility was there. She could love this man, so utterly unlike Tom.

*I'm grateful. That's all.*

Of course her gratitude was intense. He'd saved her life. He would do whatever he had to do to keep her safe. How could she not feel something powerful for him?

As the grip on her heart eased, letting her blood flow, her dizziness passed. Women must frequently imagine themselves in love with Detective Holbeck, she decided. It was likely an occupational hazard, especially for a man who looked like him.

Love. What had she been thinking?

"I'll still be next door," she said into the silence. "In fact... Well, don't feel obligated if you have other plans or you get hung up at work, but you'd be welcome to come to dinner again tomorrow night."

"Thank you," he said gruffly. "I'd appreciate it." He resumed pacing, his coiled tension reminding her how he could explode into action. And yet...he was always graceful, in the way of a prowling big cat.

Emily looked down at the quilt, no less aware of him when he passed behind her than she was when she could see him.

"It's not just your safety," he said.

She held herself very still, waiting. This time, she didn't ask what he meant. She knew.

"It's you, Emily. You must have guessed—" He mumbled something not meant for her ears. "No, forget I said that. You're not ready, are you?"

This was her chance to head him off.  And, yes, to be honest.

He stood in front of her now.  She lifted her head and met his eyes.  "I will never be ready.  Losing them both... I told you.  I would rather have died with them.  I *am* dead inside."

Muscles knotted to each side of his jaw.  "I don't believe that."

"Why would I lie?"

"Because you feel guilty to think of moving on, of really living without them."

"Of course I do!" she cried, then realized her mistake almost immediately.  "I would if I *were* thinking about it, but I'm not."

She saw purpose in the grim cast of his features.  "You screamed.  You threw yourself out the window.  You didn't want to die, Emily."

Her heartbeat almost deafened her.  "Not that way."

He studied her for a long moment, his eyes narrowing.  Then he shook his head.  "Not any way.  I think you've been healing, Emily, without realizing it."

"No!"  She stared her defiance at him.  Who was he to think he knew her so well?

"Yes."  In that confounding way he had, his voice was suddenly gentle.  "What do you think Tom would want for you?"

That had her bending her head to stare at her lap.  Tom would want her to be happy again.  Of course he would.  But, as much as she had loved him, deep inside she knew that the sharpest pain still came from Cody's death.  Her little boy, still a baby, his cheeks round, his hair as dark as hers, so soft and just a little wavy, his curiosity insatiable.  His language skills had been expanding with astounding speed, and yet his thumb still crept into his mouth when he climbed into bed for his naps, and he slept so hard his daddy could sling him over his shoulder in a fireman's carry without him so much as stirring.

Sean squatted in front of her, his forearms resting on his knees, lines cutting into his forehead.  "God, I'm sorry, Emily.  I'm a jerk to push, and now I've made you sad."

He had, but she shook her head.  She was sad most of the time without any help from him.

And despite her misery, she found herself noticing the way the fabric of his chinos pulled taut across long, powerful thigh muscles, the hair dusting equally strong forearms. His face, already marked by the things he saw day in and day out. And, most of all, his eyes, a pure, rich blue that darkened to twilight with certain moods.

"I'm not ready," she repeated, only then realizing that wasn't what she'd said the first time. She had said she would *never* be ready.

Sean searched her face with a disconcertingly perceptive gaze, and finally nodded, rising to his feet with a litheness she envied. Some days she ached as if she was an old woman.

"I need to go to bed," she said.

"Okay." He backed off, letting her stand up with the quilt clutched in her arms.

Only then he reached out a hand and touched her cheek. Just a single stroke, but she felt it to the depths of her being.

When she hurried by him, he said quietly, "Goodnight, Emily."

If she answered, she didn't remember later.

*****

The installers should be finishing right about now, giving Emily instructions on changing her passcode, on how not to trigger the alarm by accident.

Sean drove without the attention to his surroundings he should have. He'd interviewed a friend of Frank Lowe's, learning nothing of significance, and instead of brooding about the investigation that was going nowhere, he was back to thinking about Emily.

Nothing new about that. These past few weeks, she was always in his head. It was like having a piece of grit in his shoe. He could ignore the discomfort most of the time, but awareness of its presence never left him. Occasionally it presented a sharp edge to bite into the ball of his foot.

Last night...he should have kept his mouth shut. He didn't know what he'd been thinking. Did he imagine he could heal her, if only she'd sleep with him?

He made a sound in his throat.

Casual sex would only do more damage to a woman so fragile, it was easy to envision her inching along a tightrope that quivered beneath her feet. No net. Nope, if she fell, she'd plummet to jagged rocks far below.

Keeping her safe, that was what mattered. For both of them.

His thoughts kept drifting. There'd been an odd moment last night, before he'd challenged her belief that she was dead inside. It was when he asked whether she knew either of the victims. Her gaze had slid away from his just before she told him she'd heard Darryl Roff's name. Classic giveaway that she was about to lie. But then nothing she said raised any red flags. If she knew one of the men, why wouldn't she have said?

More likely, talking about two dead men and why they'd had to die had cast a shadow over her mood. It tended to work that way for most people. He spent too much time with other cops.

He had just turned east on the highway that followed Mist River from the ocean to North Fork. There wasn't much traffic at this time of day, which left his thoughts to free-float. Emily…

He saw a blur of motion ahead, at the side of the road. A man in camouflage had jumped from the shoulder of the road over a ditch and was already blending with the undergrowth.

It had to be the "scout" who had disturbed Larry. Larry didn't move like that, and would have no reason to hide when he heard a vehicle coming.

When Sean reached the spot where the man had disappeared, he parked, got out and circled his vehicle to scan the woods.

"Please come out," he called. "You don't have to come close. I just want to meet you." He held up both hands. "Say a friendly hello."

*Crack.*

He dove to the pavement at the same instant he saw bark and slivers fly from the trunk of a fir not ten feet from where he'd been standing.

That son of a bitch was firing a rifle at him. His shock and rage was supplanted by cold control. He flung himself around his vehicle and, crouched low, opened the driver side door to grab the radio.

"Shots fired," he reported. "Backup requested." He gave his location from the mile marker he saw twenty-five yards or so ahead. "I'm going after him."

Then, bending low, he returned to the shoulder, jumped the ditch in turn and flattened his back against a large evergreen, his Glock held in both hands.

Silence.

He knew he'd be dead if the guy had wanted to kill him. He'd stood there in plain sight, making a target of himself. It had been a warning shot, but Sean was still more than a little riled. What was with this guy, terrorizing Larry and now taking a potshot at a cop?

He could still, in his head, be in a war zone. Or lost in paranoia.

Alternative: he had damn good reason not to want to chat with a cop.

Sean stole a look around the tree. Nothing moved, but he had learned to trust that prickling sense of not being alone. Wearing mottled green and brown garb, his opponent had the advantage of him. Sean's olive-green cargo pants were okay, if subtly the wrong shade for these woods, but his black, long-sleeve pullover might as well have been bright red.

Taking a risk, he dodged to the next tree. Holding very still, he heard the small crunch of a branch breaking beneath a footfall, and not far away. He drew a quiet breath, preparing to make his next move—

The rifle crack came simultaneously with the sound of the bullet striking the back side of the tree he was using for cover. *Shit.*

He raised his voice. "Put your weapon down or I'm going to start shooting at you."

The rustling of branches was accompanied by the soft thud of running footsteps. Sean spun around the tree, his gaze going to a spot where leaves still quivered. He took off at a run himself, from the bulk of one large evergreen to another, but the sounds diminished and he finally stopped, swearing aloud.

He'd lost him.

He probably shouldn't have pursued in the first place.

And no, damn it, this wasn't like the chase that ended in tragedy for Emily. All he'd risked was his own life.

Yeah, but for what?

Growling, he turned back. On the way, he located the place where the son of a bitch had stood when he took that first shot. The toes of his boots had dug into the soft loam, and a couple of threads of the mottled green cotton had snagged on the rough bark.

Dead end.

He heard a siren just as he reached the ditch beside the road. He'd boosted himself over it when a patrol car screamed to a stop behind his unmarked car.

Having cut the siren and lights, Rebecca Walker jumped out and came to meet him, her gaze sweeping from his face to the woods behind him. Her hand rested on the butt of her weapon.

"You're not on nights anymore," he remarked.

She made a face. "Thank God." Then she frowned at him. "Are you going to tell me what happened?"

She listened without interruption as he did.

"What made you go after him?" she asked when he was done.

By this time, he leaned comfortably against the fender of his car. Like her, he eyed the wall of forest with its thick, perpetually damp undergrowth, looming firs and denser cedar trees with their sweeping boughs.

"Do you know Larry, the Vietnam War vet?"

A tilt of her head said he'd surprised her. "Yes, I give him a ride or slip him some money once in a while. He won't let me buy him a meal."

Sean told her what Larry had said about the advance scout pointing a rifle at him and driving him from one of his hideouts. "He's a little crazy, but not delusional. I got to worrying."

"About Larry?"

"Yes." He hesitated. "This is quite a leap, but it's these killings. You saw Frank Lowe's body."

She flinched.

"Whoever did that has killed before."

"And then you thought, what if he's ex-military?" she said slowly.

"I crossed paths with Larry not long after, and what did he do but start talking about another veteran lurking in the woods. A young guy, he said, hostile. Today, when this guy heard my car coming, he took off. I stopped, figuring I'd talk to him. Maybe get to know him, the way I do Larry. He wasn't near as friendly, though."

She let out an almost-laugh. "No, that's not what I'd call friendly."

"No. So now I'm wondering even harder."

"But he's gone."

He shrugged, as much to ease the tightness in his shoulders as anything. "He is, but probably not far. I want everyone to start watching for him. And Larry," he added. "I'd like to be sure he's okay and has the sense to stay out of this guy's way."

"Were you on your way back in?"

"I was." He tapped the hood with his knuckles and straightened. "Thanks for responding. I'll let you be on your way."

She nodded and had started to walk away when she turned back. "You didn't say what the man looks like."

Sean had to think about that. His one glimpse had been fleeting. *Could be one of Saddam's boys, or even ISIS.* Larry had seen what he expected to see.

"He's no Iraqi, I can tell you that. Brown hair, probably close to the color of mine. Hard to judge height from the one look I got of him, but he moved like lightning. He was quiet in the woods, but not as quiet as if he'd been trained to move unseen and unheard. He wore camo. I think the butt of the rifle was painted in camouflage, too. I suspect he's a good shot. He didn't hit me because he didn't mean to. It might be different next time a police officer tries to stop him."

She absorbed what he'd said and nodded. By the time he was behind the wheel and starting the engine, she was already pulling out, lifting one hand as she passed.

Sean said a very emphatic obscenity and followed.

*****

"I mean, we all knew he was just joking around." Red-faced, the boy looked down at his own, oversized feet. "You know." He stole a look up at Daniel. "But I still didn't think it was cool. He, like, picked on the kids everyone already made fun of."

"Did anyone report Mr. Roff to one of the counselors or Mrs. Grove?" Daniel asked. He hoped he didn't sound judgmental. When he'd been fifteen or sixteen, would he have had the confidence to complain to an administrator about a teacher who made fun of students for things they couldn't help? He truly didn't know. Nobody had much confidence at that age.

Mason Rose ducked his head again. "I don't know. I guess I should have, but—" There was genuine anguish in his eyes when he nerved himself to look at Daniel again. "You think one of his students killed him?"

"I don't have any reason to think that," Daniel said, and he was telling the truth. There were plenty of teenage killers, but they didn't have the skill to slice a knife across a man's throat without so much as a hint of hesitation, and do it while physically subduing him besides.

Darryl Roff wasn't a huge guy at five foot nine, lean to the point of skinny. That didn't mean he was a weakling. According to fellow teachers, he played tennis summers and racquetball winters.

He seemed to have been reasonably popular with them. Only a couple had hesitated before answering a question, or maintained an air of reserve. When Daniel asked to speak to some of his students, Linda had thought about refusing, but finally said, "I'll send some in one at a time."

Thanks to Linda, Daniel had been able to talk to teachers over the weekend. For the students, he'd pretty well had to wait until Monday morning. In a murder investigation, every delay hurt. Plus, the kids had all heard over the weekend about their teacher's death. Seeing their first reactions might have been interesting.

He'd spent all weekend reminding himself that the murder was unlikely to be linked to Roff's job. How could it be, and still tie to the killing of a defense attorney who had neither attended Cape Trouble High nor had kids who did?

A forward on the basketball team, Mason was the sixth student sent in to talk to Daniel. Daniel had been to a couple of games this winter and had been able to tell that one of the cheerleaders was his girlfriend. This wasn't a kid who someone like Roff would mock. Apparently Darryl had saved his savagery disguised as humor for a shy, especially buxom girl whose bra strap had broken in class. "Are you lopsided, Miss Dorrance?" he asked, according to another student, who said everyone had turned to stare and some of them had laughed, at which point she'd run crying from the classroom.

Taunting a boy whose acne was so bad, the teacher had suggested they put some of the pus in petri dishes and see what grew.

The guy had been a grade A asshole, in Daniel's opinion.

The question was what, if anything, that could have had to do with his murder.

Daniel sent the kid back to class, after which the principal poked her head in the small conference room.

"More?" she asked.

He shook his head. "Linda, you need to know what these kids have been telling me."

Middle-aged, sturdy and kind, she sat down across the table from him and listened, her expression increasingly dismayed.

"I'd heard a few rumors," she said. "I've talked to him a couple of times. But a lot of his students seemed to like him. Test scores have been good. There have been a few complaints from parents, but it's a rare teacher someone doesn't hate. I wish someone had told me. I've sat in on his classes, and thought he was dynamic. But if I'd known, I could have watched unobserved."

"He may genuinely have thought everyone was laughing."

She sighed. "Some of the best humor is cruel. But how could someone who chose to teach children of this age think it was fine to make the most vulnerable among them the butt of his humor?" Her mouth thinned. "It almost makes me—"

Daniel smiled. "No, it doesn't, and you know it. What you wish is that he was here for you to give him hell."

She laughed, if ruefully. "You're right, of course." A troubled look crept into her eyes. "But how can this be relevant, Daniel?"

"I don't know," he admitted, "but my gut says it is. When someone is targeted the way he was, I have to ask myself why. Why him instead of another teacher or a neighbor? This is a possible why."

"You're saying one of the students...?" She stumbled over the question.

"Not a current one." He mulled that over. "When did you say he hired on here?"

"This was his fifth year."

"He taught elsewhere?"

"Actually, no. This was a change of career for him. He did lab work at a hospital in the Portland area, but decided to go back for his teaching certification. He told me once that after a divorce, he'd done some re-evaluation of his life."

At Sean's request, she copied Roff's resume for him, although it was hard to see how anything that had happened to him before he came to Cape Trouble could be relevant, given the tie to the murder of another local man.

Walking out to his car, Daniel reached for his phone. He wished he had something more useful to share with Sean. His first thought had been that the killer might be a former student, but Roff hadn't been teaching that long, and most of his classes were for freshmen and sophomores, maybe a few juniors who were lagging. Which meant that the ones who had had him his first year at the high school were now, at most, twenty-one, maybe twenty-two.

Daniel had a flashback to Darryl Roff's body and the letters written in blood on the shower wall. Call him naïve, but he didn't buy the idea that could have been done by a kid.

They'd be a step closer to arresting a killer if they could figure out what BCD stood for.

The minor miracle was that so far they'd kept a lid on that detail. Newspaper articles and TV coverage had all focused on the glass, carefully cut out of a window. The second killing had raised public alarm to near hysteria. The phone was ringing nonstop at the police station, to Ellie's exasperation. She was doing her best to soothe fearful citizens, but nobody could escape the reality that every single one of them was vulnerable to a killer who could enter their houses in the night, unseen and unheard.

He stopped at his car, but since for once it wasn't actually raining or drizzling, he didn't get in. He wondered what Sophie was doing right this minute as he dialed Detective Sean Holbeck's number.

# CHAPTER SEVEN

Another naked body, slung obscenely over the side of the bathtub. *My bathtub*, Sean realized in shock, just as the toes curled. Movement quivered up the legs and then the spine, as if the body was being re-animated from the soles up by some mysterious and monstrous means. Before his horrified gaze, the thin shoulders hunched; it pushed itself up onto its elbows and the head slowly turned, exposing the gaping, bloody wound across the throat.

He lurched backwards, suddenly finding the door had shut behind him, closing him into the bathroom with a zombie. Only then he saw the face, smiling at him. *Emily*. Oh, God, it was Emily. Blood ran down over her breasts. Why hadn't he noticed her braid lying, sliced from her head, on the floor by her feet?

"Emily!"

His own, guttural shout pulled him out of the nightmare. He opened his eyes, discovering that he lay on his back in his bed, the room dark but for faint bands of light from the streetlamp seeping between slats in the blinds. He was panting and sweat-soaked.

When he blinked, the sight of her, grotesque and bloody, seemed imprinted on his eyelids instead of fading as dreams and even nightmares usually did.

"Shit," he muttered, scraping both unsteady hands across his face. That was all he'd needed, an invasion on the little sleep he was managing to get.

*Emily*. He stiffened. Had he heard something that triggered the nightmare? He launched himself from bed and ran to the window, yanking the cord to raise the blind. As usual, she'd left half the lights in her house on and every set of her blinds closed. He waited, unmoving but for the painfully fast thud of his heart, but nothing and nobody stirred.

Sean swore again and turned back to his bed, glaring at his clock. He should have slept for another couple hours, but no way was he going back to bed. His skin crawled at the horror his mind had conjured.

Hot shower, coffee. He had his laptop and could study his timeline and notes. Maybe some anomaly he had so far missed would catch his eye.

He couldn't call it a surprise that his subconscious had melded his fear for Emily with the two ugly murders that preoccupied him in between thinking about her.

He shuddered and wondered if he'd ever sleep again.

*****

They needed ideas, and they needed them now. Sean didn't delude himself that collectively they would be any smarter than they were individually, but nonetheless he'd made some calls yesterday to form an unofficial task force. They'd all agreed to meet this morning.

Voices came from the conference room down the hall from the bullpen, so he knew some of the others had already arrived. Folder in one hand, coffee cup in the other, he had almost reached the doorway when he saw Wilcynski coming from the other direction. It seemed courteous to wait, but he was sorry when the lieutenant's eyebrows rose as his gaze took in Sean's face.

"You look like hell. I hope you didn't go on a bender."

"I don't go on benders." And, yeah, he let his irritation show.

Hard not to, considering how on edge he felt.

"This investigation getting to you?"

"No." Yes, but he wasn't about to admit it. He knew he'd be cooler if it weren't for the threat to Emily. Yeah, and it would help if he could sleep through the night.

Like any detective, he'd investigated crimes he never solved. He didn't like it, but it happened. The faces of those victims stayed with him even more than most. This time, his gut churned because he knew this killer wouldn't stop until they caught him.

And then there was Emily.

The lieutenant didn't move. He looked as if he had no plans to move out of Sean's way any time in the foreseeable future. Close to

Sean's height, he was as solid as the broad bole of a giant Douglas fir.

Succumbing to the silent pressure, Sean admitted, "Just…not sleeping well."

Understanding showed in those dark eyes. "Your neighbor?"

"She had a home security system installed, but I keep waiting for a rerun anyway. Makes for restless nights." He hadn't told anyone that she'd stayed at his house for four nights – five, counting the hours after the break in.

"You're functioning?"

"Yes," he said shortly.

With a nod, Wilcynski preceded him into the conference room, where Daniel Colburn sat talking to Jason Payne while two other men listened. Sean had invited Rey Mendoza, a detective with North Fork P.D., in hopes of building cooperation and giving him a head start in case murder number three happened in his jurisdiction. He and Sean had played basketball together over the winter, and Sean thought they could work together. As his name suggested, he was dark-haired and dark-eyed.

Sean was glad to see that Alex Mackay was here. As sheriff, Mackay had been handling press conferences and media questions about Frank's murder and its potential ties to Darryl Roff's with practiced ease. In that role, he needed to stay on top of the investigation anyway, but beyond that, he was a knowledgeable, hands-on cop, not just a figurehead. Sean had found him to be professionally approachable even as, without ever saying so, Mackay made it clear he did not welcome personal questions. All Sean knew was that he had suffered a major injury that had ended his career with Portland P.D. Word was, he'd been inside or standing next to a car that blew up, although no one really knew for sure, only that he walked stiffly, appeared to be in chronic pain, and had visible burn scars above the collar of his shirt. If anyone in the department had done a search online for his name, Sean hadn't heard about it. He hoped no one had.

Mackay's eyes, as dark as Lieutenant Wilcynski's, surveyed Sean briefly and left him wondering whether his boss had employed skull-penetrating radar.

The seat at the head of the table stood empty. Since it seemed to be expected, he took it. "Thanks for coming, everyone. I have no groundbreaking news. My intent is to keep everyone informed." He had a thought. "Does everyone know Detective Mendoza from North Fork P.D.?"

Wilcynski introduced himself. Apparently the others already had.

"Good. Let me say first that, according to Frank Lowe's law partner, Roff was never a client. He could have called, decided not to retain him, or they had an informal consultation, but it's sounding unlikely. Otherwise, why don't you start, Daniel," Sean suggested. "Something in Roff's life has to intersect with Frank's."

Nothing Daniel had to say was new to Sean. The others listened intently, however.

Before moving to Cape Trouble, Darryl had worked at Oregon Health and Science University's Doernbecher Children's Hospital in Portland, where his research had focused on blood disorders. He'd claimed a divorce had triggered the career change. Daniel had managed to get in touch with the ex-wife, who was shocked to hear about his death and agreed that he had been getting bored with his job.

"She insisted they had just drifted apart, no big betrayals. She did say he could be 'mean' when she annoyed him."

He repeated what he'd learned at the high school two days ago, then got up to write a list of Darryl's hobbies and favorite hangouts. Everyone in the room studied them, then looked at Sean, who shook his head.

"Frank Lowe and his wife liked fine wines and could afford them. They took long weekends to visit wineries in the Willamette Valley and over the Columbia River to Walla Walla. Their last real vacation, they spent a week in the Napa Valley, tasting and buying. They belonged to wine clubs. Beyond that, he was obsessive about doing the New York Times crossword puzzle every day, come hell or high water. Their friends were money market managers, county commissioners, the North Fork Hospital administrator. A cardiologist there."

"People with influence?" Mendoza suggested.

Sean shook his head again. "People who liked fancy wines. Lieutenant, you saw the wine cellar."

Wilcynski grunted. "Basement, half again as big as the house. The house was custom built, and his wife says that's why. There are hundreds if not thousands of bottles of wine down there, kept at a perfectly controlled temperature."

Jason's lip curled. "Makes you wonder what some of the clients he didn't keep from prison would think about it." Evidently, he wasn't a wine guy.

"But how would they know about it?" Daniel asked.

"Odds are, they wouldn't," Sean said. "Rita Lowe made it sound like a bank vault filled with valuable artwork. A few of their friends might have been taken on a tour. I doubt either of them mentioned it to anyone else."

"Do wines hold their value on a secondary market?" Mackay asked, sounding bemused.

"No idea." Sean looked around, and saw a lot of heads shaking. "It's something to keep in mind, but we have to remember the killer made no apparent attempt to access the wine cellar or, in fact, to steal anything else. He didn't hurt Rita."

"Lucky she didn't wake up," Jason muttered.

"That's safe to say."

"By the way, I finally found Barry Rollins," Jason said. "Given the second victim, his whereabouts are probably irrelevant, but turns out a friend of his has been paying him to help work on a cabin near Crater Lake. The friend says they've both been staying there. I checked with the nearest small store slash gas station, and the owner remembers seeing them." He shrugged, apparently philosophical about having wasted his time.

Detectives wasted a lot of time following leads that ended up going nowhere.

They discussed the timing – five days between the two murders. Did that mean they should expect another murder tomorrow? Since the spacing between only two events wasn't enough to suggest a pattern, they moved on quickly.

Sean shared his thoughts about the killer having a military background and told them about his encounter with the young guy wearing camo who'd scared Larry. Turned out they all knew Larry except Rey Mendoza, who both lived and worked in North Fork, which was apparently outside of Larry's range, and Lieutenant Wilcynski because he was so new in the area.

Nobody disagreed that the murders suggested a level of expertise beyond the norm, although Mendoza threw out the idea that the guy could be a surgeon, work at the morgue, even be a butcher at Safeway, Fred Meyer or Mist River Meat.

"Farmers and ranchers must get kinda good at cutting throats, too," Mackay offered. "Still, the timing when this new homeless man showed up is suggestive."

"Identifying him should be a priority," Sean said.

Nods all around.

Wilcynski rolled a pen between his fingers. "Let's not forget the BCD he writes in blood. He's trying to tell us something with it."

"Why be so obscure if the message is for us?" Daniel asked. "I wonder if he isn't expressing something private to him."

Jason leaned forward. "Why would he bother if it's just for him? He knows the body will be found, that cops will see what he's written."

Mackay raised an eyebrow. "Maybe it doesn't mean jack shit. It's a random configuration of letters. Maybe he's playing us, liking the idea we're wasting our time trying to figure out what it means."

"There's a thought," Sean grumbled.

"I don't believe it." The speaker was Jason again. "For one thing, if that was the case I'd have expected him to choose different letters with the second killing." He shook his head. "I think he's expressing something important about the victims. Partly for himself, but partly for our benefit. He's saying, 'Here's why he deserved to die.'"

Sean's gut feeling said the same. He was a little surprised at how boldly Jason had spoken out, given how new he was on the job. He wasn't shy, and he'd been using his head. Sean thought the lieutenant's expression suggested approval, too.

They threw around a few more ideas before the meeting broke up. Mendoza thanked Sean for including him, without mentioning whether Chief Lundy knew he'd involved himself in in a county-wide task force. His last words were, "Keep me posted," and Sean nodded.

He hated knowing they were really waiting for another murder to happen, in hopes this time the killer would make a mistake.

*****

Emily hated her new security system. When she'd initially agreed to this, she had pictured some invisible network of wires, the only obvious presence the keypad where she turned the whole thing on and off. But she'd been informed that in-the-walls, wired security systems were most practical for new construction or when a homeowner was already doing a major remodel. Otherwise, it would mean a lot of holes in her walls.

So she had opted for the wireless system, which meant receiver along with door and window sensors, a keypad and a remote control, which she kept eyeing as if it was a coiled snake because she was so afraid of pushing the wrong button. The plus side was that she could disable individual sensors in case she ever worked up the nerve again to open a window for some fresh air. But holding onto what sense of security the whole system gave her meant she didn't dare disable any part of it, or there would be a chink in her armor.

Instead of feeling safe, she felt even more isolated than she had.

She could tell Sean hadn't been a hundred percent satisfied, which made her uneasy.

"No system is perfect," he had said with a shrug. "But if you use it faithfully, this one is hard to defeat."

He came for dinner Tuesday, but seemed preoccupied. She had a feeling there was a lot he wasn't telling her about his day. She asked if he was working a new crime, and he shook his head.

"I'm concentrating on this one and winding up some others. I have a court appearance Thursday, which means reviewing my notes." His mouth quirked. "And dressing up."

"A suit and tie?"

"I know some guys who throw on a sport coat and call it good, but I go for a suit. I want to look at least as professional as the attorneys."

She laughed at that, but saw his point.

He commented on how helpful it would be if they could find a single person who had known both Frank Lowe and Darryl Roff. "There must be somebody," he grumbled. "Besides the murderer. Damn it, they have to have something in common."

"Or someone," she heard herself say.

His gaze sharpened. "You're right."

"You think there'll be more murders, don't you?"

"I do," he said quietly, his expression darkening. "It's possible this was a one-two punch, but I don't think so."

"Or...or the other people he wants to kill live somewhere else."

"That's possible, too."

"If nothing more happens, what will you do?" Emily knew what she was really asking. When would he give up? Underlying it was the parallels to her own situation: what if a week went by, a month, six months, and no one tried to break in to her house? When could she believe it was a one-time thing and she no longer had to worry?

His expression was entirely unreadable when he said, "Put the investigation on the back burner, but keep an ear to the ground. People get careless."

Her blood seemed to chill. Would she ever feel safe enough to become careless?

And why was she so afraid when she'd been convinced she wouldn't mind if death came for her? Was Sean right? Had some kind of life force reawakened in her without her noticing? Or had it reawakened when she noticed *him*?

And...why him, so unlike the one man she had loved?

But even she knew that was a silly question. She had changed. Once upon a time, she'd been happy and optimistic, with no dark undercurrents or foreboding. Now, she was layer upon layer of complications. Grief and guilt had destroyed any faith she'd once had. Even if she wanted another family, how would she live with the fear?

How did cops who saw so much tragedy fall in love, marry, have children? Did they live in constant terror? Or could they compartmentalize so well, they didn't allow the misery they saw on the job to color their personal lives?

She couldn't believe that. She was so close to asking Sean, her lips parted, but she thought better of it in time. He might see a question like that as encouragement. He might think she'd begun wondering whether happiness was possible even if you already knew how quickly it could be shattered.

The way he watched her so thoughtfully left her sure he'd seen her struggle with herself, but he didn't say anything.

When she refused his help at cleaning the kitchen, he thanked her for dinner and left with only one last look she couldn't interpret.

Alone in her possibly-breachable fortress, Emily knew she wouldn't be sleeping any better tonight than she ever had. Once she had the dishwasher running, she plugged in her iron and went to her work table, where she'd already piled a selection of fabrics. Some of the simplest patterns were the most popular with buyers. She laid several fabrics atop each other on the mat, carefully placed her ruler and picked up her rotary cutter.

Later, when her concentration flagged to the point where she might make mistakes, she'd switch to hand-quilting.

\*\*\*\*\*

At the sound of a throat being cleared, Sean lifted his eyes from his computer monitor. Looking stolid, Mike Stoffel stood in front of the desk. Heading toward retirement, Mike had spent his entire career as a uniformed deputy. His belly sagged over his pants and he had jowls and broken veins in his nose, but he was good with people.

"Heard you wanted to know if we saw Larry or that new vet."

"I do," Sean said, sitting back in his chair.

"Saw Larry a couple of days ago. I asked about this other dude, and Larry said he's avoiding him. I tried to get him to tell me where we might find the guy, but he wasn't about to."

Sean nodded, thinking about it. "Even if he doesn't like him, Larry might be feeling protective. He's pretty mellow himself now, but he's had a lot of years to recover."

Stoffel nodded. "I went to Vietnam myself. Came home feeling raw. Drove my first wife away. This guy you saw may just not be ready to mix with people at all."

Annoyed as he was at having been shot at, Sean had to concede the point. Watching Stoffel walk away, he was struck by how much more human the deputy had become to him in the last two minutes or so.

*Came home feeling raw.*

Instead of returning his attention to the court records he'd been scanning, Sean brooded over how all-American and normal and happy his childhood had been until the day that changed everything.

Nothing was the same after Matt was killed. And, God knows, Sean had seen too much heartbreak and tragedy since then, if one step removed.

What stunned him now was to realize that, in the back of his mind, he'd still seen himself someday having a family like the one he'd grown up in. A mom and dad who stayed in love and were best friends, a couple of kids able to grow up with the knowledge their family was solid. Happy, no complexities.

Emily couldn't be that mom. If she ever had other children, every day would have her balancing on a knife edge, her terror of losing them doing war with her awareness that, because she loved them, she had to give them confidence and an occasional gentle push out into the world.

And, sure, Sean thought with a frown, even thinking like that was premature, but he needed to figure out what he did want from her before he was stupid enough to make some kind of move he'd regret. Worse, did something that would hurt her.

Because of that uncertainty, he'd kept his distance these past couple days beyond a quick call each morning and stopping by her house briefly on Thursday to see with his own eyes that she was okay. Renewed strain had been visible on her face, which didn't help his own lousy mood or inability to sleep for more than fleeting stretches. Even when he didn't have a nightmare, he had taken to waking every hour or two as if he'd been poked with a cattle prod, electricity buzzing through his body as he listened hard for whatever sound might have disturbed him.

His bedroom window faced hers, more or less, albeit with a fence between them, so he left his open a few inches to increase his chance of hearing anything out of the ordinary from her house.

So far, there hadn't been anything.

He wasn't reassured, and he could tell she wasn't, either. Sean kept circling back to his belief that, whatever the purpose of the break-in, it hadn't been fulfilled. If what happened had been a typical attempt to grab some stuff to pawn, a repeat was on the scale of unlikely to hell-no. A teenager would have had the shit scared out of him. No way he'd come back for an encore.

But the man who had shoved his way into Emily's bedroom even as she screamed louder than the coastal tsunami warning siren, would he give up? Sean didn't believe it.

His thoughts reverted to his attraction to her.

She claimed a part of her had died when she lost her husband and child, but that implied she'd been numb since then. He wondered if her new norm hadn't been more the way Mike Stoffel had described feeling. Had she been so raw she couldn't bear the thought of being touched, physically or emotionally? If so...most of the Vietnam War vets had recovered eventually, hadn't they?

But they'd seen friends blown up, not their loved ones.

Her husband and child hadn't died right in front of her.

Like a slideshow, Sean saw face after face from the notifications he'd done, heard himself say with as much sympathy as he could muster, *I'm sorry for your loss.* Remembered his mother's anguished cry. He wasn't so sure being told might not be worse than seeing the deaths yourself. Deep inside, would you be convinced that the people you loved really were dead and gone? Or would you dream about them, turn eagerly at the sound of a certain footfall, a baby's cry in the grocery store, a glimpse from the corner of your eye?

Sean gave himself a shake. Crap. He was sitting here staring into space, which might be excusable if he had been thinking deep thoughts about an investigation. But him? He was stuck thinking about a woman.

He groaned, rubbed a hand over his face, and wondered if the nice, uncomplicated, sunny woman he'd vaguely imagined loving would even interest him anymore. If a woman as complex, damaged and afraid as Emily Drake worked up the courage to love again, the man she'd chosen should be awed and honored, because her love wouldn't be ordinary or easy.

*I don't know her well enough to be in love with her*, he thought in shock. But he felt something unfamiliar, he knew that. He had from the first time he set eyes on her.

Somehow, in a matter of a week or two, his priorities had been turned on end.

Protect and serve, he thought – but he was being torn two ways.

He flipped open a folder on his desk to look down at a chart he'd been trying to construct, one with lines that refused to intersect because he still didn't know what the two murder victims had in common. It wasn't teenagers, lab work, gym membership, the law or wine. Nobody who knew Frank Lowe well had ever so much as heard Darryl Roff's name, and vice versa.

Unless someone was lying.

And, damn, a full week had now passed since Daniel found Roff's body. Did that mean their killer was done? Or was there no rhyme nor reason for the intervals between murders?

He slapped the folder closed, making a decision. He wasn't accomplishing a damn thing, and he needed to see Emily. He picked up his phone. When she answered, he said, "Hey, you up for a run?"

*****

The moon was almost full, the pale light making the crest of the waves and the sea foam shimmer with a beauty that was almost unearthly.

Emily had never run in the dark before. When they started out, a spectacular, fiery sunset over the ocean had distracted her from thinking about the night that would follow. She wouldn't have wanted to be navigating curbs or tree roots, but the hard-packed, wet sand at the ocean's edge was as smooth as the surface of the high school track. Moonlight allowed her to see well enough to avoid stepping on the occasional darker strand of seaweed or kelp. And…with Sean running easily beside her, she felt completely safe. He wouldn't let her fall.

They talked intermittently, idly, comparing what they had on their iPods – mostly folk, alternative and some old rock on hers, harder driving sounds on his. Talking to Daniel Colburn about the biology teacher had gotten Sean to thinking about high school, and he wanted to know what she'd been like as a teenager, whether she'd been a conformist or a rebel or something else altogether.

She gave it some thought before answering. "I suppose…an independent. I had friends and a boyfriend and I didn't flout rules, but I didn't rush to buy the newest brand of jeans because everyone else was. I stayed interested in quilting, too, even though it was something *old ladies* did."

He laughed at the way she said that. When she asked what he'd been like, it was a couple minutes before he said anything, and what she could see of his face was more reflective than the question deserved.

"Until Matt died, I was a typical teenage boy," he said finally. "I was a jock – I played football and baseball, and probably would have done basketball, too, if there wasn't so much overlap. Thought about girls a lot, had a stupid sense of humor and a reckless streak, because how else is a guy supposed to show off his manliness?"

She laughed. "I'll bet you did more than think about girls."

"Yeah, I had a couple of girlfriends—" the gleam of white teeth let her know he was grinning "—but nothing very serious. A couple buddies of mine married their high school girlfriends." He shook his head. "I know I'm glad I didn't commit myself for a lifetime when I was only eighteen years old."

"The marriages might not last a lifetime," she retorted.

"That's true, but these two have so far."

Looking at the unearthly beauty ahead, the whole world painted in silver and black edged with the opalescent white crest of waves, she asked, "Were you a good student?"

It was a mistake to express so much curiosity about him, she knew. It was a bigger mistake to be curious.

"Yeah, actually I was. My parents had expectations. You know. I never really defied them."

"Because you loved them."

"Yeah," he said gruffly. "That was part of it." That last almost two years at home, he had been desperate to be everything they could want in a son, because he had to make up for the other son who was gone.

When he asked, she told him more about her grandparents rather than her parents, maybe because they'd meant so much to her. She never put on her thimble or threaded a needle without seeing Nanna's face or at least feeling…she didn't know. A hint of warmth otherwise so conspicuously absent from her life now. Brow crinkling, she put into words something she hadn't consciously thought about before. What she felt was a hug. Not real, of course. Imagined, or perhaps an echo of the comfort Nanna offered so unstintingly.

There was a sting, too, of course. Quilts were a women's art that stitched together generations. Nanna had made a crib quilt for Emily when she was born. Mom had kept it, passing it on when Cody was born. When she laid him to sleep in his crib and pulled the quilt over him, Emily remembered smiling softly as she thought about how carefully she would put it away once her children had outgrown it, and how they would use it when *they* had children, making real the existence of a great-great grandma those kids would never know in any other way. But now…now she had no one to pass that quilt down to, and never would. The history of her family would be snipped off.

As she talked, though, she suppressed that constant ache and lived in the now.

Sean said nothing about her intruder, her security system or his investigation. That had to be deliberate. Grateful, Emily realized she felt better than she had in days. More like herself.

No, she thought in faint shock – more like the woman she'd been Before.

Dumb thought. Running was supposed to release endorphins that boosted a person's mood. Easy explanation.

Quiet now, they slowed to a jog, then a walk for their cool-down, finally strolling over the loose sand until they found the opening between dunes that would lead them back to his SUV.

"Thank you," Emily surprised herself by saying. "I mean, for suggesting this. I've been feeling really closed-in."

"I'm not surprised. Have you set the alarm off by accident yet?"

"Yet?" She laughed. "Is it inevitable?"

"Pretty much." He unlocked with his remote. "Common, anyway."

"I admit, I'm afraid to push a button."

"And if you don't push it at the right time…"

She made a horrible face at him that he wouldn't be able to see. "After this pep talk, I'll be paralyzed."

His laugh was deep and rich. "You'll get the hang of it."

During the short drive back to town, he suggested they go out to dinner. Emily tentatively offered to cook, but he turned his head to smile at her.

"Nope, you deserve an outing. We can do fancy, if you want, or grab a pizza or burger and fries. Whatever appeals to you."

Compared to the idea of going home and shutting herself in again, anything sounded good.

"I need to shower first."

She saw him take a cautious sniff of his underarm.

"Yeah, good idea." He turned into his driveway. "I'll walk you home first."

Emily opened her mouth to tell him he didn't need to, but closed it. The sidewalk was reasonably well-lit, but her yard was very dark. Especially, she saw, since she'd forgotten to turn on her porch light. So all she did was say meekly, "Thank you."

As they walked the short distance, she felt a burst of thankfulness to know he wasn't just leaving her. Part of the sense of security he gave her was physical – he was so big, his shoulders so broad. But she was also very aware of his readiness – his head turning as he unceasingly scanned their surroundings, his body balanced in a way that would allow him to move fast.

It was more than that, though, she knew. It was just him. His need to protect ran deep. Confidence was a big part of him, but it wasn't the shallow cockiness that defined so many men. The fact that he cared so intensely about victims and doing his job well was what felt like a balm to Emily.

The way he had of laying his hand on her back…was not soothing, although she found herself wanting to lean into it.

She'd unlocked her front door and tapped in her passcode to turn off the security system when she glanced past Sean to see Louella Shoop hurrying across the street.

"Mrs. Drake!" she called. "Yoo-hoo! Mrs. Drake!"

Sean had already spotted her and shifted just enough to put himself in front of Emily.

She poked his wide, rock-hard back. "It's just Mrs. Shoop."

She actually wasn't sure whether there had ever been a Mr. Shoop, but that's what everyone called her.

"Just?" he muttered, but stepped to one side and laid a hand on the small of her back as they went to meet her elderly neighbor.

"Mrs. Drake. Detective."

They both greeted her.

"Is something wrong, Mrs. Shoop?" she asked politely.

"I'm a little slower than I used to be, but I can't complain," she said. "I see as well as ever now that I've had those cataracts taken care of. And good thing, too." She sounded energized. "I was watching for you, because I saw something earlier."

Louella Shoop was the nosiest woman in town. Emily had let the shrubs along the front of her yard grow thick and tall in part to prevent Louella from watching her every move. Now…God. She'd been thinking about tearing them out.

Beside her, Sean stiffened. "Something?"

"First I thought it was a dog," she said, "but I grabbed my binoculars real quick and got a better look after he jumped your fence into Mr. Vandehee's yard."

Sean's house was on one side of Emily's, Robert Vandehee's on the other. Emily scarcely knew him. He was the general manager of the Safeway store, unmarried, and, while pleasant enough when Emily had spoken to him over their common fence, otherwise kept to himself. He must be a constant source of frustration to Louella, who liked to know all.

And why was she thinking about Louella?

Because she didn't want to think about who he was that had jumped her fence.

"I still couldn't see him very well." Louella sounded regretful. "He had to be wearing all black, and maybe a hat, too?" There was a doubtful note in her voice. "He disappeared behind that big old rhododendron in Mr. Vandehee's yard, but a minute later I saw someone on a bicycle riding away fast, right down the street."

"When you first saw movement, where was it?"

She nodded toward the gap between Emily's house and Sean's. "You don't have a gate on the other side, do you?"

Emily shook her head.

"I wouldn't have seen him if I hadn't been watching closely, but I'm quite sure he crossed in front of your house." Satisfaction tinged her voice. "It's only neighborly to keep an eye out for each other. After what happened last week, I thought you should know someone was lurking."

"He…he might have been someone looking for a dog, or…" Emily trailed off, knowing how idiotic that sounded.

Two sets of eyes regarded her with pity. It was Louella who sniffed and then said, "Then you'd think he would have been calling for it."

She bit her lip hard. "Yes."

"I would have dialled 911, but he was gone so fast and you know how long it would have taken one of those officers to get here." She sniffed. "I've complained to Chief Colburn several times about the response time."

All those happy endorphins had gone over a cliff like lemmings, leaving Emily feeling hollow. "Thank you for telling me, Mrs. Shoop. And…and watching out for me."

"It's simply not in my nature to do anything less," she declared. "I'm so glad we have a police officer living right here on our block now."

Sean thanked her as well and said, "If you'll excuse us now, Mrs. Shoop, I believe this has been a shock to Ms. Drake."

With clear reluctance, she retreated.

Emily wasn't sure she'd have moved on her own, but Sean propelled her gently back to her house and pushed her in.

"Let me walk through quick." He did, leaving her with her back to the front door. When he returned he said, "Take your shower, and we'll talk about this over dinner."

His voice was so gentle, she would have been fooled if she hadn't looked up at his face to see rage that, oddly, reassured her.

She nodded like a child. "Okay."

"Damn, Emily." Taking her utterly by surprise, he slid a hand beneath her braid and kissed her. Briefly, but hard, conveying a depth of emotion that stunned her. Then he turned and bounded down the porch steps, only stopping then to say, "Lock up. Security system."

Lips tingling, she nodded again and closed the door. She had no doubt at all that Sean waited until he heard the beep of her system resetting itself.

# CHAPTER EIGHT

Sean wasn't sleeping anyway when his phone rang at 6:24 a.m.

He'd wanted Emily to move back into his spare bedroom, and hadn't liked her refusal.

"If…if he still has his eye on me, he may have just been confirming that I really have a security system. You know, you can buy stickers that claim you do. Businesses have them, too. But if he looked in any of my windows, he might have been able to see one of the window sensors, so now he knows."

Sean had ground his molars together. He didn't say, *Why is he back? What does he want so bad?* She was scared enough already, and she had no more answers than he did.

Not long after he'd left her locked in her house, he had heard the hum of her sewing machine. Her living room light never had gone out last night. Either she hadn't gone to bed at all, or she'd felt safer with her house brightly lit. Maybe the light was a decoy. *I'm awake, so don't think you can sneak up on me.*

She wasn't the only one who hadn't slept worth shit. His mind reached new creative heights with harrowing nightmares.

The minute he picked up the phone and saw the caller's name, his edgy disquiet hardened into dread. He'd only added Rey Mendoza to his contacts list last week.

"Holbeck," he said.

"You were right." Mendoza's voice was hushed, as if he didn't want to be overheard. "The guy has struck again."

Feeling sick, Sean braced himself. "Who's the victim?"

Mendoza sighed. "Charles Tranor."

Tranor was the presiding judge of the local circuit court. He was famous – or was it infamous? – for a conservative, tough-on-crime stance that made him popular among a segment of the law enforcement community. Sean considered him too rigid and preferred the other circuit court judge, a woman.

"At least he ties to Frank Lowe," he said.

"Yeah, not much help there. How many thousand times has Lowe appeared before Judge Tranor?"

"But if we can draw a line between Tranor and Darryl Roff..."

"That would help. Uh...I only have a minute. I stepped outside. Chief Lundy is in the house, probably contaminating my crime scene, so I'll talk fast. Tranor lives alone, but it turns out he had a lady friend. She's distraught, but because she's an attorney, she's also worrying about whether we'll be willing or able to keep her presence quiet."

Fat chance of that. Then Sean's eyes narrowed. "Not Sandra Graafstra."

"That would have been convenient, but no." Mendoza hesitated, but finally said, "Janet Taylor."

How many times had *she* appeared before by-the-book Judge Tranor? Plus, there was a significant age gap. Yeah, their affair would be a major scandal by Burris County standards.

"Same deal as at the Lowe's, except Ms. Taylor never woke up at all until her alarm went off. She had it set for five, planned to shower and be out of there before the neighbors stirred and anybody saw her. She was surprised Charles was already up, went in the bathroom and found him."

"BCD?"

"Nope. This time it says DD."

"Dishonorable discharge," Sean said slowly. Had to be. Question answered.

"That's my guess. A bad conduct discharge means you did something crummy, but a dishonorable one is a lot worse."

"That's not subtle. He hates Tranor more than the previous victims."

Mendoza grunted his agreement.

"You know we've kept the messages out of the news. It would be good if we can keep it that way."

"I'll talk to my chief," the other detective said. Sean heard voices in the background. Mendoza muttered, "Shit, got to go," and the call was over.

Another murder.

*If I'd done my job better...* Sean grappled with the unreasoning belief that he had to be better at his job than anyone else, have X-ray vision that cut through walls, be able to leap two-story buildings as if they were no higher than the hurdles on the high school track. Fortunately, common sense won. He had done every damn thing he could think of to figure out who murdered Frank Lowe. Even so, he'd missed something. What?

Consternation would sweep through the legal community once this got out. Human nature being what it was, people had wanted to assume Frank had been killed for some reason unrelated to his job, but now they'd all start picturing targets on their own backs.

And maybe, Sean thought, some of them really were wearing them.

So who would be next? A prosecutor? A cop? A juror?

His hunting instinct latched onto the last possibility. What if Darryl Roff had done jury duty? Or had been a witness in a particular trial?

Sean showered, got dressed and drank his first cup of coffee before starting to make calls, Lieutenant Wylcynski first, Colburn next. Wilcynski sounded wide awake, but it was Colburn's fiancé who answered his mobile phone.

"He's in the shower," she told him. "I'll tell him to call you."

"Sorry if I woke you up."

"Oh, I was awake." A certain note in her voice told him why she was awake. He wished like hell he'd been lucky enough to wake up with a pretty woman cuddled up to him.

Not just any pretty woman. Emily.

Was she finally sleeping? he wondered. With daylight, it was harder to tell which lights were still on in her house behind those blinds. If she finally had conked out, he didn't want to awaken her, but he knew he wouldn't be able to concentrate on anything else until he saw her.

For the first time ever, he was glad Louella Shoop lived across the street. He had a feeling her binoculars would be trained on Emily's house as close to twenty-four/seven as she could manage from here on out. This was the opportunity of a lifetime for a woman who, with her energy and ambition, really should be an army general. His mouth quirked. Or a police detective.

Not that the creep would go after Emily in daylight hours, Sean reflected, not if he had any brains. It would have been different if all the near neighbors were working people, but as it happened, several were retirees, including the owners of two houses right across the street. Anyone watching Emily would have noticed.

Sean wished he felt reassured.

He took his time eating breakfast, locked up and went to her front door where he rang the bell.

She appeared quick enough, she couldn't have been in bed. While she tapped in her alarm code, Sean was distracted by the thin knit pants she wore with an equally thin tank top – and nothing under either. The sight of her face looking hollow-eyed almost quelled his lust. Strands of dark hair had escaped from last night's braid, curving over her cheek and clinging to her long, pale throat.

"You didn't sleep," he said.

She made a face. "Not much."

She would have slept fine in his spare bedroom, he knew, but he also understood her stubbornness. Going home with him would mean she was succumbing to fear and allowing herself to be driven out of her house.

He could suggest she go spend a couple weeks with her grandparents, but tracking her down wouldn't be hard for someone who was determined. And Nanna and Grandad probably didn't have a home security system.

That wasn't even his first objection, Sean admitted privately. The truth was, he would go crazy if he couldn't watch out for her. A daily phone call wouldn't cut it.

He was freaking obsessed.

"Try to nap today," he said quietly.

She forced a smile. "I will." Her forehead creased. "You're up early."

He barely hesitated. He could trust her not to talk. "We have another murder. This one is in North Fork, so it's not my jurisdiction, but we're all working together. It should give us some new avenues to investigate."

She gripped the doorframe. "Can you tell me who?"

"A judge. Charles Tranor."

Did she look relieved? "I've seen his name in the newspaper, but I'm sure I don't know him. Oh, but you must."

"I've testified in his courtroom. That doesn't make for a very personal relationship."

"No." Her eyes widened, the color so extraordinary, he couldn't look away. "There aren't that many detectives around here, are there? What if…" Her voice faltered. "What if he wants to kill you?"

The odds were against it. Was a cop on the to-do list? Maybe. Sean kept in mind, though, that whatever grudge the killer held might just as well have to do with a misdemeanor crime, civil case or a custody hearing as a major criminal trial.

"If Roff had been a juror or witness in a trial where I testified, I'd remember him," he said. "I'm good with faces and names."

"Oh." She relaxed. "Okay."

He couldn't help himself. He lifted his hand to stroke the silky skin of her cheek with his knuckles, then gently tuck one of those wayward locks of hair behind her ear.

Her eyes darkened. "Sean…"

He shook his head and made himself back up. "Dinner? I'd suggest a run, but it's supposed to rain."

She looked past him at the sky and nodded, expression wary but also… He wasn't sure.

"I'd be happy to cook again," she offered.

What could she say after he'd put her on the spot? But he'd take what he could get anyway. "If you mean it."

"I mean it."

"Six? If it looks like I'll be late, I'll call."

As he walked back to his own driveway, he discovered he'd paid more attention to the lush shape of her breasts and hips beneath the thin fabric than he'd realized. His hands tingled with awareness of how her breasts and the firm, round globes of her butt would feel cupped in them. And damned if he wasn't getting aroused.

It was probably a good thing his drive would take twenty minutes or more.

\*\*\*\*\*

An hour later, Emily's doorbell rang. Her hand jerked, spilling coffee hot enough to make her gasp.

Living in a state of fear could not be good for her blood pressure, she thought, going to one of the windows to peek between blinds before she dared open the door.

To her astonishment, it was Sophie Thomsen who stood on her porch. What did the police chief's fiancé want with her?

Glad she'd showered and gotten dressed right after Sean left, Emily unlocked and opened the door. "Sophie! It's been ages."

Blonde hair bundled on the back of her head, Sophie was maybe five foot five or six, which meant she was several inches shorter than Emily. She was fine-boned, but not so petite as to make Emily feel like the Hulk, as she had so often in school, when she towered over all the other girls and most of the boys.

"I know you work at home and, even if it's Saturday, I'm probably interrupting you, but I was hoping you could take a break for coffee. Daniel keeps worrying about your break-in. I thought maybe it would help to talk to someone who's been there."

Emily stepped back. "I was actually sitting at the kitchen table brooding over a cup of coffee, so your timing is perfect."

It took them awhile to reach the kitchen, since Sophie stopped to ooh and aah over half-completed quilts, including the one in the frame.

"This is stunning," she said. "I love the really modern quilts, but I have to admit to especially coveting the traditional ones." Her fingertips trailed over the curves of a hand-pieced wedding ring as she studied the quilt still in the frame. "I don't suppose it will be for sale."

Emily didn't remember seeing the diamond ring on Sophie's left hand the last time they'd met. She smiled. "I think it might be a wedding gift, if the bride doesn't mind not being surprised."

She lifted her head. "You mean… Oh, you can't be serious. The work in this boggles my mind! You could surely sell it for a ton, and it is your livelihood."

"It's actually not." Emily tried to keep her sadness at bay. "The quilting keeps me busy, that's all. Lucky for me, Tom carried generous life insurance, and the county where the accident occurred offered a settlement, too." Her mouth twisted. "They acknowledged that much fault, anyway."

The other woman's eyes held compassion. "I'm sorry to remind you."

"I never forget," she said simply, and led the way to the kitchen. "It would give me great pleasure to know that quilt would be loved."

"I can promise you that." Sophie sniffed, laughed and swiped at her eyes all at the same time. "Darn it, I'm not usually so emotional."

"Is there a reason?"

Their eyes met. "I think so," Sophie said ruefully. "I haven't even told Daniel yet. You won't say anything, will you?"

"Of course not." Hit painfully by the memory of the magical moment when she had first suspected she was pregnant, Emily struggled to sound pleased and to hide her grief. Joy was there, too, though, for a woman who had come so close to not having a chance at love or family. Surprising herself, Emily gave her a quick hug. "Congratulations. On the wedding and your secret."

This time, Sophie's laugh was less complicated. "Thank you. And to think I came by to find out how you're holding up."

Over coffee, Emily surprised herself again by being more open than she'd been with anybody but Sean in a long time. Why it helped to hear what Sophie had gone through was a mystery. Misery loves company?

"I still have nightmares," Sophie admitted, "but so much good came out of the whole experience, I count my blessings."

"Daniel."

"He's number one. But finding out my mother didn't commit suicide, that she was murdered and would never have left me by choice, that means more to me than I can tell you."

Emily nodded, feeling a sting of tears in her own eyes now.

"The auction was a huge success, and we saved Misty Beach, and that means a lot to me because it was so important to my aunt." Whose murder, Emily knew, had started Sophie Thomsen's ordeal. "But what I really came here to tell you is that I found out I'm stronger than I ever believed I could be. Without Daniel, that monster would have killed me anyway. But I didn't make it easy for him. Knowing I'm capable of fighting back has changed the way I see myself."

Emily found her head bobbing. "I…hadn't thought of it that way, but I thought—" she smiled crookedly "—and moved fast enough to save myself. Although I've never been so glad to see anyone in my life as Sean." Her cheeks warmed. "Sean Holbeck. He's a detective with the sheriff's department. He only moved in next door a month ago. Before that, the house was empty for ages."

Sophie frowned. "Daniel says there's some suggestion the guy may have been back casing your place, trying to figure out whether he could get in again."

"Louella Shoop claims to have seen someone."

Sophie wrinkled her nose, but said, "I've never heard her make anything up."

Emily hoped her shiver wasn't obvious. "Why would he even think about coming back? It doesn't make sense. And…do you know how creepy that is?"

"Oh, I can imagine." Sophie reached across the table to squeeze Emily's hand. "Part of me thinks you should take a Caribbean vacation right now. But…"

At her hesitation, Emily said, "I'd have to come home eventually."

"Yes."

They looked at each other, and Emily suspected her own gaze was as troubled as Sophie's.

\*\*\*\*\*

Sean was in Daniel's office when the jury coordinator for Burris County returned his call, which was great timing as well as a minor miracle, given that this was Saturday. He'd found her home phone, and she'd volunteered to go into the office to do the search for him.

What she had to say wasn't so great.

"It doesn't appear we've ever sent Mr. Roff a summons. He certainly hasn't actually served on a jury," she told Sean. "Not in this county. He hasn't been resident here very long."

"Five years."

"I'm sorry," she said, now sounding tentative. "Isn't he that high school teacher who was murdered?"

"Yes." Frustrated beyond belief, he thanked her and ended the call. "You caught that?" he asked Daniel.

"Unfortunately. Which leaves us no further ahead where motive is concerned."

Daniel had already asked Roff's friends and fellow teachers whether he might have witnessed a crime or had occasion to testify as an expert witness. Everyone had been quite sure he hadn't. "That's the kind of thing you talk about in the break room," as one of the teachers said.

"Bev Sheahan from CAU called, by the way," Daniel continued. "No surprise, my scene was as clean as yours. This guy almost has to be covering himself head to toe. I'd say a Tyvek suit, except I've never seen one that wasn't bright white."

Sean agreed. "I've been thinking about that. What about a wetsuit? He could move well in it, and if it's black he'd blend right into the night. Once he walks away from the house, he could pull down the hood, whip on jeans and a sweatshirt right over it, and who would look at him twice?"

Daniel grunted. "You heard any more from Mendoza?"

"He suggested a lunch meeting tomorrow. That's partly why I stopped by. I was hoping you'd want to join us."

"I take it his boss doesn't know?"

Sean shook his head. "He'll be fired if Chief Lundy finds out he's leaking information to us."

"That guy is an idiot," Daniel said flatly. "But I have to tell you, after taking this job, I figured out pretty quick that most of my predecessors were idiots, too. The cream of the crop does not always end up in small town police departments."

Sean grimaced in agreement. "Rural sheriff's departments, either."

"You stick just because you grew up around here?"

"I can't think of a better place to live," he said simply. "After the academy, I became a deputy for Washington County, which mixes urban and rural." Washington County took in Portland and its environs. "I drove home to Cannon Beach on a lot of my days off, and a couple of years along, I decided I'd be happier living over here on the coast. Tillamook County didn't happen to have an opening around then, but Burris County did." He shrugged. "We don't have the same amount of excitement, but I can't say I miss it."

Daniel rolled his shoulders. "No. I was trying to ditch the excitement when I took this job. I had no idea what a pain in the ass it would be trying to keep the department staffed, though."

"Which is why a lot of small agencies take whatever they can get."

"Unfortunately." Colburn sighed. "Back to the investigation. I'm stymied for the moment. I'll keep digging into Roff's background, but my gut says I'm wasting my time."

"Mine agrees. I'm getting desperate enough to have bothered to find out where Frank Lowe liked to fill his gas tank, what he usually ordered for lunch and, hey, speaking of guts, that he'd been gobbling antacids like jelly beans, but none of that is useful."

Daniel raised his eyebrows. "Ulcer?"

"The ME can't believe he wasn't puking blood."

Daniel laughed. "On that note, who's hungry?"

\*\*\*\*\*

"Mind if I turn this on?" Sean asked, already reaching for the power button on the small TV that sat at one end of Emily's kitchen counter. He'd just arrived. In the nick of time, Emily told him, since the lasagna was ready to come out of the oven.

"Of course not," she said, reaching for a pair of potholders. "Oh. The local news is on, isn't it?"

"I want to know what they're saying about this latest murder."

Lundy liked any excuse to hold a press conference and posture for the cameras. Sean prayed he was capable of some discretion.

A commercial finished, followed by an anchorman looking somber. "Another brutal murder in Burris County," he intoned. Some still photos rolled as he talked. Traynor in his judicial robes. An outside view of the courthouse and then the judge's home. "Jennifer Whitburn attended a press conference held just an hour ago, where North Fork Police Chief Howard Lundy issued a statement and answered questions. Jennifer, what did you learn?"

After the usual brief pause, the attractive blonde said gravely, "The murder of Circuit Court Presiding Judge Charles Tranor is unquestionably linked to the two recent killings in this county that have already raised alarm. That much was clear from Chief Lundy's remarks. Once again, a pane of glass was cut from a window, allowing the killer to reach in and open that window. Chief Lundy shared a further, horrifying detail with us."

Oh, shit. "No, no, no," Sean groaned.

Uselessly. That self-important ass Lundy appeared behind a podium, a forest of microphones in front of him. His forehead was creased with concern, or a pretence at deep thought.

"Two letters were written in blood on the wall above the bathtub," he said. "DD."

A voice shouted out a question.

"I cannot comment on the investigations being conducted by other law enforcement agencies. I can tell you that the similarities at each scene have been significant."

Sean stared in disbelief as he pontificated on about how they were all searching for one killer – or perhaps a pair of killers. The significance of the two letters was not yet known, although there was speculation that they stood for dishonorable discharge.

Emily touched his arm. "I'm sorry."

"Is he really that stupid?" He snorted and answered himself. "No, he's that self-important. Wants to look smarter than everyone else. I know damn sure he's never investigated a homicide in his life."

The anchorman reappeared, made a few comments while looking deeply worried, and then said, "When we return from a commercial break…" Sean stabbed the power button. The TV went dark.

His phone rang. Wilcynski.

He answered. "I saw it. I'm still stunned."

The lieutenant was steaming. He vented for several minutes about Lundy before saying resignedly, "What's done is done. The sheriff is going to be seriously pissed, though."

"He can join the crowd," Sean growled.

*****

Daniel understood the choice of restaurant, even though he'd have rather eaten at the Sea Watch Café or gone home to have a sandwich with Sophie. The Waves, attached to the Surfside hotel, served conventional American food in its heaviest and blandest form. The benefit here was that Sean had been able to reserve the back room, where they could talk privately as they ate. Plus, Chief Lundy didn't appear often in Cape Trouble.

Sean had arrived before Daniel. Otherwise, they straggled in by ones and twos. Sheriff Mackay walked in with Lieutenant Wilcynski, Detective Payne on his own, and Mendoza last, looking harried. Full attendance, and on a Sunday. Workaholics, one and all, Daniel thought.

"I appreciate you all driving down here to meet me," Rey Mendoza said as he pulled out a chair. "As you know, my chief doesn't see any reason we can't keep our investigation in-house." He shook his head. "With a serial killer operating, sharing information is critical."

When the waitress appeared to take orders, they talked idly about the projected opening of the fancy new resort being built just the other side of the point and a fatality accident that had happened the previous weekend south on 101. The minute the door closed behind her, Mendoza said, "I suppose you all saw the press conference."

"We saw it," Sheriff Mackay said tersely. "I had words with your boss last night. He claims he had no idea we were trying to hold back that detail."

"How could he not?" Wilcynski muttered.

"I begged him not to go public with the letters," Mendoza exploded before visibly collecting himself. "That's not why I wanted this meeting, though." The smallest pause ensured all eyes were on him. "We have a witness."

"What?" That was Detective Payne, but someone else sucked in a breath and all of them leaned forward, waiting.

"I should have said, a witness of sorts. A woman a couple doors down called in a report about a prowler," the North Fork detective said. "Her dog started to bark, she looked out the window and saw someone running across her back yard and vaulting the fence. In response to her call, a patrol unit came by, the officer walked around her house, then let her know the trespasser seemed to be long gone."

"What time did she call it in?" Sean asked.

"3:08. The responding unit arrived at 3:15." He shrugged. "Given seven minutes, the guy could have been half a mile away by then."

"Not if he was on foot," Payne argued.

Sean shook his head. "He didn't walk to Frank Lowe's neighborhood. And look how far apart the three scenes are. The guy's got transportation."

"Wouldn't the woman who made the call have noticed if a car started up nearby?" Daniel said. "After seeing the guy, she had to have been on alert."

Mendoza was already shaking his head. "She swears she didn't hear anything."

"Nobody remembers hearing a car at the time of the other murders, either," Lieutenant Wilcynski said thoughtfully.

Sean looked the most tired and frustrated of any of them, but Daniel knew that had more to do with his neighbor's problems than it did with this investigation. Now he shook his head. "You know he has a vehicle, probably parked out at the highway for the first two murders."

"It would have been easy to walk that distance from the Lowe's house," Wilcynski said. "He'd have stood out a little more in Cape Trouble."

"Maybe, maybe not. Not many people awake in the middle of the night, and most people throw a slipper at their dog if his barking wakes them up."

"Could the woman give any kind of description?" Daniel asked.

"A man." Mendoza let out a tired breath. "She seems sure of that. Tall. Dressed in black, or at least a dark color. Either dark-haired or wearing something like a stocking cap."

Sean's eyes met Daniel's. They were thinking the same thing. Hood, very possibly of a wet suit.

"She says she wouldn't have been able to see him at all, except he passed in front of their garden shed, which is painted white. With moonlight providing enough contrast, she got a good look. Her guess is that the guy jumped into her yard over the fence, too, and shook it enough to rattle the gate. That would have been an unusual enough sound at night to get her dog worked up."

"The responding officer didn't happen to pass a walker, biker, car coming out of the neighborhood…?" It was Sheriff Mackay, who had been silent until now.

"Unfortunately, the officer approached from the opposite direction. He did cruise slowly through the neighborhood after looking around her place, but didn't see anyone."

"Guy's a fucking ghost," Payne observed.

Muscles bulged in Sean's jaw. "Not a ghost. This time, somebody saw him. If a patrol car had happened to be a couple blocks away, we might have had him, or at least an I.D."

The arrival of the waitress carrying a tray brought the discussion to a close. They were able to talk more as they ate, but mostly throwing out information that didn't seem to be new to anyone. The sheriff looked intrigued at the name of Judge Tranor's much-younger lover, but he didn't say why. When it was just the two of them, Daniel would ask him more. In the almost two years since he'd taken the job in Cape Trouble, he and Alex Mackay had become friends. Daniel felt comfortable enough with Sean to call him a friend, too.

Mendoza and Wilcynski, he didn't know at all. So far, so good with Mendoza; at least he had the balls to take an end-around his boss when it was the right thing to do. Daniel hadn't made up his mind about Jason Payne, except it was obvious he was green. In a larger law enforcement agency, he wouldn't have made detective for years, given his relative inexperience. The thought afforded Daniel some amusement when he remembered what Sean had said. And, yeah, he'd been right. They did take what they could get.

Which made Daniel wonder a whole lot about Lieutenant B.J. Wilcynski, whose credentials would have gotten him hired just about anywhere. So why here? Another question to ask Mackay. Probably Wilcynski was a case of burn-out, as Daniel himself had been, but Daniel liked to know people he worked with. Payne was smart, but also an eager beaver and cocky as hell. Wilcynski, though, was a harder read.

"Something that's been worrying me," Sean said abruptly. "Probably unrelated, but I thought I'd throw it out."

He had everyone's attention.

"Most of you know my next-door neighbor, Emily Drake, had a break-in."

Daniel had an immediate, horrified understanding of where Sean was going, and he didn't know why he hadn't made the same leap.

Sean told them the basics, including what Louella Shoop had reported seeing. Dark shape circling Emily's house. Probably wearing something over his head. Getaway on a bicycle.

There was a long silence.

Wilcynski broke it. "What could possibly connect her to the three victims we have?"

"What connects Roff to the others?" Sean countered, face grim. "And no, there's nothing obvious here, either. She says she didn't know any of the victims. She's an artist, a businesswoman. The only attorney she's ever hired was the one who handled her husband's estate after his death."

*She says.* Did Sean doubt she was telling the truth? Daniel wondered.

"Most burglars wear dark clothing and case homes," Alex said mildly.

"That's true," Daniel said, "but this guy was dead-set on getting his hands on Emily, not anything in her house."

Jason appeared appalled, Lieutenant Wilcynski impassive, the others interested but not necessarily convinced.

Sean pushed his plate away. His lack of appetite showed in how much food he'd left and the sharper jut of his cheekbones. "Like I said, there probably isn't a connection. I don't want to believe there is. But...it crossed my mind."

They broke up shortly after, Daniel leaving most of his fries uneaten. He didn't need a lump of undigested concrete in his belly all afternoon.

# CHAPTER NINE

"You're quiet tonight," Emily said tentatively, mid-way through dinner Monday night. Sharing at least this much of their day was becoming a habit. "Is there something…well, more wrong than usual?"

The somber expression Sean had worn since he walked in the door cleared when he laughed. "I guess with my job, there is always something wrong, isn't there?"

Her mouth curved too. "By the time your average homicide detective reaches retirement age, I don't suppose he's a very jolly fellow."

Sean chuckled again. "You might be surprised. There's plenty of dark humor, at least. Without some sense of humor, who could cut it? And you should hear what my parents think is funny. I swear, medical people tell the most grisly jokes."

Emily made a face. "I heard some from Tom. The kind where you feel awful because you couldn't help laughing. Um…do you want coffee?"

"If you don't mind." His gaze rested thoughtfully on her face. "I've been mooching off you."

"I…look forward to you coming home."

*Home?* she thought with a burst of alarm, pushing back from the table to busy herself starting the coffee. Whose home was she talking about?

And, oh, she hated admitting even to herself how much she did anticipate his knock on the door. Hours before she expected him, she'd find herself lifting her head at the sound of any passing vehicle, feeling disappointment when she realized it wasn't his. He made her feel safe while he was here, but that wasn't all of it.

He'd pushed back his own chair enough to stretch out his legs. When she glanced over her shoulder after setting mugs on the counter, it was to find him watching her.

"You're a great cook," he said. "I'm getting spoiled."

She came back to the table. "If anyone's in the debt column, it's me. You saved my life."

A shutter closed over his expression. "That's why you're feeding me?"

Panic fluttered in her chest. If she said yes, he'd refuse future invitations. She knew he would.

"No." Her breathing came too fast. "I like talking to you. Having you…" She gave a small shrug. "Here. You know."

His smile was wry, but it did soften his face again. "And I like being here."

*I like you. You like me.* That almost sounded like…oh, some kind of beginning. Scary thought. But, despite her panic, she discovered that the idea of going back to being utterly alone was unimaginably bleak.

Not that she'd have to be. If she allowed herself friends, they would be here for her. Sophie Thomsen could be one, she thought. Hannah Moss, who owned a combined bookstore and fudge shop a block from The Sandpiper, had made overtures. And then there were the friends Emily had driven away.

But the panic remained, and she knew why. She wanted more than friends. She wanted Sean in her life.

And, oh boy, but that scared her, too, because her feelings for him went beyond friendship.

"You never answered my question," she said hastily, needing to divert them both. "About why you're all broody tonight."

One side of his mouth tilted again. "Like a hen on her eggs?" The hint of humor vanished from his face. "Not a bad comparison. I keep waiting for another egg to break."

"You mean, another murder."

His eyes seemed to darken. "Maybe. Maybe something else."

"Like…what?" It came out as a near-whisper.

He only shook his head.

Somehow the tension in the room increased with his silence. Talking, she wasn't so aware of him physically. Without that distraction, she'd fixate on his hands, so much larger than hers, the sinewy power of his forearms, the evening stubble shadowing lean cheeks. The penetrating blue of his eyes.

His mouth.

After his last swallow of coffee, he insisted on helping clear the table and get the dishwasher loaded. They did the dance, stepping past each other, as if they'd done it hundreds of times, she thought, disconcerted. He already knew where everything went in her cupboards.

Tonight, as she put away leftovers, he washed pans. She hadn't known he was finished until she shut the refrigerator door and, turning, bumped into him. He wasn't supposed to be so close.

He caught her with his hands on her upper arms. "Emily."

The rough, deep texture of his voice resonated with something inside her. She swallowed and lifted her gaze to meet his.

"I'm going to kiss you."

She opened her mouth, but her lips refused to frame the word 'no'. *Because I want this*, she realized with shock.

When she didn't say anything, didn't retreat, Sean slid a hand beneath her braid and gently squeezed. Then he stroked her neck, the rasp from his calluses an erotic contrast to the delicacy of his touch. Goosebumps tiptoed down her spine. With his free hand, he cupped her jaw.

Unlike the only other time he'd kissed her, he started softly, even sweetly, his lips brushing hers, nibbling, testing. Asking instead of making a statement or demanding. Emily stood completely still, overwhelmed by sensations she'd almost forgotten. It was like diving into the surf, feeling the wave crash over her. In the churning depths, she couldn't seem to think, only feel. The teasing touch of his mouth wasn't enough. She pushed up on tiptoe to deepen the kiss.

Beneath her hands – when had she put them there? – his chest vibrated with a groan. An arm came hard around her, and he took advantage of her parted lips to stroke inside her mouth with his tongue. Hers met it. Her knees wobbled even as heat ran through her veins.

She heard a sound that could have been a whimper. *Me. I whimpered.*

She did it again. Her hands crept around his neck. Her fingers dove into the coarse silk of his hair, making him shiver.

His tongue slid rhythmically against hers. The hard bar of his erection pressed against her belly. One of his hands moved restlessly up and down her back, finally gripping her hip to lift her. She felt something cool and hard at her back. The refrigerator. He'd backed her up a couple of steps. Her body fit against his miraculously well, but she needed…wanted...

He tore his mouth from hers. "Emily. God." Panting, he rested his forehead against hers. "Give me a minute."

The last thing she wanted was him to stop, but…she couldn't do this. Could she? With his body still pressed against hers, the throbbing between her legs, it was hard to clear her mind, but she struggled to think.

"Are you ready, Emily?" he asked hoarsely. "If not, you have to say so now."

She'd told him she would never be ready. A fireball burst in her chest. "No." Her arms dropped and she squirmed sideways, escaping the cage of his body. "No. I can't…" She clapped a hand over her mouth. Around it, she whispered, "What was I *thinking*?"

Every stark angle of his face seemed sharpened, as if passion and anger had honed his features. "You're attracted to me." He was mad, and not hiding it. "You have needs you've been suppressing." Then, miraculously, his voice softened. "You trust me."

She felt herself sag even as her eyes widened in renewed shock. She did trust him. She liked him. She might even…more than like him.

Wrapping her arms tightly in front of herself, she said, "Yes. You're right. I'm sorry. It's just…"

His eyes were the bluest she'd ever seen them, and the large hand that engulfed her cheek was inexplicably comforting. "We kissed, Emily. That's all. This is why I stopped. I need you to be sure before we go any further."

She couldn't look away from him. A nod was all she could manage.

"Good." He smiled ruefully, gave her a tender kiss and said, "It's time for me to go home."

*Don't go. Please don't go.* Emily bit back the plea. Now it was fear talking – and the unexpected wish that home for him was here, with her.

Once again, she nodded.  Like a civil hostess, she walked him to the door and even came up with a smile of sorts.  "You triggered a panic attack," she said lightly.  "I apologize."

"Not surprising."  This smile was crooked, too.  "Can I take you out to dinner tomorrow night?  Or am I pushing it?"

Yes.  Yes, he was.  He had some definite bulldozer tendencies.  But if he hadn't pushed...  She'd still be alone.

"I don't mind cooking again," she heard herself say.  "But if you'd rather..."

"I want to make things easier for you," he said quietly.  "I've loved every dinner you made.  Whatever you prefer."

"Then...here," she decided.

After a last, lingering look but no more touches, he was gone.

Setting the alarm, Emily pondered how it was that eating together every night had come to be expected.  Their norm.  As if...

She wasn't ready to finish that sentence.

*****

With a rush of adrenaline, Emily came awake, opening her eyes to pitch darkness.  She shot to a sitting position, trying to understand why there were no bedcovers over her.

On an adrenaline-laced rush, she remembered.  In the early days – the first year, at least – she had come into Cody's room daily to sit on the bed and try desperately to believe she felt his presence.  She rarely did anymore, but last night sleep had seemed impossible.  Instead of getting into her own bed, she'd crossed the hall in the dark.

But she had fallen asleep, after all, because she was curled up now on the bed.  It was the strangeness of where she was that had awakened her.  No, she was cold.  Or...she'd had a nightmare.  What else would—

A floorboard creaked.  In her hall.  Barely outside Cody's bedroom door, which she had left ajar.  The sound was very faint, but she knew it.

Rational thought dissolved into instant terror.  *I have to get out.*

She slipped from the bed, never tearing her eyes from the half-open door.  She had no protection at all, not even the dining room chair she'd been propping beneath her doorknob in her own room every night before she went to bed.

Once he realized she wasn't in her own bed...

She could close the door, shove the small bookcase in front of it, like she had the other time. Heart hammering, she thought, no. He'd been in the living room then, picking himself up off the floor. Her door had already been closed.

Tonight...he was so close. Staring down at her empty bed, maybe. Slipping silently into her bathroom. The first sound would tell him where she was.

She crossed as quietly as she could the few feet to the window and unlocked it, wincing at the tiny click. Maybe she'd imagined that creak. She could have been dreaming. Maybe...

She strained to hear anything at all that would tell her she was no longer alone in the house. Her own panting sounded loud to her ears.

*Don't take a chance. Get out.*

Emily thrust the window sash upward. A scream split the night as she kicked at the screen. The alarm.

She heard running footsteps just as she plunged through the opening. A butterfly bush here had grown partially in front of the window. Branches snagged her pajamas and scraped her skin. She scrabbled out of it on her hands and knees, turning her head wildly. An ominous, black shape stood at the open window. He'd follow her any second. Screaming herself now, even though no one would hear her over the alarm, she ran, driven by instinct to go around the back of the house instead of toward the street. If he went out the front door instead of the window, he'd be there to meet her.

Or he was right behind her.

Not daring to look back, she tore around behind the house, past her bedroom window until she reached the gate. Her skin prickled with horror. She'd feel his hands any second.

She fumbled with the latch, sobbing with relief when it swung open. Instinct had her thrusting it closed behind her, even though, oh, God, he could be waiting here, too. He'd seen which way she went.

*Keep going.*

She pushed past an old lilac bush and collided with a hard body. A hand closed over her mouth. Mindless with fear, she fought wildly.

"Emily, it's me. It's me," Sean said urgently.

She gasped with relief. He was always there to save her. "He's in my house. I don't know how, but he got in again."

"Come with me." He grabbed her hand and pulled her with him toward her front yard.

She wanted to dig in her heels but let herself be towed. He didn't want to leave her alone, she realized. Good thought. She didn't want to cower alone in the yard, searching the darkness.

They both heard…something. Whirring?

"Shit!" The one explosive word, and Sean dropped her hand and ran full-out toward the street through the open gate in her picket fence.

The one that was usually closed.

Emily chased after him, and saw a bicyclist pass under the streetlight half a block away. Head-down, Sean tore after it, passing a minute later under the same pool of light.

Suddenly freezing cold, shaking, Emily stood with her toes curled on the gritty sidewalk. Even through her shock, she was aware that porch lights had come on in neighboring houses and worried voices called out.

The alarm kept screaming.

Dimly, she thought, Somebody else's alarm is going off, too, but the next second realized it was an approaching siren. Somebody must have called. Maybe everybody in earshot of the alarm had called.

No, she guessed, Sean would have had the presence of mind to dial 911 even as he sprang from bed.

Suddenly, she wasn't alone. A person materialized from the darkness and tenderly draped a blanket around her shoulders.

"You must be freezing." Of course, it was Louella Shoop, but she sounded so kind, Emily turned instinctively toward her, and let herself be embraced by wiry, strong arms. "There, there. You're safe now."

Her teeth chattered. "I should shut that off."

"Do you know how?"

"Yes, I think…"

"That sounds like a good idea," Louella said encouragingly. "Let's do it."

She never took her arm from around Emily's shoulders as they made their way through the gate and up to the porch. Emily's hand shook, but she managed to type in the code.

In the sudden cessation of sound, her ears continued to ring. Louella kept patting her and murmuring words of comfort. Emily stared down the street, waiting with all her being for Sean to reappear.

The siren had been turned off, too, she realized. Her heart clenched. What if the officer had seen Sean running down the street with a gun in his hand? What if he'd tackled him, hand-cuffed him…shot him? No, no, she would have heard that.

Would she, over the alarm? She, who never prayed anymore, did just that. *Keep him safe. Dear God, please. Please, please, please.*

A squad car rolled to the curb in front of her house. No siren, and the rack of lights weren't flashing. The passenger side door opened and Sean got out.

A sob of relief escaped Emily, and, still clutching the blanket, she ran down the steps and walkway to meet him. Something like desperation on his face, he snatched her into his arms and held her so tight it hurt.

*****

Sean was incredibly grateful that Daniel Colburn had been taking a night shift. His response time had been lightning fast. Once he picked Sean up, they drove up one street and down the next, both sharp-eyed, but the son-of-a-bitch was gone.

*Guy's a fucking ghost.*

No, damn it! Sean had seen him.

Trouble was, between streetlights was too much darkness. Old houses meant huge old shrubs, big trees. Backyard fences, detached garages, cars parked along the street. Too damn many places to hide.

A sheriff's deputy had been buying a cup of coffee at the all-night convenience store on the highway. He was still driving slowly through town, watching for traffic of any kind.

Sean heard Colburn reassuring the neighbors and persuading Louella Shoop to go home. Emily pulled away from Sean to give Louella a big hug.

"Thank you," she murmured.

"You let your detective take care of you now, honey," the old busybody told her.

Maybe she wasn't so bad after all.

"She has a good heart," Daniel said in a low voice.

Emily nodded. She was still shaking, and Sean pulled her back to his side. By God, he was never letting go of her again.

She drew a shuddering breath and looked up at him, her eyes so dark they dominated a face that was pinched and paper-white. "He was in my house. I saw him. How did he do that?"

"That's a damn good question," Sean said. "Let's go in and find out."

He steered her into the living room, but she balked at the head of the hall. Horror in her eyes, she stared toward the bedrooms.

"Do you want to wait here?" Sean asked her.

A shudder passed through her, but she shook her head. The two of them followed Daniel down the hall.

All three bedroom doors stood open. They all felt the cold coming from the first room, where she stored fabric and batting and quilts in progress. Daniel nudged the door farther open, turned on the light and murmured an expletive.

"But..." Emily gaped. "But...I'm sure the alarm was on."

Setting her to one side, just inside the room, Sean went with Daniel to inspect the window. The glass in the entire lower sash was missing.

Sean leaned out. "Jesus. He cut it."

Daniel took a look, too, at the large pane of glass leaning against the house side. Just as the smaller piece of glass had been left outside the French doors into the master bedroom at Frank Lowe's house.

"Cut?" Emily whispered. "Isn't that like...?"

She didn't want to say it. Sean didn't blame her. The terrifying knowledge had already rooted beneath his breastbone. The man who had killed three men in barely two weeks wanted Emily dead, too. He'd come back twice now. He wouldn't give up.

"Yeah," he said hoarsely. "It is."

The horror in Emily's eyes didn't abate as she gaped at the window. "But I have an alarm system. Why didn't it go off?" Her whisper rose to an outraged cry. "It was supposed to go off!"

"The window sensors react to the window opening, or the glass breaking. If the glass is cut carefully enough, maybe cushioned somehow so there's not much vibration, the sensor doesn't react. He could have used something like a suction cup to stabilize the piece he was cutting out."

She looked like a woman betrayed. "But when he climbed in…"

"I don't know where you left it, but the sensor is right there. He probably disabled it once he could get a hand on it," Daniel said. "We'll figure it out."

"Oh, God." Emily spun abruptly, turning her back on them. "I shouldn't have had it sitting on the window sill. I never dreamed—"

"None of us did." Sean crossed the room and squeezed her shoulders, gently massaging until her rigidity eased. "How did you know he was in the house, Emily?" he asked. "Were you awake?"

She shook her head. "But I wasn't in my own bed. If I'd been—" Suddenly, she began to shake. Sean pulled her against him, hoping his embrace made her feel safe, and let her burrow.

When the worst of the shudders passed, he murmured, "If you weren't in bed, where were you?"

"Cody's room. I went in to sit and…I guess I fell asleep."

He hated the picture that formed in his mind of her sitting in the dark on the edge of her dead son's bed, remembering the nights when she'd tucked him in. Sung to him, kissed him softly. Had she rocked herself? Cried?

Her teeth chattered. "There's a place in the hall. The floorboard squeaks." She pulled away from him and went out into the hall, going a few feet toward what he knew to be her son's bedroom. Sean heard a small creak.

So little, to have saved her life.

"It's not very loud, but— For a minute, I thought I might have had a nightmare. But, really, I knew."

Fighting for control, he closed his eyes, picturing her alone, petrified. A killer so close.

"So I got out of bed, being as quiet as I could, and I unlocked the window, only I started thinking maybe I'd dreamed the sound." She shot him an apologetic look. "Denial is one of my specialties."

"No." He sounded harsh and didn't care. "You were quick and smart. Don't start thinking you should have done anything differently."

Her teeth closed on her lower lip. After a moment she nodded.

"I decided I'd rather feel stupid than die. I threw up the window and dove out." She hugged herself tight and still trembled. "I looked over my shoulder and saw him. Just a shape, standing at the window. So I ran. And...and you know the rest."

He knew that this time the guy had done the smart thing and taken off.

*The better to try again.*

Emily waited in the hall while he and Daniel checked out her bedroom, but there was no sign anyone had been here. Even the covers remained smooth.

Only the pane of cut glass told its story.

Fear felt like ice in Sean's veins, circulating throughout his entire body.

When he looked back at her, waiting in the hall, Sean saw her teeth chatter. He picked up her slippers from beside her bed and opened drawers until he found a sweatshirt. Maybe the husband's again; right now, Sean didn't care.

He crouched in front of her and lifted each foot in turn to put on the slippers as if she was a child, then gently unwound the blanket, letting it drop. The sweatshirt went over her head. After pulling her fat braid free of the neckline, he helped her get her arms into the sleeves. Then he cocooned her in the blanket again.

"Better?" he asked, and her head bobbed.

"I'm taking her home," he said without even looking at Daniel. "I'd tell you to lock up when you're done, but I guess that wouldn't serve much purpose."

Not even looking back, Sean steered her down the hall.

*****

Emily had never seen Sean look so grim.

Last night, after bringing her home, he'd made her a cup of hot cocoa and refused to talk about their new knowledge.

"Morning is soon enough," he said. He insisted she get into his bed. Leaving on the sweatpants and T-shirt he'd been wearing, he'd set his big, black handgun on the stand where he could reach it and climbed in with her. She hadn't even been able to make herself protest. His arms around her felt too good. She had rested her head on his shoulder, closed her eyes and relived the terror and the inexplicable knowledge that a serial killer had *her* on his list until, astonishingly, she'd fallen asleep. Now she thought it had to have been the shock. Her brain had simply shut down.

She had woken up alone, but known he wouldn't have left her. Once again, he had fed her breakfast. Suppressed rage showed in his body language, but it was the determination in his eyes that persuaded her to eat the food he set in front of her. She had a suspicion he'd shovel bites in her mouth himself if she didn't do it.

Once her plate was empty, he poured coffee for both of them, then looked at her across the table.

She bent her head and went utterly still, resisting the desire to stick her fingers in her ears. She did not want to talk about this.

As if denial had ever done her any good.

"You've watched the news. You know the facts. In each of the three murders we've linked, the killer got in the house by cutting out a piece of window glass," he said, in that same implacable voice. "It has to be the same guy, Emily." And yes, that was regret in his eyes now, or even pity. "What we have to figure out is why you."

"I'm...I didn't know any of them!"

"So you said."

Struggling with her fear, it took her a moment to hear in his voice that he hadn't believed her.

"You think I'm lying."

The lines in his forehead deepened, letting her see his weariness and worry. "No, Emily. But I do think you know something. You had a thought when I asked you about Darryl Roff. Whatever it was, you didn't want to share."

She bowed her head, focusing on the coffee in her mug. She had to tell him.

"I never met him. That's the truth."

"But?"

"I…Tom and I fostered a teenage boy briefly." She made herself look at him. "It was something Tom had always wanted to do. His best friend as a kid lived in a foster home. When he contacted social services, they asked if we'd consider taking a teenager instead of the younger child we'd been picturing. They had a boy whose mother had just died. We agreed."

She wasn't sure Sean was so much as blinking.

"Um…his name was Braden. Braden Wilson."

He frowned, as if the name had tickled his memory.

"Braden stuttered. Supposedly it had been a problem when he was younger but he'd overcome it, only after his mom died, he reverted. Kids made fun of him, but that wasn't the worst. He had biology with Mr. Roff. Braden hated him. Every day in class, Mr. Roff made a point of using this fake stutter to give directions. Then he'd say something to the whole class like, 'To make sure Mr. Wilson understands these instructions, too.' Or, 'Since Mr. Wilson's English isn't yet fluent.' Of course, everyone would laugh."

"Son of a bitch," Sean muttered.

"The thing is, we'd only had him a few weeks when Tom and Cody were killed. Braden is part of the reason I hadn't gone with them to visit Tom's parents. They…didn't know we'd taken in a foster child, and Tom expected them to disapprove. We didn't want to spring him on them." The shame she still felt rose in waves of heat that were probably painting her cheeks red. "After…" She swallowed back nausea. "I fell apart. I called social services and asked them to find another place for Braden. I couldn't take care of another human being. I wasn't taking care of myself."

Compassion in his eyes, he reached across the table and clasped her hand. "That's understandable, Emily."

"If I'd had another child of my own, I wouldn't have given him away."

"Not the same thing."

She shook her head. "Maybe it should have been. I'll never forget the way he looked at me when I told him he couldn't stay." The betrayal on his face had penetrated her devastation, but only briefly. Too briefly. She'd been so relieved when he was gone, but even that vanished in the bottomless well of pain that was her reality. "All I know is, I let him down. I never heard what happened to him after that. I never asked or tried to find out. But…it's because of Braden I knew something about Mr. Roff."

"He's the key. He has to be." Sean went utterly still, then made a strange sound, as if he'd taken a blow and air was escaping. "Oh, Christ. I know that name."

## CHAPTER TEN

"What? Tell me," Emily demanded.

Sean hesitated, because, damn, he didn't want to. But keeping Braden's fate quiet was hopeless. She needed to know why she'd been targeted by a killer.

"You're lucky you didn't keep him," he said tersely. "Braden raped a girl, Emily. He was tried and convicted, but as he was being led out, he managed to grab a gun from a guard in the courtroom. Another deputy shot and killed him."

Shock widened her eyes. "Oh, no. I remember that." She released a ragged breath. "Vaguely. Did the news report his name?"

"Since he was a juvenile, they probably didn't initially."

As if she hadn't heard him, she said, "Oh, my God. That was Braden?"

"Oh, yeah." Puzzle pieces were slotting into place as if moved by an invisible hand. "And what do you want to bet Frank Lowe was his attorney and Judge Tranor presided at the trial?"

Her forehead crinkled. "But…if he's dead…?"

"Oh, he's dead, all right."

He saw that Emily got it. "Somebody cared about him," she said slowly. "And…he intends to murder every single person who ever hurt Braden." Despite a shudder, she somehow kept her voice steady. "And I'm one of them."

He took her hand again. "You can't blame yourself."

Her eyes met his. "Can't I?" she said with simple dignity.

"Emily…"

She shook her head. "You have a job to do."

They had to talk about this. She didn't need to be haunted by one more death, but Sean recognized in frustration that this wasn't the time. She had retreated emotionally, and he had to let her.

"I can't leave you alone."

"You can drop me off at The Sandpiper. I'll stay there all day. I promise."

He didn't like even that idea. He wanted her where he could see her, but could just imagine what Lieutenant Wilcynski would say if she became a permanent ride-along partner.

"You won't be alone there?"

"I promise."

She'd still be too vulnerable. As ruthless as this bastard had proved himself to be, he might be willing to kill another woman just to get at Emily. Sean had to remind himself that, after his last failure, the guy had retreated to regroup. Yeah, and chosen to take out another of his targets before working his way back around to Emily.

And so far, he'd operated only at night.

Because he had a nine-to-five job and had to keep up appearances? Sean speculated. Or because he was a crazy, homeless veteran who could pass unseen at night, but whose appearance would turn heads during the day?

"Yeah," he said, his voice only a little rough. "I'll drop you and pick you up."

He went so far as to walk her into her store, relieved to see that two other women greeted her in surprise and studied him with interest. Emily promised again not to set foot outside until he picked her up. Sean checked the back door, reassured that the deadbolt was already locked.

Then he made calls, summoning everyone on his task force to a meeting. The sheriff was the only one he failed to reach.

Even Rey Mendoza showed up. Sean brought them up to date, first with the night's events, then what he'd learned from Emily.

"I pulled up what I could on the trial. Braden Wilson was accused of raping a girl named Kimberly Fisk, who also attended Cape Trouble High School. Sure enough, Lowe represented the boy and Tranor presided. We know from Ms. Drake that Braden hated Darryl Roff. As I see it, we have two immediate priorities. One is to determine other possible targets and provide protection. Second, now that we know he's connected to Braden, is to figure out who this guy is." He glanced at his notes. "Braden was prosecuted by Mike Emerson."

Even Wilcynski had likely encountered Emerson by now. His title was Assistant Chief Deputy District Attorney. If the killer was angry at the presiding judge, he would harbor as much rage at the man who had prosecuted Braden.

"Was he prosecuted as an adult?" Daniel asked, reminding Sean he had only been in Cape Trouble for something like a year and a half.

"No, thank God. Not much in this qualifies as good news, but Braden being a minor is a silver lining."

"No jury," Mendoza murmured. "Otherwise, we'd be looking at twelve more potential targets."

Sean continued, "We need to get social service records. First, because the social worker – or workers – who supervised this kid in his foster homes is at high risk."

"And then there are the other foster parents," Wilcynski said.

"Maybe multiples. It's possible there was only one other home, but if Braden was already troubled, odds are good that in two years he was moved around. Then there's the girl he raped. Was she a classmate? A random target? Braden claimed she lied, that the sex was consensual."

Someone snorted. "Don't they all?"

"As far as the killer is concerned," Sean said, "she may be the brass ring. It's all her fault."

"Oh, I'd think there would be two brass rings. Who shot and killed him?" Wilcynski asked.

"One of our deputies. Byron Saunders. Having to kill a kid really hit him hard. I remember him saying he had a boy of his own not that much younger."

"Was there any question about whether the use of force was appropriate?" Jason asked.

Sean remembered that Jason wouldn't have been around then either. "Not that I recall," he said. "Once the boy lunged and got his hands on the other deputy's weapon, and right in the middle of the courtroom, there weren't a lot of options."

Wilcynski lifted his eyebrows. "Let's find out as much as we can about the incident. If the shooting wasn't a hundred percent necessary, that might explain the level of rage the killer is displaying."

A ball of anger lodged in Sean's gut. "How does it explain him wanting to kill a woman whose only sin was not being able to function as a foster parent when her own husband and child were killed?"

"He might think everything else that went wrong is her fault," Jason suggested. "Especially if it turns out the kid was abused in a later foster home."

Sean's jaw was clenched so tight, he was about to crack some teeth. It was probably just as well he didn't respond.

Daniel glanced at him, then said, "Let's not speculate ahead of the facts. The boy may already have had behavioral issues that just hadn't manifested yet. Remember, he was new on the social services radar. Do we know how the mother died?"

"No," Sean managed to say. "That's a question we need to ask. More important is finding out what other family Braden Wilson had. It's hard to imagine some buddy caring enough to carry out a lethal vendetta. Where was the father when the kid needed him? Were there siblings? Other relatives? An attempt would have been made to locate relatives before placing a kid in foster care."

He passed out assignments, reserving the Department of Human Services for himself.

Wilcynski promised to get a warrant in the works in case they needed it. "I'll talk to Byron Saunders as well as his direct supervisor, too," he said.

Mendoza grimaced. "If I were him, I'd take the whole family on a vacation. Say, a Caribbean cruise. It'd be hard to get to him on a cruise ship."

There were sounds of agreement.

Jason volunteered to track down the rape victim and her family. Mendoza would talk to Mike Emerson with the D.A.'s office.

"Then we have a plan," Sean said. "Stay in touch. We'll meet again tomorrow morning, same time. In the meantime, let me know what you learn and I'll disseminate it as necessary."

After swift agreement, the room cleared.

*****

Sean's visit to the local Department of Human Services produced the expected consternation. If Braden had still been alive and in the system, he'd have met more resistance to opening the boy's records.  As it was, he was funneled almost immediately to a sturdy, middle-aged woman named Jeanette Kelley, who had been Braden Wilson's caseworker.  She was scared, but maintained enough self-possession to remind him that she dealt on a daily basis with angry teenagers and troubled adults.  In fact, she told him, she'd been assaulted twice in her career.

She remembered Braden well, and not only because of his violent death.

"After we removed him from Mrs. Drake's house at her request, we placed him with a family whose last name was Fisk."  She saw Sean's expression.  "I see you understand the significance."

"They had a daughter."  Oh, crap.  The dots had all seemed so random, but now a kindergartner could have drawn lines between them.

"That's correct.  Braden was later accused of, and convicted of, raping Kimberly Fisk."  She sighed.  "Braden inexplicably became 'clumsy' shortly after going to live with the Fisks.  There was a broken arm, a cracked cheekbone and black eye.  His stuttering worsened.  I became suspicious immediately, but Braden denied abuse initially and, of course, had been struggling over his mother's death and going into the foster care system.  After several ER visits, I removed him from the home.  At that time, he admitted that Mr. Fisk had been physically abusive.  Braden said Kimberly was the little princess and could do no wrong, while everything Braden did or said brought a blow.  The Fisks had previously fostered a girl who turned eighteen only a few months later.  That went fine."  Her lips thinned.  "Why they agreed to take a boy, I have no idea.  Braden was a big kid – taller than Mr. Fisk and already strongly built.  I can only guess that Mr. Fisk felt threatened by him in some subliminal way.  I regret not understanding what was happening in that home faster than I did."

"Hindsight is a wonderful thing," he said dryly.

She sighed.  "Yes.  Sadly, matters did not improve for Braden. There are never enough foster homes for teenagers, and I didn't have one available at that point.  I had to put him in a group home."

She told him which, and Sean nodded.  Unfortunately, the Elk Creek Home for Boys existed to take in kids who already displayed significant behavioral issues.  He cringed at imagining Braden

Wilson, traumatized and stuttering badly, plunked down in the middle of a bunch of tough kids angry at the world.

Hell, he thought; how many names were on the killer's list?

"Do your notes indicate whether any particular boy tormented him? What about the supervisors?"

Mrs. Kelley opened Braden's file, printing out the original work-up while she browsed her own notes.

Sean focused on the family information. Father: David Wilson. He'd abandoned his family when Braden was a baby and Braden didn't know if he was alive. The complete lack of contact made it unlikely he'd now set out to avenge every perceived wrong done to his son.

Braden had an older brother, he had insisted, but not a blood relation. His mother had lived with a man for some years who had died in an industrial accident. The 'brother' was Aaron Voight. Braden called him AJ. He wasn't asked, or hadn't said, what the middle initial J stood for. Supposedly, Aaron had promised he'd take care of Braden, who had been certain this guy would rush to his rescue. Unfortunately, it turned out he was in the army, and when Mrs. Kelley contacted him, he was on the verge of deployment to Afghanistan.

Career military and unmarried, she had noted. Unable to provide stable living situation for a minor.

And there, Sean thought, was the military connection.

Aaron had told Braden to hang tight and said when his current enlistment ended he wouldn't re-up so he could bring Braden to live with him.

Two years later, Braden was dead. Mrs. Kelley had attempted to contact Aaron, but found his email address and mobile phone number both invalid. She had tried to inform him via Army channels, only to be told they could find no records that matched the information she had supplied.

*Guy's a fucking ghost.*

On a rush of frustration, Sean rejected the thought again. No, the guy was living and deadly – and somewhere within Burris County. Sean had no doubt this "brother" was their killer. He had the skill set. He had made promises to Braden he hadn't kept. Guilt might as well have been a trip line for an IED. Because he couldn't accept his own failure, he had to blame someone else for Braden's descent into hell.

Not someone: everyone else.

Sean recognized that he might be indulging in psychobabble, but thought he was right.

He'd mount a search for an A.J. Voight, but knew it would be futile.

Mrs. Kelley gave him copies of key information to take with him, after which they discussed her vulnerability. He suggested she get the hell out of Dodge. He had no doubt her supervisor would gladly okay extended vacation time. Sean mentioned the idea of a cruise, which she jumped right on.

"My husband is retired. We can pack and go to my mother's in Portland tonight. We've talked about taking a Panama Canal cruise." She smiled weakly. "What better time?"

Sean asked her to stay in touch, and left with her personal email address that she promised to check wherever she went.

His phone had vibrated twice while he was with her. As soon as he reached his car, he checked messages.

The first was from the lieutenant. Sean returned it.

"Saunders is furious, scared shitless and resistant to the idea of going into hiding," Wilcynski reported. "He'll sleep with a gun under his pillow, he says. Goes without saying that he's outraged at any suggestion he didn't have to shoot to kill." He sounded weary. "I have to agree. I read up on the incident and talked to a couple of other people, too. He aimed for mid-torso. If he'd tried anything fancy, he'd have risked hitting someone behind the kid."

He listened to what Sean had learned, then said, "I'll pursue the military angle. There may have just been a screw-up when DHS asked about this Aaron Voight. Or the inquiry might have been blocked for some reason. Say, he was special forces."

"Worth trying," Sean agreed, then mentioned his speculations regarding A.J.'s legal name. "He could have changed it along the way, of course, but what if his legal last name never was Voight?"

"You're saying his parents weren't married."

"Right. He could have gone by Voight just because he lived with his dad and sometimes that's easiest, but the last name on his birth certificate was his mother's. Easy to go back to. In fact, he'd have *had* to use his legal name when he enlisted."

Wilcynski expressed his frustration, which Sean shared. Following the trail of Braden and his mother had become even more critical.

The second caller had been Rey Mendoza. Emerson from the D.A.'s office said he was threatened all the time and had had a top-of-the-line home security system installed when he had his house built. "Turns out Emerson lives in North Fork. I approached Chief Lundy about getting round the clock surveillance on him, and I think he might go for it." His tone became sardonic. "He likes the idea of North Fork P.D. making the arrest."

Listening to the message, Sean gave a sharp laugh. That sounded like Lundy. A police officer parked in front of the Assistant Chief Deputy District Attorney's house might protect him, but an arrest? This guy was too smart to stroll right by the patrol car, inviting capture.

Back at his desk, it took Sean barely a minute to discover that the Fisks, unbelievably enough, were still in the same house. Apparently they felt no shame. He doubted the daughter still lived at home, though. She'd be nineteen now. In college? Conceivably even married, he supposed.

As if he'd conjured it, his phone rang and he saw that Payne was the caller.

"Kimberly Fisk is a student at Oregon Coast Community College in Newport," he said. "Didn't know there was a college there."

"There are three community colleges here on the coast," Sean said. "Coos Bay and Tillamook, too. Did you get an address?"

"Yeah, sounds like a typical off-campus dump she shares with a bunch of students."

"Did you contact her directly?"

"No. Should I?"

"Let me think about it." Remembering that Jason didn't know Kimberly Fisk's father had also been Braden's foster parent, Sean updated him, adding, "We don't want her to run home, that's for sure."

"That would be convenient, wouldn't it? Two for the price of one." After a moment, Payne grunted. "Maybe three for the price of one. Depends on whether the mother did a damn thing to stop her asshole of a husband from beating on the boy."

"Husband might be abusing her, too," Sean suggested.

"Then he'd likely be beating on the daughter, too. And if that's the case, why was Braden so angry at her?"

Sean remembered what Mrs. Kelley had said. Kimberly was the little princess and could do no wrong. Abused kids usually kept their heads down to avoid notice. Kimberly had either been full of herself, or the apple of her daddy's eye. Or both. Neither sounded like he hurt her.

Sean said, "We might get a feel when we talk to the Fisks. They live here in Cape Trouble." Which made them technically Daniel's problem.

The group home, he had determined, was in Jasper Beach. The small community had grown up around the cove on the other side of the point that reared above Cape Trouble. The long-since deactivated lighthouse could be seen from both sides. Jasper Beach was something of an artists' colony, with a number of studios, a gallery and a small grocery store/gas station. Kids from there attended Cape Trouble schools.

Several of the wealthiest early settlers had built big Victorian houses on the Jasper Beach side of the point. Even aging, they stood proudly separate from the plebeian cottages that otherwise made up the community.

Cape Trouble police officers occasionally responded to calls from Jasper Beach if sheriff's deputies were too far away, but it was part of unincorporated Burris County, and thus the sheriff's department responsibility.

Making a decision, Sean said, "Contact Coos Bay P.D. Ask if they can keep an eye on Kimberly's house just for tonight. My gut feeling is we need to put her into hiding, but I'd rather make a solid plan than do something too fast. Tell them she doesn't know what's happening, so they don't want to be too obvious."

"Will do."

"After that, see what you can find out about Braden's mother and their lives before she died." Sean would have liked to pursue this thread himself, but he had to delegate. Keeping the likely targets alive had to come first. "Unless Braden was on his own for a while," he said, "they probably lived here in Burris County. How long had she been sick? Did she work? Where? If we're lucky, you'll find neighbors who remember the man she lived with. We need his name and history if we're going to find his son."

"I'm on it." A thread of energy in his voice suggested that Jason knew how important this was.

Next, Sean called Daniel, who answered right away.

"Well, hell," he said in response to the update and the news that yet another target of a deranged killer resided in his town, which hadn't proved to be as peaceful as he'd expected it to be.

"Have you had any contact with the Fisks?"

"Not that I recall." Daniel sounded thoughtful. "I think I'll call Linda Grove at the high school and see what she can tell me about the family."

"That would be interesting," Sean agreed. "Given the rape, she'll remember the daughter for sure. She might have some insights."

"Do you suppose there is a chance in hell the Fisks still have the same computer? Assuming Braden used it for emailing and didn't have his own."

"It's only been a little over two years. So there's a chance. Huh. I should check for a Facebook page."

Daniel waited while he did just that.

"If he had one, it's been taken down. Probably he didn't bother. It doesn't sound like he had any friends."

"He had to be in regular contact with his brother, or the guy wouldn't know who to hold responsible for Braden's problems. He could have found out about Frank Lowe and Judge Tranor from news articles, but not Emily and the teacher."

"No. With his brother deployed, email is likeliest."

"I agree. And while reading what he said would be interesting, we already have a good idea who is on the hate list."

Sean felt unease stir. "Unless there are people who aren't so obvious. If Roff wasn't already dead, he wouldn't have crossed our radar."

"And we'd still be completely mystified, because nothing Emily told us would have connected her to Lowe or Tranor." Daniel sounded as grim as Sean felt. "Shit. You're right."

"Do you suppose the guy has been saving the best for last?"

"You mean the abusive foster dad, the girl and the cop who killed Braden? That seems likely."

"Which leaves Emerson and Mrs. Kelley that we can be pretty confident are also targets."

"And Emily," Daniel said, almost gently. "He's not going to see failure as a successful outcome. She may have been almost incidental to start with, but now he's pissed. You know he is."

Sean squeezed the bridge of his nose until cartilage creaked. "I do know."

The last thing Daniel said was, "Take care of her."

\*\*\*\*\*

Midmorning Tuesday, Emily retreated to the office at the back of the store and pretended to concentrate on financials. Both her store manager, Cheryl Sizemore, and the clerk working today, Maria Gutierrez, knew about the two break-ins at Emily's house. This was a small town, after all. They had fussed and asked questions, many of which she couldn't answer. Why had he come back? That's what they really wanted to know.

Of course, she couldn't tell them. Even if Sean had been okay with it, she didn't want to tell anyone.

How could she have done that to a boy who'd just lost his mother?

The awful thing was, beyond that one moment of shock when she told him the social worker was coming to get him, she could barely picture Braden's face. He'd had that little importance in her life. A creeping sense of discomfort layered over long-held guilt made her wonder if she had really wanted to take him in at all. Had she felt the compassion she should have once he was in their home? Tried to like him?

She'd agreed readily enough when Tom talked about adding foster kids to their family, but somehow a hulking teenager wasn't what she'd pictured.

As if height and the need to shave hadn't allowed her to see the child he still was.

She thought now he'd scared her a little. When she tried to talk to Tom about it, he'd laughed at her.

"Cody will shoot past your height by the time he's fifteen, too, you know," he'd pointed out. "And he'll need to shave and speak in mumbles when he isn't responding with grunts."

"Were you like that?" she had asked, and he'd hugged her and said, "Of course."

And still, she hadn't felt comfortable with Braden's brooding silences.

When really, she thought unhappily, the poor boy was afraid to open his mouth because he knew how dreadfully he'd struggle to get the simplest words out.

Had she been the tiniest bit apprehensive and even angry when she was left alone with him that weekend?

She closed her eyes, appalled to understand that afterward, however unconsciously, she'd believed she would have gone with Tom and Cody if not for Braden. Magically, everything would have been different. They wouldn't have died.

After receiving the news, she could hardly even look at him.

When the truth was, she dreaded visiting Tom's parents and might have secretly been relieved that Braden gave her an excuse not to go.

She'd needed to blame everyone else for a tragedy that she couldn't accept as random.

In a weird way, she could identify with a killer who needed to blame everyone else but himself. Whatever his relationship had been to Braden, he wasn't there when Braden needed him. Accepting your own failures and inadequacies was a hard thing to do.

Emily remembered telling Sean about the accident. Blaming the cops. She'd been so angry, her skin had felt tight and hot. Now, ashamed, she thought, the patrol officer might really have made an error in judgment. But...people did. Sean had been willing to agree that cops screwed up, too. Had she really felt better to blame other people for Tom and Cody's deaths?

No.

And, oh God, poor Braden.

But as the day went on, she circled back to remembering her own devastation. She had been utterly shattered. When she slept at all, she would wake up in the morning and stare at the ceiling, ignoring her need to use the toilet, unable to imagine eating or returning a call. In those first weeks, she scarcely showered. Sometimes, her eyes had burned and she would realize that she had forgotten to blink. She'd been an automaton. When she eventually became able to resume a semblance of a daily routine, it was to find she'd lost so much weight, her clothes hung on her body.

Because the maternal instinct drove women to extraordinary lengths, she knew she would have managed somehow to be a parent if she'd had another child. Braden, still a near stranger, hadn't been enough to pull her from her agony.

She was ashamed she hadn't been strong enough to see how much he'd needed her, but understood why she had believed he would be better off with another family. Dealing with the loss of his mother was enough for a boy that age. After Tom and Cody were killed, Emily had walked in grief for so long, she hadn't noticed when hours at a time, even days, would pass without the pain grabbing her and shaking her in its teeth. Braden hadn't needed to take that walk with her.

She heard herself make a funny sound that might almost have been a laugh. Sean was right. She had been healing.

Which didn't actually mean she was ready to risk her heart again.

But then, he hadn't asked for her heart or offered his. His main interest might be sex.

Oh, yeah, and keeping her alive.

Emily remembered Sophie Thomsen talking about silver linings, and it occurred to her she, too, had already found several, first among which was the realization that she did not want to die.

And then there was Sean.

They hadn't talked about where she would stay tonight, but maybe they hadn't had to. She wanted to be in his bed, with his arms around her.

Because he made her feel safe…and not safe at all.

# CHAPTER ELEVEN

That evening, Sean lowered himself to one end of the sofa, facing the chair where Emily sat with her quilting hoop. Different quilt in it, he'd noted. He stretched out his legs in a semblance of relaxation that lasted for thirty seconds, tops, before he rose to his feet to complete another circuit around the living room.

The limited space made him feel like a hamster on a wheel, frantically running in tight circles. As an outlet for intense stress, this wasn't working.

Sex would.

"You're making me nervous," Emily said.

He stopped where he could see her from the front. She'd lowered the hoop to her lap and was watching him, worry shadowing her face.

"I'm sorry. I'm not good at sitting even at the best of times. Damn it, I wish I'd gotten a run in today."

"You don't have a treadmill?"

He shook his head. "If it's raining, I usually stop at the gym."

It was definitely raining. Not hammering on the roof, but coming down steadily. Typical March day on the Oregon coast. Spring hadn't made much of an appearance yet. No way he could have stopped at the gym. He'd been too anxious to pick up Emily.

"I do have one," she reminded him. "We could go over to my house—"

He was already shaking his head. "I don't want to get wet." Or usher her through the dark night, even for such a short distance.

"You think he might break in here."

Sean exhaled hard. "No. I don't think he's that stupid."

"But he kept coming after me that first time even after I'd started screaming."

"Okay, you're right. But that wasn't stupid planning, it was panic on his part."

Emily nodded slowly, her eyes grave. "Do you always get so…I don't know, worked up about investigations?"

"Worked up? What's that supposed to mean?"

Wrinkles appeared in her forehead. "You said it was making you crazy."

"I said you were making me crazy," he shot back. And, God help him, it was all he could do to stand in one place right now. The need to move, to do something, consumed him.

He had to get the idea of making desperate, life-altering love to her out of his head. It wasn't happening. Not when she wouldn't admit she wasn't still in deep mourning.

"You didn't even know me when this started," she continued. "And even so, you were willing to do almost anything to protect me." She was thinking hard, which made him uneasy.

"I'm a cop."

"You've gone way above and beyond."

He couldn't argue, since he had every intention of insisting she sleep again in his bed. Yeah, there was an exercise in stress reduction.

He also couldn't say, *I think I'm in love with you.* It was too soon, and while she was in danger and dependent on him for her safety was no time for him to get pushy about their personal relationship.

All he had to do was imagine her reaction if he said that word: relationship. Forget 'love'.

But he had to be honest, at least to a point. "You were never just a neighbor, like Gus Rumbaugh or Mrs. Shoop," he said. "You caught my interest from the beginning. By the time of the first break-in, we'd spent some time together."

Was her mouth curving, just a little bit? "That first time we ran together, would you have left me behind on the beach if I'd been gasping for air half a mile along?"

Sean grinned, some of his tension waning. "Probably not."

"I had a suspicion," she said drily – then nothing else. She just kept watching him, her hands idle. She wasn't satisfied.

He rolled his shoulders in a futile attempt to release tension. "You…triggered something in me," he said finally.

Her cheeks were pink, but she said, "Lust?"

He forced himself to return to the sofa. Once he'd sat down, instead of pretending to relax, he leaned forward, elbows braced on his thighs, hands dangling. "Definitely lust. And more." *You weren't going there, remember?* "But that's not what I was talking about." He cleared his throat. "I mean, about the trigger. I guess this is the first time since my brother was killed that someone I really care about has been in danger."

The smile had faded from Emily's lips by the time he finished that little speech. He felt twitchy again at the way she was looking at him, as if she could see well beneath the surface.

"You knew ahead of time that he was in danger," she said.

Either he'd betrayed more than he meant to, or she was a mind-reader.

He let his head fall forward for a minute. "Yeah," he said. "The asshole who killed him had been making threats." Then he frowned and looked up. "Sorry for the language."

She only shook her head. "What kind of threats? Had your brother gone to the police?"

"Once. The guy had graduated from the high school a couple years before, but was still hanging around. Living at home, working at an auto body shop. Wherever Dani was, he popped up."

"He was stalking her."

"Yes, but he hadn't done anything overtly threatening. He stared a lot. A couple of times he approached her, said he missed her and she should dump the other guy. If she didn't, she'd be sorry." He grimaced. "She interpreted that as, 'You'll miss me as much as I miss you' instead of 'Blood will flow.'"

"I take it she's the one who broke up with him."

"Yeah." Sean had never seen what Matt did in Dani. Truth was, once the boyfriend had graduated, she'd lost interest and hooked up with Matt instead. Quarterback of the football team, smart guy who was aiming for Stanford and, eventually, medical school. He and Sean had looked enough alike people saw that they were brothers, but Matt was the handsome one. Smarter, too, Sean thought, without any sting. "I don't think either Matt or Dani were all that serious. Matt felt protective. He was more afraid for Dani than for himself."

Emily nodded. "I can see why he'd assume she was one in danger if either of them was."

"Rich—" Sean stopped, then said with loathing, "His name is Rich Latimer. He apparently imagined himself in love with her 'til death do them part."

Emily winced.

"Apparently it wasn't his death he had in mind," Sean said in a hard voice.

"Do you want to tell me what happened?" Emily asked softly.

He was suddenly on his feet without making a conscious decision to stand up. "It was late in football season." He'd never forget the date. The time. "I'd been at practice, too, but..." God, he hoped she didn't notice his hesitation. "I stayed to hang out with some people." To flirt with Chloe Wardell. "Mom called to check on us. Matt should have been home long since, so one of my buddies took me to check out the parking lot at the high school, then drive home the way we both usually did. We found his car at a stop sign." Fuck. He was back to pacing. "He'd been dragged out, beaten to death. The police later figured out Rich had used a tire iron. Found it in his trunk with traces of Matt's blood he'd failed to hose off."

"Oh, Sean," Emily whispered. "For you to be the one to find him…"

"Yeah," he said hoarsely. "It was…" He shook his head, refusing to finish the sentence.

The way she studied him, he felt like a crystal ball. She was the witch.

"You feel guilty," she said slowly, as if a vision was taking on substance before her eyes. Then her eyes sharpened on him. "Why?"

He'd never told his parents this part of the story. Not the police. Not anyone. But…Emily had opened herself to him in ways that had to be excruciating. If he wanted…whatever he wanted with her, how could he do less?

"I was supposed to be with him." It came out abrupt, and just hung there in the air, his secret shame.

She blinked. "You mean, you usually got a ride with him?"

He shook his head, nodded, then yanked viciously at his hair. "I had my own car. Yeah, we drove together sometimes. But after Rich started getting down and dirty with his threats, I promised Matt I'd have his back. We either went to and from together, or if I had my own car for some reason, I rode his bumper home. That day— That day, I made a joke. Said, 'You can make it by yourself, can't you?' Because this girl I'd had my eye on was hanging around. And—" his throat had clogged "—I was tired of playing bodyguard. I'd decided Rich was all talk."

Emily rose in a rush, dropping quilt and hoop to the floor, and came to him. She grabbed his hand and held on tight, compassion he hadn't known he craved in her eyes. "You were a boy. How long had you been guarding him?"

"Weeks. I don't know." He shook his head, hating the burn in his sinuses. "Long enough, I could blow him off. My own brother."

"Did he say anything? Or...do anything?"

"You mean, look reproachful? Betrayed? No." He swallowed hard. "He kind of shrugged and said, 'Yeah, I think I can handle it.'"

Words burned into his memory.

"Oh, Sean." Emily wrapped her arms around his torso and laid her head against his shoulder.

He put his arms around her, too, and rested his cheek on the top of her head. Closing his eyes, he breathed her in. The hint of sweetness, the herbal tang. And something he could only define as her. Her warmth penetrated where he was cold. She was both taut and soft against him. Everything he needed. They stood there for a long time, not speaking.

He heard a mumble at last, and lifted his head. "What?"

"I said, you know that Rich person was just waiting for his chance. If you'd been there that day, another day would have come when you couldn't be, or when he tricked your brother into meeting him."

Sean started to stiffen, but she squeezed him.

"Think like an adult, not a guilt-ravaged boy."

He didn't really have to. Rationally, he knew she was right. Some of his anger the day Arianna Keezer had gone missing had been directed at her friends, none of whom had gone to a parent or teacher and said, I'm scared for my friend. The frustration that hit him had been…an echo, maybe, of his own guilt. He and Matt genuinely had believed the threat from Rich Latimer was real. So what did they do? Go to their parents? Talk to their coach, who'd known Rich, too? Follow up with the cops and say, We think he means it? Hell, no. All macho swagger, they'd determined they could handle it. Sixteen- and seventeen-year-old boys.

He discovered he was breathing easier, and, miraculously, hadn't actually leaked any tears. In the nature of an experiment, he let himself see Matt in a way he usually blocked. That last, eye-rolling look. Had Matt ever really believed he needed backup, or had Sean thrown himself heart and soul into the role because, yeah, he was a teenager, with all the drama that implied?

Maybe, he thought cautiously, but couldn't entirely let go of the knowledge that he had failed his brother. He'd made a promise he didn't keep, and swore he'd never let anyone down again.

Especially, he thought now, this woman.

Was it some kind of karma? Here he finally loved, and it had to be a woman whose life was threatened? Maybe in a cosmic sense he was being given a do-over.

Losing Matt had altered the course of his life. Losing Emily, he thought, would bring him down.

And he'd wondered why she couldn't just get over the deaths of her husband and son? It was almost funny.

He tried to ease back. Feeling her body melting into his had had the inevitable consequence, and he didn't want her to notice. But her arms tightened, as if she refused to let him go.

The next moment, as if it had occurred to her that he sought to escape, she let her arms fall and took a hasty backwards step. Sean couldn't seem to make himself release her entirely. His hands had settled on her upper arms. His fingers flexed, and he ached.

He hated to see her expression, but when he made himself meet her gaze, it was to see her hazel eyes darkened, heavy-lidded, her cheeks rosy. Her face was a perfect oval, bones just defined enough to let him know she'd stay beautiful with age.

He'd meant to apologize. Instead, voice husky, he said, "Emily?"

Her tongue touched her lips. She was going to say, *I'm not ready*. How many times had she used the same words?

"Will you kiss me?"

It took him a second to take in what she'd said. He kneaded her upper arms, sweating at the idea of having to let her go—

Awareness slammed into him. She hadn't said no. She'd asked him to kiss her.

"Yeah." His voice was barely recognizable as his own. "I can't think of anything I want to do more."

He bent his head slowly, drinking in the sight of her face tilted up to his, slumberous with arousal. Be gentle, he told himself, and instead took her mouth with fierce, hungry need that she answered. She kissed him with as much urgency, using lips, tongue and teeth. As he gripped her hips, lifting her, she locked her arms around his neck. He'd never gone up so fast. Her hips rocked, and, desperate, he ground himself against her.

He managed to free one hand to wrench the hem of her shirt up. He got it as far as her armpits before it sank in that he'd have to back off to pull it over her head, and he wasn't about to do that. So he abandoned the shirt in favor of unhooking her bra. God, he loved the feel of her back, long and sleek, silky and strong, the underlying structure delicate. His hand kept moving, beneath the band of her stretchy yoga pants as well as her panties, until he cupped one round cheek of her butt. He squeezed, and she made that little, whimpering sound he remembered from their last kiss. It had to be the single sexiest sound he'd ever heard.

He scooped her up and started for the bedroom, to hell with the lights. Locks were something he didn't have to worry about; he checked them compulsively these days, never went in or out of a door without locking.

Her braid flopped over his arm, and he got even harder at the idea of freeing that mass of thick, dark silk. She kissed his throat. He'd have sworn he felt the damp touch of her tongue.

But instead of laying her on his bed, he let her slip out of his arms onto her own two feet. Then he took a hard grip on his libido and lifted his head.

"Emily."

She looked up, dazed. Her slender, strong hands kneaded his shoulders.

"Are you sure about this?"

He saw her blinking, trying to comprehend. Fear seized him as he waited while her expression cleared. God, if she asked him to stop—

But, suddenly shy, she nodded.

Exultant, he grinned, lifted her again and damn near threw her onto the bed, coming down beside her. Before he knew it, she climbed on top of him, laughing. This time it was his heart that clenched. She was happy. He wanted to keep her happy. Forever.

Then she wriggled a little, enough to straddle him so that she rode his erection. Lust swamped his brain. He yanked her shirt over her head, taking the already loose bra with it and tossed them aside, then just let himself look.

"Perfect," he whispered, lifting his hands to her generous breasts. Her nipples pressed against his palms and she let her head fall back so she made a glorious, sensual sight. Long, white torso, slim and tight with smooth muscles, lusciously full breasts with dark, hard peaks, slim shoulders and a graceful neck.

The fat braid lay across his arm.

Somehow he persuaded himself to release her breasts, tug the elastic from the end of the braid, and begin combing his fingers through her hair, separating the twined strands until he reached her nape. She had lifted her head so she could watch him, her lips slightly parted, the green-gold of her eyes a witch's brew. He'd have sworn she didn't so much as blink.

When he was done, the whole mass of curls tumbled over her shoulders and breasts, over his hands and arms. It had to be waist-long. He kept sliding his fingers through it, reveling in the texture. Her breasts peeked through the dark waterfall. She was the sexiest thing he'd ever seen.

Suddenly, his patience snapped and he pulled her down for a voracious kiss, wet and frantic. He flipped her so he was on top, then flipped them again, his hips surging up when her thighs tightened around him.

Should have gotten her naked first.

Should have gotten himself naked first.

This kiss exploded until he was too damn close to coming. He flipped her one more time and went to work on her shoes, socks, then stretchy pants and skimpy black panties. The sight of the silky dark triangle of hair over her mound maddened him.

All the while he was stripping her, Emily half-sat and did the same for him. As she eased the zipper down, he sucked in his belly and gritted his teeth. The delicate dance of fingers felt so good he went utterly still for a moment. When she found bare skin, he didn't dare let her stroke his full length more than once before he said gutturally, "No more," and slid off the bed. He wrenched off shoes without even untying them, followed by pants and shorts, then had the small remaining brain power to scrabble in the drawer of his bedside stand for a condom.

As unblinking as she'd been when he freed her hair, she watched him sheath himself. Once he was done, her eyes heavy-lidded and dreamy, Emily held her arms out for him in a welcome that felt better than anything ever had in his life.

He took one of her nipples into his mouth, the rhythmic tug making her hips rise to press against him. Sean moved to the other breast, his hand slipping down to stroke between her folds. He pressed a finger into her, then two. Little cries broke from her throat. He couldn't wait for another second.

She was tight, but so ready he slid right in, pushing deep, then doing it again. Her thighs clasped him tight and her heels dug into the bed as she lifted her whole body to meet each thrust. Head back, eyes closed, she whimpered, the little sound almost more than he could stand.

He gritted his teeth, trying to hold on, wait, wait…

Suddenly her eyes opened. "Sean? Please. That feels— Ohhh."

Her body convulsed around him, and he sank into her and let himself go, hearing himself call her name as a shuddering release went on forever.

\*\*\*\*\*

Emily knew when Sean got out of bed, presumably to get rid of the condom, although then she heard him pad down the hall. Lights, her sleepy brain provided. He had left the bathroom light on, the door ajar an inch or two as a sort of nightlight, just as he'd done the other night she slept in his bed. When he came back, he set something down on the bedside stand with a soft thump. The glow from the bathroom allowed her to see that he'd placed his gun within reach. Once that would have horrified her. Now, it was reassuring.

Still naked, he slipped back beneath the covers and gathered her into his arms. Snuggling close, she reveled in his heat and the powerful muscles in his chest and those arms that held her. She'd lain alone on her own side of the bed for so long, the comfort of a man's embrace was only a distant memory.

The thought gave her a sharp twinge. Oh, Tom... But she knew in her heart that Tom would be smiling, because she'd had at least a glimpse of happiness for the first time in too long.

"Sleep tight, sweetheart," Sean murmured, pressing a kiss to the top of her head.

She tried to respond, but it came out as an indecipherable mumble that made his chest vibrate with a silent laugh. She felt...odd, as if she'd been wound tight like a top for years and years, and suddenly freed to spin and spin until there was no more tension left. Head pillowed on Sean's shoulder, Emily let herself sink into the beckoning darkness of sleep.

A burbling sound brought her shooting out of sleep as fast as she'd fallen into it.

"What...?" she mumbled, sitting up.

"Phone," the man in bed with her said.

Sean. She was in his bed. Had made love with him. Emily grappled with all that as he fumbled for his phone and finally brought it to his ear.

"Holbeck."

She couldn't quite make out what the other person said, only that the caller was male.

Whatever it was had Sean going on instant alert. After a minute, he said, "Good thing she didn't dawdle getting out of there."

The caller asked something.

"I don't think I told anyone. Mrs. Kelley's husband is retired. She was going straight home to pack and take off."

More talk. Sean said a few unrevealing things like "Uh huh" and "Yeah," then, finally, "Still eight o'clock."

After dropping the phone on the bedside table again right next to his gun, he frowned into space for a minute.

"Sean?"

He shook his head. "Give me a minute."

His minute was spent visiting the bathroom. Her bladder made itself known. Clearly, she'd need to do the same before she could fall back asleep. But first she wanted to know who had called in the middle of the night and why.

He came back, still naked, but grabbed his chinos from the floor and pulled them on. "I'm going to do a walk-around," he said, and grabbed the gun.

Emily whisked into the bathroom while he was gone. They met back at the bed.

"No unexpected openings in any of your windows?" she asked, knowing she was going for frivolous to counter the fear that pressed at her ribcage.

"Nope. All's quiet." Those lines in his forehead had deepened again. "I'm sorry you got woken up."

Emily climbed under the covers and tugged the covers high. "Who was that?"

"My lieutenant." He hesitated. "You knew Jeanette Kelley?"

Her heartbeat picked up speed. "The caseworker? Yes. She was really nice. Oh, God. She wasn't killed, was she?"

He sat on the side of the bed. "No, but only because she followed my advice without wasting any time."

Emily remembered his side of the conversation. "She went into hiding."

"Right. If she'd packed in preparation for leaving in the morning…"

Emily shuddered. "She'd be dead."

"Probably."

"Do you think she'll be safe now?"

"If we can catch this son of a bitch," Sean said with quiet force. He gusted out a breath. "I don't think I can go back to sleep. I'll leave you in peace."

She reached out and laid a tentative hand on his thigh. The muscle tightened and she felt a warm curl low in her belly. Shirtless, he was an impressive sight. And…she could be wrong, but thought right now he needed her.

"You could stay," she suggested, voice momentarily throaty, then on a burst of embarrassment whisked her hand back under the covers. He was bound to think she was offering her body because she was scared to be alone.

Sean planted a hand on the mattress and bent over her. The pale band of light from the bathroom cast interesting shadows on his face, but let her see a glint in his eyes. "You're really awake, huh?"

She nodded and let the covers slide down, freeing her arms. "If there's something you need to do…"

"I'd probably just brood." He slid his other hand beneath her hair, cupping the back of her head. "My eggs can wait."

His eggs could wait? What? Then she remembered. Broody. Hen on eggs. Emily was smiling when his mouth captured hers.

# CHAPTER TWELVE

"A couple of interesting pieces of news," Wilcynski said, shortly after the morning meeting had convened the next day. He started by telling everyone who didn't know about the break-in at the social worker's empty house.

A next-door neighbor had had back surgery two days before and wasn't sleeping well. He'd gotten up to take more pain killers, then decided to read in the living room until they took effect so he didn't keep his wife awake, too. Before he turned on the living room light, he looked out and saw a dark shape hop out of a window at the Kelley's house. He'd called 911 immediately. As was common in a county as sprawling as this one, the responding unit arrived fifteen minutes later. The intruder was long gone.

However, upon circling the house, the deputy saw that not only did a window stand open, a six inch square of glass had been carefully cut out of it to allow a hand to reach in. The glass had been left in the flower bed beneath the window.

The neighbor who called had told him the Kelleys had loaded their car that evening and left for what they told him was a vacation. Nonetheless, the deputy called for backup, and, once another deputy arrived, they had gone in to be sure the house really was empty.

"We knew Jeanette Kelley was likely to be on the guy's list," Jason remarked.

"Yes, but I talked to her yesterday morning," Sean said. "For him to go after her that same night?"

"What if he was watching the DHS offices?" Rey Mendoza suggested.

"Why would he?"

"Is her address and phone number unlisted?"

Wilcynski grabbed a local phone directory and Sean typed in a query on his laptop. The answer was yes; for obvious reasons, the Kelleys had chosen to stay off the grid.

Not much liking coincidences, Sean still wasn't satisfied with the explanation but supposed it was possible. The guy had been staking out DHS so he could follow Mrs. Kelley home. If he'd happened to see Sean going in or out, he might have feared she'd been warned. Damn sure he'd been following the news, which meant he'd have seen Sean in the background at the initial press conference and recognized him. Hell, the sheriff had named him as primary.

But why would the killer had been watching DHS in the middle of the day?

"You said you had a couple of interesting pieces of news," he said, looking at the lieutenant. "What's number two?" He was prepared to be pissed if this was something Wilcynski should already have shared with him. He'd woken up amazingly relaxed this morning, but not any more caught up on sleep.

"I talked to Dean Driscoll this morning." Driscoll was Wilcynski's counterpart on the patrol side. "Deputies have reported a couple of sightings of the young veteran."

"Really? Where?"

Wilcynski laid out a county map on the table. He'd already marked two red crosses on it, surprisingly far apart given Sean's assumption that the homeless guy was on foot. Presumably homeless, Sean corrected himself. It was never smart to jump to conclusions. After handing the marker to Sean, the lieutenant said, "Not exactly sure where your encounter with him took place."

Sean added a cross, then studied the map. Larry stuck to Cape Trouble and environs; in contrast, this guy was ranging county wide at least.

Thinking aloud, he said, "He's either hitchhiking or he has transportation of some kind."

Daniel raised an eyebrow. "Say, a bike?"

"If so, you'd think he'd be spotted more often."

"If he's wearing camo, yeah. Otherwise, if he obeys traffic laws, why would a patrol officer pay any attention?"

Unfortunately, Daniel was right. In Sean's opinion, the Pacific Coast Highway, with too many curves and narrow shoulders, was dangerous for bike travel, but it was scenic enough to attract frequent group rides anyway. It would get worse come summer. Sometimes a hundred or more riders would be strung out over a couple of miles of winding road shared by rubber-necking tourists. An occasional car versus bicycle duel to the death didn't seem to deter anyone.

Plus, there were plenty of serious bicyclists who lived in this area, seen in all weathers in their spandex or rain gear. Some of them commuted to work on their bikes. And if the veteran rode at night, maybe moved off the road when he saw a car coming…

"Do you have dates and times for the sightings?" Sean asked Wilcynski.

"I do. This one—" he pointed "—was yesterday afternoon."

Which placed the possibly homeless veteran within a mile or two of the Kelley's house.

"I want him picked up," he grumbled.

The lieutenant shook his head. "Neither of the deputies who saw him even got close. He seems to have eyes in the back of his head. Got to say, I don't want one of them killed because he's pursuing on his own."

Sean agreed, and suggested they move on.

"I talked to the Fisks," Daniel said. "He's not a pleasant man. He told me what a slimy little worm Braden was, 'accidently' walking into the bathroom when Kimberly was showering, even peeking in her window. He got really angry, says he never hit the kid."

Sean glanced around the table to see expressions that were hard, even angry. They'd all dealt too often with abusers who invariably denied their behavior or justified it, and sometimes both, as Ed Fisk had done.

"I had the impression he's scared for his daughter, but doesn't believe anyone related to Braden would have the balls to take him on." His eyebrows twitched. "His words."

"It's almost enough to make you hope the guy does," Jason said in a hard voice.

The lieutenant glared at him. "We protect the citizens of our county whether we like them or not. Got it?"

The muscles in Jason's jaw knotted, but he gave a curt not.

No one else said anything. The truth is, they'd probably all been thinking the same thing he'd said aloud.

Good time to change the subject. Sean looked at Daniel. "Did you ask about the computer?"

"They didn't have one. Do now so his wife can email with Kimberly. Apparently Kimberly had a laptop back then, but he doesn't think she'd have let Braden use it. Doesn't much matter, because she's replaced it since. He says Braden went to the library a lot, so he may have emailed from one of those computers." He shook his head. "Without knowing Braden or his brother's email addresses, there's no point in even contacting the server."

Sean was forced to nod agreement.

"I have what may qualify as good news," Mendoza told them. "Chief Lundy authorized around-the-clock surveillance of Mike Emerson's house for the coming week, continuation to be dependent on events."

Jason looked interested. "I don't suppose we have the manpower to do the same for county residents on the list?"

Wilcynski's glance was dismissive. He didn't say, Grow up, baby cop, but he might as well have.

Sean saw a flash of anger on Jason's face, and didn't blame him.

When the silence continued, however, the lieutenant said grudgingly, "I'll speak to Sheriff Mackay."

Hell, Sean thought, maybe he was just more conscious of budget realities than the rest of them. The sheriff's department, like many police agencies, was always stretched thin given their inadequate funding.

"I have my officers including Jasper Beach in their patrols at night, just in case the group home is a target," Daniel said. "We're doing regular drive-bys of the Fisk's house, too." Then he looked at Sean. "Do we have a plan for the girl?"

"Deputy Walker is prepared to take her in." The idea had come to Sean yesterday. He'd talked to her, then cleared it with the lieutenant. Kimberly Fisk was frightened enough to have agreed with the arrangement. And, damn, he'd be glad when she was safely tucked away. "I'll move her today."

"Walker?" Mendoza asked.

"A female deputy."

"Jason, have you had a chance to find out anything about Braden's history before he went into the foster system?"

"Just a beginning. He and his mother had an apartment in North Fork." He mentioned the complex, and Mendoza nodded. "According to the manager, they'd only been there a few months. He's supposed to find me the rental contract. I'm hoping she had to give references. Otherwise, you know what kind of turnover places like that have."

"You want me to take that over?" Mendoza asked.

Jason shook his head. "Following up with the manager won't take long."

Sean looked around. "Anything else?"

Nobody lingered.

Yesterday morning at this same time, Sean had felt optimistic. Today? They had nothing on this guy. Not even a name. There could be targets they hadn't identified, and several they had identified remained vulnerable.

And then there was Emily.

*****

"I thought it was all over," the girl in the back seat whimpered. "I mean, he's *dead*."

It was hard to know how to offer comfort, Emily thought. She understood why a rape victim would have been relieved that her attacker was dead rather than in prison. Putting the assault behind her would be even harder if she had to worry about the possibility of the rapist getting out of prison someday. Since Braden Wilson had been tried as a juvenile, that day wouldn't have been far down the road.

Kimberly Fisk was so sunk in self-pity, however, she mostly ignored anything Sean or Emily said. Plus, she kept repeating herself. She was having trouble believing this could possibly be happening to her, of all people in the world.

Of course, Kimberly was only nineteen, Emily reminded herself. A teenager. Hormones equalled self-absorption.

As relieved as Emily had been when Sean suggested picking her up from the gallery so she could ride along with him to pick up Kimberly and transport her to a 'safe house', she was beginning to wish she'd declined. Unfortunately, Newport was a fair drive from

Cape Trouble, especially given the two-lane highway. Sean had growled under his breath several times when they'd gotten stuck behind someone driving really slow, with no opportunity to pass until they reached a straight stretch of road.

The lure to persuade her to accompany him was his promise when they were done to take her to the gym so they could both use the treadmill. Running on the beach would have been better, but despite the lack of rain he'd shaken his head tersely without telling her why that wasn't an option. She hadn't argued.

Emily saw Sean glance in the rearview mirror at their passenger. "Kimberly, your father said you recently bought a new laptop."

"Well...*yeah*." Her expression suggested he was dumb or maybe just old. "I mean, I couldn't go to college with my old one."

Sean rolled his eyes at Emily, who hid her smile.

"Did you ever let Braden use your computer?"

"No!" Her eyes narrowed. "He'd better not have."

"Any chance you held onto the old one?"

"Why would I?" After a minute, she added, "I know you aren't supposed to throw computers in the garbage, but since mine was just a laptop, that's what I did."

His fingers tightened on the steering wheel, a minor symptom of his exasperation. Or was it frustration, because the investigation seemed to have stalled again?

Behind them, Kimberly mumbled, "This is completely unreal. I'm going to get behind in classes, and I have a boyfriend! I don't understand why I can't tell him where I am. He could visit..."

"And the man who wants to kill you could follow him." Sean didn't pull his punches. "Kimberly, you can't tell anyone at all where you are. Not your parents, not your best friend." He sounded all cop, grim and inflexible. "Do you understand me?"

"Yes!" she cried. "But it's not fair!"

Fair? Only the young could say it that way. How *fair* had it been that Tom and Cody had died the way they did, as unavoidably and unexpectedly as if they'd been struck by a lightning bolt? That boy who'd been caught by a huge, rogue wave on the beach a few months back; was it *fair* he'd died?

But Emily's flare of anger died quickly. Kimberly had been raped when she was only seventeen. And she was right; what was fair about that?

Trying to calm herself, Emily turned her head to look past Sean at the endless gray of the Pacific Ocean. With the cloud cover, she could hardly tell where sky met water. It was sometimes possible to see a freighter off the coast, or more rarely even a humpback whale, but not today.

"We'll catch this guy," Sean said. "All you have to do is be patient."

"I still don't understand why you think Braden's brother would come after me," Kimberly said. "I mean, he's the one who hurt me, not the other way around."

"During the trial, Braden claimed the sex was consensual." Ignoring her sputtering protest, he continued, "I think we can assume that's what he told his brother as well. Braden may not have had the chance after the arrest to contact his step-brother. But there ended up being quite a bit written about the trial. If the brother bought into everything Braden had been telling him, he'd believe his claim that it wasn't rape, too. If he's convinced you lied to the police and in your testimony, to his point of view, that makes Braden's death your fault."

"He deserved to die!" she spat, with a vitriol that had Emily turning her head to see her face. "I'm *glad* he died."

She was not a pretty young woman at that moment, her face twisted with hate. Emily understood her feelings and even sympathized, but also found she didn't really like Kimberly Fisk. She could very well have been her parents' little princess, disdainful of the strange boy they had imported into her home. Emily wondered whether she'd made up stories about Braden to be sure her daddy never favored him instead of her.

Emily shook her head. She was making big assumptions. Not being fair.

That thought had her mouth curving humorlessly.

It was a huge relief to finally arrive at the log cabin in the woods where the female deputy Sean had mentioned lived. Emily liked Rebecca Walker on sight. She exuded warmth that proved irresistible. Emily bet she was really good in her role as police negotiator. Kimberly immediately latched on to her, probably certain Rebecca would understand her woes when those two awful people who'd driven her here from Newport didn't.

There was silence in Sean's SUV as they drove down the long, dirt lane from the cabin. He was the first one to speak.

"Wonder whether the chicken or the egg came first."

"Are we back to brooding?" Emily asked with interest.

He gave a shout of laughter before sobering. "No, just trying to decide whether she was full of herself and unlikeable before the rape, or whether we're seeing the consequences of it."

"I'd say there's no way of knowing, except…"

"For Jeanette Kelley's description of her as daddy's little princess."

Emily nodded. He frowned ahead as he steered onto the narrow road that had led them east from the Coast Highway into the foothills of the coastal mountain range. Mailboxes and dirt or gravel driveways appeared every few hundred yards, but the damp woods prevented them from seeing the homes.

"It's pretty out here," Emily said, thinking of the woman and girl they'd just left, "but I wouldn't want to be this isolated."

"Rebecca is a cop, and a good one. I suspect she forgets that as a woman she has some vulnerability the rest of us don't."

"We look enough alike to be sisters." It just popped out.

Sean glanced at her in surprise. "Do you?"

"You weren't ever, I don't know, interested in her?"

"Never crossed my mind." He sounded as if he was telling the truth. "Even if it had, I can't imagine getting involved with another cop. Especially one in my own department."

Emily nodded. Any workplace romance could present difficulties, but in law enforcement, they might be involved together in something like a shootout, where a distraction could be deadly.

*Let it drop*, she told herself, disconcerted by her sudden insecurity. She couldn't doubt Sean was really attracted to her. It wasn't as if she had forgotten the way his gaze narrowed the first time they met. She'd felt as if a weapon system had just locked onto her.

"Do we still have time to stop at the gym?" she asked.

He glanced at the dashboard clock. "Sure."

"Will you tell me why we can't go to Misty Beach?"

His sidelong glance was wary. "I don't want to scare you."

She swiveled in her seat to stare incredulously at him. "Like I'm not already scared?"

"Okay, I don't want you even more scared."

Reaching a logical conclusion wasn't hard.

"You think someone might…what? Ambush us? Or shoot from a distance, like a sniper?" She thought about that. "But don't…don't murderers stick to an M.O.? Isn't that the term?"

"Mode of operation." The furrows in his forehead had deepened, as they always did when he was troubled. "To answer your question, yes and no. What counts to a killer is meeting his objectives. If rape is central, that will always be part of his assault. In this case, our guy hasn't deviated from his method so far. Because Mrs. Lowe heard voices, we believe the killer had something he wanted to say to his victim before he killed him. He might get off from taunting him, but my guess is that he's recounting what he sees as the victim's sins."

"Here's why you're going to die," she said slowly, a horrible knot tying itself in her belly.

"That's what I'm thinking." Sean reached across the console and covered her hands, which she had been squeezing together. "And because he's determined to speak to each victim, he went with a silent method of killing close at hand. Gave him a chance to leave a message for investigators, too, but he might figure that we've gotten the point by now."

She closed her eyes. "You're saying that now everyone knows why he's after them, there's no need for him to talk to them in person. Or…or kill them the same way. But…how can he know we all know?" Awful sentence, but she didn't care.

"We can't be sure he does. If not, he'll probably stick to his pattern. But we've been interviewing his potential targets. If he's watching any of them, he'll have seen us. Plus, people like to talk. The targets themselves, because they're rattled. Cops, dispatchers, forensic technicians, they all gossip. The media has been sniffing at our heels. He could have overheard someone talking in the next booth at a diner, in line at the grocery store. If so, he'll be happy. Everybody he hates is living in fear."

Emily made a sound that was almost a laugh, even as she curled forward because of the cramps in her stomach. "Anticipation is half the pleasure."

"Emily—"

She shook her head fiercely. "I'd rather know."

He let out a long breath. "All right. If he's aware of what we know, he may be increasingly nervous about breaking in during the night the way he has been. We might have prepared traps. His victims are forewarned. Some of them are probably armed. He's had the couple of close calls already when he went after you. For you, especially, I doubt he'll try the same approach again. You're already scared, you already know what he blames you for, so it makes sense for him to avoid risk while, uh, achieving his objective."

Killing her, was what he meant.

"We're assuming he's former military," Sean added, tension threading every word. "He could have had sniper training."

A small sound escaped her, as well as all the remaining air in her lungs. Any time she was outside, she could be in the crosshairs of a rifle sight. Even the thought made her skin crawl. She wanted to duck down and crouch on the floor instead of sitting here, exposed.

"I don't even dare go out to get my mail," she said, sounding more numb than she felt.

"I don't want you outside any more than we can help," Sean agreed, more grim than she'd ever heard him.

All she could do was nod. Unlike Kimberly, she didn't whimper, Why me? Because she knew. She knew.

Suddenly gentle, Sean said, "I'm sorry," and she could only nod.

*****

Sean hated to wake her up, but the alarm he'd earlier set on his phone had buzzed, letting him know it was time for the great stakeout. Since he'd laid down beside her fully dressed, all he had to do was shove his feet in his athletic shoes and tie laces. "Emily."

"I'm awake," she said tensely.

"I have to go." But, man, he didn't like leaving her alone. When Daniel had asked him for backup, he hadn't been able to say no. Given the level of trust and respect they shared, how could he have? But right now, Sean wished he had told him to find someone else.

Emily already had his instructions. Lock herself in the hall bathroom, which had no window, and sit in the bathtub where she wouldn't be vulnerable to a shot through the door. Keep his backup gun within reach. Shoot anyone who tried to come through the door without satisfactorily identifying him- or herself.

She had to be scared, but she nodded, grabbed the comforter from the bed and scuttled for the bathroom. He waited for the door to close and the lock to click, then hopped out the bedroom window in an attempt to keep his departure unseen – just in case Daniel was wrong and the killer was here, watching his house.

Then he set off jogging, having allowed himself plenty of time to cover the half mile or so across town to where the Fisks lived.

*****

Damn, he was getting cold. Hiding behind a lilac bush in the Fisk's backyard, Daniel had moved only enough to keep from stiffening up like a rusted piece of machinery. He'd forgotten how much he hated stakeouts. The boredom was bad enough, but mostly he had trouble staying still for long. The twitchiness overcoming him, he gave himself permission to rise carefully from a crouch to standing upright.

Really, he doubted he could be seen by anyone more than a couple feet away. With the moon behind the cloud cover, it was next thing to pitch black beyond the limited reach of the street lamps. His bigger worry was whether he would see the killer should he appear.

Daniel rolled his shoulders, flexed and unflexed muscles, curled and uncurled toes and fingers. If the moment came, he didn't want to fall flat on his face because his limbs wouldn't obey nervous-system commands.

He'd left Sophie behind at home stewing. He doubted she would sleep until he was home. She'd argued against his plan until he had literally closed the front door in her face. He didn't like scaring her, but he had to do his job. And, while he'd sympathized with Detective Payne's feelings about Ed Fisk, Daniel also shared Lieutenant Wilcynski's beliefs. God knew there were plenty of Cape Trouble citizens Daniel didn't much like. He'd been hired to protect and serve. His oath of office didn't say, protect and serve the decent folks and forget the rest.

Fortunately, Sean agreed with him. He was serving as backup tonight, waiting a block away in the shadow of a currently unoccupied house. They'd decided this yard was too damn small for two of them to lurk unseen.

His head turned when headlights appeared on the street. Approaching slowly, the vehicle came to a near stop in front of the Fisk's before continuing on. The patrol drive-by Daniel had ordered. This was the third time he'd seen the CTPD unit pass. The intervals were about forty-five minutes. His young officer was following instructions. As the sound of the engine receded, Daniel regretted not adding a second officer to work this night shift. It would be just his luck if Diaz was doing the extra lap through Jasper Beach at the wrong time.

Too late.

Daniel listened hard. He couldn't hear any other traffic. Only the ever-present roar of the surf kept the quiet from being absolute. That wasn't unusual; not much happened at night in Cape Trouble.

Not a creature was stirring…

He pushed a button on his watch to check the time. 1:56. Daniel felt a prickling sense of awareness that hadn't been there a minute before. *If I were going to do it, now is when I'd pick.*

He scanned the back of the house, then the one side he could see from this position. His eyes had long since adjusted as much as possible to the limited light. By now, he knew the shape of every bush in the yard.

A dark figure separated itself from one of those bushes, stopping right below a bedroom window.

*****

An hour or more had passed. Worrying about Emily had occupied Sean for the first while, but boredom brought sleepiness in its wake. Despite his half doze, he snapped instantly awake when his phone vibrated. He pulled it from his pocket.

The text had only one word: *Now*.

Sean ran, sticking to lawns where he could to muffle his footsteps.

The initial silence as he approached the Fisks' had him slowing to a jog. He searched the darkness. Had Daniel made his move yet? Damn, Sean didn't want to be responsible for spooking their target.

Then a voice cut through the night. "Police! Don't move!"

\*\*\*\*\*

Shockingly fast, the man twisted and dove for Daniel, hitting him before he could pull the trigger. Icy pain shot down his arm as he fell back. His Glock dropped from his nerveless hand.

Daniel managed to flip his attacker so he came out on top, and he got in a punch on a masked face. Light glinted off a blade that stabbed his chest.

They rolled again, fighting wordlessly, the only sounds grunts as blows landed. Where was Sean, damn it? Daniel felt himself weakening. His head rang. Maybe blood loss.

Just when the blade lifted above him again, he heard the hard pound of running footsteps.

The raised arm and knife went still; the guy launched himself off Daniel and took off into the deeper darkness behind the house. The back fence rattled, and Daniel swore aloud.

\*\*\*\*\*

It was so goddamn dark back here, Sean almost fell over the man sitting hunched on the ground. Before he could switch on his flashlight, a light came on in the house above them. It let him see Daniel Colburn, clutching his arm and swearing.

"The bastard cut me."

"No shit. You're bleeding like a stuck pig." Blood spilled between Daniel's fingers, covering the wound. Other slices through his shirt let Sean see the Kevlar vest beneath.

The window scraped open. A man leaned out the window, snarling, "Who the hell are you, and what's going on out here?"

Had to be Ed Fisk.

"Cops." Sean held up his shield even as he lifted his phone. He called 911, asking for police backup and an ambulance.

"Is there anything I can do?" Fisk sounded shaken. As well he should. If not for the stakeout, chances were good he'd be dead by now.

"Can you toss a couple of hand towels down?"

The guy disappeared.

"He went over the back fence," Daniel mumbled.

"I thought you were going to wait for me."

"He was going in the window. How he heard me, I don't know. I was going to grab his legs and yank his ass down. And then, damn, it all happened so fast."

Sean spotted the handgun. "Did he touch it?"

"No." Grimacing, Daniel swore some more. Had to hurt. "Wore gloves."

Of course he had. Sean picked up the gun and slid it into Daniel's shoulder holster.

Something landed softly almost on his lap. Towels. He folded one and pressed it to the wound, not looking up when Ed Fisk started complaining because they'd let the guy get away.

"What kind of incompetent...?"

Sean really wanted to shoot him.

*****

With no light at all in the bathroom, Emily's eyes couldn't adjust. The blackness was absolute. It was like being shut in a coffin, buried alive.

*Don't get hysterical*, she ordered herself. She'd known Sean would be gone for up to several hours. She should have been able to sleep.

A rap on the bathroom door sent a jolt through her body. Emily went as still as a mouse that sees a prowling cat.

"It's me," Sean said. "Let me in."

Oh, thank God, thank God. He was back. Safe.

"Okay." She untangled herself from the comforter and climbed out of the bathtub, opening the door. He switched on the light, momentarily blinding her anew. She blinked a couple of times, ready to wrap her arms around him...until she saw the blood. "Oh, my God. You're hurt."

He shook his head. "Daniel's blood. The scumbag cut him before I could get there."

She recognized the anger and frustration thinning his mouth and darkening his eyes. "It was him?"

"Oh, yeah. Shit." He yanked his bloody shirt off, the motion jerky and violent. "If there'd been two of us there—"

Emily hesitated, then laid a hand on his arm. "Daniel could have brought in an officer from his own department, or one of the others from your task force."

"Yeah." He let his head fall forward and squeezed the back of his neck. "You mind if we go to the hospital?"

Her breath froze in her lungs. "How badly is he hurt?" she whispered. "Does Sophie know?"

"He was wearing a vest. He has a hell of a slice on his arm, though. And, yeah, I called her. She should be there by now."

Emily stepped forward and wrapped her arms around him. For just a second, he didn't move, but then he grabbed onto her, bent his head to rest against hers, and held her until some of the tension in his body eased.

# CHAPTER THIRTEEN

During the short drive, Sean called his lieutenant. Voice terse, he described events in more detail than he'd yet told Emily, and said he was on the way to the hospital.

He listened, then said, "With Fisk hanging out the window listening, we couldn't talk. If Daniel had recognized the guy or been able to give any kind of useful description, he'd have said so. Anything else can wait until he gets stitched up." Emily could just hear a rumbling voice, but not make out words. "The CTPD patrol officer got there fast. He's still driving patterns, keeping his eye out, but he hasn't seen anyone on foot or bike yet. I called dispatch for any patrols we had nearby, but the closest was twenty minutes out." A moment later he laid the phone on the console and then reached for Emily's hand, seeming to know where it was without even looking.

"Your boss?"

"Yeah, Wilcynski. Guess you'll get to meet him. He says he's coming to the hospital, too."

She couldn't make out his face very well with only dashboard lights. "You don't sound thrilled."

"He's okay."

There was something in his voice that alerted her. He hadn't expressed doubt before about the lieutenant, but it was there now. Or maybe just irritation? She couldn't tell.

At the hospital, he pulled into a parking slot marked for official vehicles that was only steps from the emergency room doors. Picking up her purse from the floorboards, she was momentarily startled by the weight. It would take some getting used to.

Once she'd admitted to having done some target shooting with her grandfather, Sean had decided she should carry with her at all times his usual backup gun, a small semi-automatic, the one she'd clutched while she was in the bathtub waiting for him. He hadn't bent even when she pointed out the likelihood of the safety getting bumped off in her cluttered handbag and accidentally firing.

He kept her slightly in front of him as he ushered her the short distance, his head turning nonstop. As they passed through the automatic doors, she was disturbed by the flat look in his eyes. He feared the killer would have guessed that he would be bringing her with him to the hospital, she realized with a thrill of fear. Or had followed them here.

The waiting room was empty. Sean spoke quietly to the woman behind the counter, who used her phone and a moment later unlocked the doors to let them go back into the ER proper.

This was a small hospital, and there were only half a dozen glass-fronted rooms back here. Emily saw that most were empty, like the waiting room. She and Sean passed one that was occupied by a young couple, the man holding a fretful, flushed baby. Two darkened rooms separated them from the one bustling with activity. Sophie hovered just inside, watching as a doctor worked over Daniel, who lay on the bed.

Seeing Sean and Emily, he said, "You didn't have to come. I'm not dying here—" His body jerked. "Damn it, that hurts!" He glared at the doctor.

"Sorry. Tugged a little too hard." She bent to her task.

Emily hurried to hug Sophie and felt the way the other woman's body shook.

"Men are such idiots," Sophie mumbled.

Emily laughed, but shakily, her eyes following Sean as he ambled closer to watch the stitches being set. "Some of them are a little more reckless than others." How ironic that Tom, who hadn't been reckless at all, was the one who had died.

"Aren't we lucky." Sophie sighed, then separated herself. "Thank you. I feel better."

Emily didn't. Someday, that might be Sean. Probably would be Sean. His was a dangerous job. He gave her such a sense of security, she was able to forget. If their relationship lasted, she would have to live with a low level of fear for him.

Or not so low, given that she knew how it felt to lose the people she loved most.

Shock speared her. *I don't love him. How can I? It's way too soon.*

She'd dated Tom for months before accepting that he was the one. Falling in love with him had been a slow, natural process. A feather floating gently down.

This wasn't like that at all. Even so, she knew with stunning certainty. She wasn't the same woman she'd been then. Sean wasn't the same kind of man. The circumstances were as different as they could be.

She had responded to his intensely protective nature, and to the tenderness that was such a contrast. A contrast to what she'd known, too; Tom had been kind to everyone, including her. He'd been a contented, gentle man not given to much expression of emotions. The depth of understanding she sometimes saw in Sean's eyes was new to her, along with the focus on *her*. And then there was the passion, shatteringly different than anything she'd known.

Watching Sean laugh at something Daniel Colburn said, Emily discovered she, too, was trembling. Someday... She might get a call. A knock on the door.

She couldn't seem to draw a breath. *I can't do this again*, she thought as her lungs seized, but discovered in an instant that she was just as afraid of going back to the lonely, empty life she had wanted to believe was enough.

And...it was too late anyway, she realized in shock.

"Room for one more in here?" a voice said behind her.

She turned to see a man of a similar height and breadth as Sean, with hair as dark as her own and eyes a deep, espresso brown. Weary lines aged his face. He had to be in his late thirties, if not early forties. He didn't look as if he smiled often.

Daniel grunted a greeting. Sean came back to Emily's side, placing a proprietary hand on her back.

"Lieutenant Wilcynski, meet Sophie Thomsen, Daniel's fiancé, and Emily Drake."

Those dark eyes skimmed over Sophie, then settled with more interest on Emily. She didn't love the way he scrutinized her, as if he found her wanting.

She decided she had to have been imagining it, since he greeted both of them pleasantly.

Then his gaze met Sean's. "Was it smart to bring her?"

"Would it have been smart to leave her alone?"

The lieutenant jerked his head toward the broad hall. "I need a minute."

Sean squeezed her arm in brief reassurance and went. The two men walked far enough away they presumably believed she wouldn't be able to hear what was said. They were wrong. She didn't catch everything, but enough.

"What the hell were you thinking, bringing your girlfriend along when you picked up the Fisk girl?"

With his back to her, Sean's reply was unintelligible.

"And now, tonight? Are you going to start taking her to work with you every day?"

"I'm thinking keeping Emily alive is a priority." Sean must have been mad, because she heard him this time.

"We have half a dozen other potential victims. You haven't requisitioned a bus so you can haul all of them along everywhere you go."

Sean said something. Emily could tell from Lieutenant Wilcynski's face that he didn't like it.

"You're a good detective." His voice was hard, unrelenting. "Don't risk your job."

Face enraged, Sean turned to walk away. He took all of two steps before he snarled over his shoulder, "If that has to be my choice, fuck the job."

Oh, God. What was he doing? Had he just quit, over her? Glaring past him at his boss, she hurried to meet him.

"Don't do this. I can go away, like Mrs. Kelley did. I'll quit being a handicap. I'll—"

Sean shook his head. His eyes were turbulent and a nerve jerked in his cheek, but his mouth had softened. "No. I need you where I can be sure you're safe. I wouldn't be able to concentrate if you weren't here."

"But—" Her sudden understanding had her stopping mid-sentence. The last time someone he loved had been threatened, the ending had been devastating. He couldn't let himself fail again. It was no surprise that he'd go so far as to throw over his job if he had to, to keep her safe. She might even represent a form of redemption for him.

Her protesting wouldn't stop him. He needed to guard her, which meant she had to let him.

So to hell with Lieutenant Wilcynski, who was watching them with narrowed eyes.

"We'll talk about it later," Sean said. Gripping her arm, he steered her back into the room.

She followed his example in ignoring his boss.

The young, female doctor was just stripping off her gloves and smiling at Sophie, who now held Daniel's hand. "Big, tough guys are the worst whiners."

"Hey!" he exclaimed.

"A nurse will be in shortly to put on a dressing and give you information on wound care. Definitely don't get it wet for several days. Make an appointment with your regular doctor in ten days to have the sutures removed." She looked at Sophie. "Any redness, exceptional soreness, numbness or fever, take him for medical attention."

Sophie nodded. "Thank you."

"I'm still here," Daniel grumbled.

Feeling sick at being the source of the confrontation out in the hall, Emily had no choice about where she went. Propelled by Sean, she found herself on the other side of the bed from Sophie.

Emily glanced down at Daniel's bared forearm, sinewy and strong. In the harsh light, the dusting of hair glinted. A strip had been shaved, she saw. She couldn't help evaluating the doctor's work. "Those are really neat stitches. I couldn't have done better myself."

He gave a choked laugh, eyes almost as blue as Sean's showing enough amusement she suspected some of his grumpiness with the ER doc had been staged.

Then he looked toward the foot of the bed. "Wilcynski. I didn't expect you here."

"Sean called me. I was hoping you got close enough to this guy to be able to tell us something useful."

"I got close, all right." He didn't seem to notice that Sophie had shuddered. His voice was grim, his expression focused. "Most of what I can tell you, we already suspected. He was…rubberized. I couldn't get a good grip on him. There wasn't a lot of light, but I'd have seen some sheen if he'd worn spandex. Felt like a wetsuit."

The other two men nodded. Emily was as riveted as they were, but felt internal quakes at the same time. They were talking about the man who had twice gotten within feet of her, with only the bedroom door between them. This was the man who seemed absolutely set on killing her with the same knife he had used to slice nearly the length of Daniel's forearm.

"It may have extended over his head," Daniel continued, "but he also wore what I'd guess was a ski mask, too. Other than that…hell. He had to be somewhere around my size. Athletic, strong. Unbelievably quick with that goddamn knife. I hate knives."

Sophie's teeth actually chattered. She was holding onto Daniel's hand so hard her knuckles turned white. He didn't protest.

"For what it's worth, not a smoker," Daniel added slowly. "That smell tends to cling."

"Could you make out his eyes?" the lieutenant asked.

He shook his head, but Emily thought she wasn't the only one who saw some doubt on his face. "I should have been able to hold onto him." Typical male, it figured that he was fixated on his failure to capture the man he'd set out to ambush. "My arm just quit functioning after he cut it." They all watched as he managed to curl his fingers into a loose fist, but could tell it wasn't happening easily.

"He'd have done some real damage if you hadn't been wearing a vest," Sean observed.

Emily let the point of her elbow planted just below his rib cage suggest he should have kept his mouth shut. He looked down at her in surprise, then up at Sophie, whose face had blanched.

"Uh…sorry."

"The thought had already occurred to me," she said tartly. "I told him this was an idiotic plan. That he shouldn't have staked out the house by himself."

"Hiding two of us in a small yard increased the risk of being seen," Daniel argued. "Sean wasn't far away. He was alerted to be there fast."

"Apparently this particular suspect is even faster." Red spots flared on Sophie's cheeks. "Or smarter." Her glare transferred from Sean to Daniel, who winced.

Lieutenant Wilcynski cleared his throat. Emily would have suspected he was swallowing a laugh if she'd seen any sign he had a sense of humor.

Daniel stared at the ceiling, clearly an unhappy man. "We still have nothing."

"Maybe not, but this was interesting." Sean sounded thoughtful rather than discouraged. "Did he go after Fisk because he has a predetermined order and it was his turn? Or did he somehow know Fisk was the most vulnerable of the possibles we believe are on his list?"

"If we hadn't moved the girl, she'd have been as vulnerable. He may be saving her for last, though." At least Daniel looked interested now. He had what Emily was beginning to think of as a cop's dispassionate view of the world. In this mode, people were pawns to be moved from square to square.

She knew both Daniel and Sean felt for victims. Sean had let her see a range of powerful emotions. But he seemed able to switch them off, too, so as not to cloud his thinking.

"Because she's, er—" Lieutenant Wilcynski joined the conversation, but cast wary glances at the women. He shrugged and apparently finished the thought. "The brass ring."

The brass ring? *Oh.*

"Or he knows she's gone." Daniel said flatly.

The silence that ensued felt uneasy to Emily. Sean frowned at a wall, Daniel at the glass front of the cubicle, the lieutenant at his feet. It was as if they were all thinking hard, but none of them wanted to share those thoughts with the others.

And *that* scared her.

*****

The next day, Sean was in the act of parking a couple of slots away when he saw Jason Payne none-too-gently yanking someone from the backseat of his unmarked county car.

Sean focused on the detainee as he staggered and snarled at Jason. Brown hair, camouflage pants and shirt, the kind of flexible tactical boots military guys and some cops liked to wear. Mid-twenties, maybe, dirty and raging mad. Right age to be A.J. Voight.

Sean got out, locked with a press of his thumb on the remote, and walked over.

Payne glared at his captive. "I asked my questions nicely, and what did the asshole do? He hit me."

Blood trickled down a swollen, already bruised cheek. The bruising ran under his left eye.

The vet let loose of a stream of invective. The gist seemed to be that the cop was a lying piece of shit.

"That so?" Sean said. "You shot at me."

Muddy brown eyes burned holes in him. "If I'd wanted you to be dead, you'd be dead."

Even though he'd never had any doubt that was true, Sean let his eyebrows flicker in a visual 'yeah, sure, if you say so'. Then he dropped back a couple of steps in case Payne's prisoner made a break for freedom despite being cuffed with plastic behind his back.

Payne steered the guy into department headquarters and, ultimately, an empty interview room. As he pulled out a pair of metal cuffs to secure him to the chair that was bolted to the floor, the prisoner erupted. It took Sean and Jason both to hold him down, and he managed to head-butt Sean, whose nose gushed blood.

"Son of a bitch," he growled, holding on until the cuff clicked closed.

The guy screamed and fought like a crazy man, his eyes wild.

Backing away, Sean pressed his forearm to his nose, trying to stop the flow. His eyes stung and his whole face hurt like hell. Even so...something like pity squeezed him.

Out in the parking lot, the homeless man – if that's what he was – had been furious and defiant, but not nuts. Jesus, Sean thought, was there any chance he'd been captured over there at some point and brutally interrogated? Of course he'd flash back under these circumstances.

Nonetheless, Sean backed out of the room with Jason, who took a last look through the glass, then said, "We'd better clean up. You're a mess."

Sean ended up sitting on a toilet, head tipped back, a cold, wet paper towel pressed to his nose. Water kept running at the sink as Jason presumably rinsed off blood.

"How'd you find him?" Sean managed to ask.

"I've gotten to be buddies with Larry. I played the veteran card. We reminisced. Turns out he knew all along where this guy's crib was. Kind of built into a hillside. Could have walked right by it and not seen it. Couple of sheets of corrugated metal as a roof, but they were covered with moss and branches. Metal chimney." He shrugged. "Not the coziest place on earth, but I've slept in worse. Except the climate over there isn't so wet."

Examining his feelings, Sean discovered he was annoyed for more than one reason. Patrol officers had been alerted to watch for the man in camouflage. Finding him wasn't Jason's job. He was supposed to have been concentrating on finding the name of the man Braden's mother had lived with. What, had he gotten bored?

Sean was a little chagrined that part of his irritation stemmed from the knowledge that brash new Detective Payne had been able to bring this guy in when he couldn't. Stupid, when he hadn't been looking for him except idly, when he was on the road. He had a few too many other things on his plate.

Like Emily.

His temper heated at the thought of her, a boiler being fed with fresh fuel. If Wilcynski wanted to fire him, let him try.

He sighed and pushed himself to his feet. Jason still looked like he'd taken a couple of serious punches. The black eye was already in full bloom.

"Better?" he asked.

"Yeah." Sean dropped the wet paper towels in the trash, then tentatively touched his nose. "Looks like I've quit bleeding."

"You'd better put some ice on it, though."

"You, too." Sean assessed him. "You've already got a shiner."

Jason grimaced. "I noticed."

Sean detoured to grab two ice packs from the break room. Arms crossed, Wilcynski was waiting in the hall. Not much choice but to accept his invitation to join him in his office. Jason already had one of the not-so-comfortable chairs facing the lieutenants desk. Sean handed him one of the ice packs, then activated the other and held it to his nose.

Wilcynski sat in his big desk chair and studied the two of them. "Good work finding him," he said finally to Jason. "From the looks of you two, we have an excuse to hold him until we figure out who he is."

"No I.D.?" Sean asked.

"Not that I found in a quick pat down," Jason said. "Wasn't sure whether I should search his hut without a warrant."

"You'll have to pinpoint where it is," the lieutenant said. "Once we know whose land he was on, we can get the warrant if we need one." He switched his gaze to Sean. "What do you think?"

"We could call Colburn, ask him to come take a look. It might be interesting to see how he reacts when he sees Daniel."

Wilcynski nodded.

"He's the right age, the right experience." Sean gingerly shifted the pack on his nose. Sooner or later, he'd get numb – but, damn, in the meantime ice hurt worse than the original injury. "We're reaching here," he said finally. "Unless we find I.D. that says his last name is Voigt, how will we tie him to Braden?"

"And?"

"He can't be over – what? – five nine? Maybe five ten? Kind of skinny, too."

"But strong and quick," put in Jason, who had reason to know.

"Granted. Still. You heard what Daniel said last night."

Wilcynski inclined his head. Jason hadn't, so Sean explained.

He went on. "The other thing is, he's off his rocker right now. Yeah, the first time he broke into Emily's house, he pushed it when he should have disappeared. But otherwise, every crime scene has been clean. Those murders were well-planned and meticulously performed. His failures since weren't because he screwed up. Whatever he feels inside, the killer has to be able to compartmentalize, stay completely in control of himself. Is this guy capable of that level of planning and care? I don't know."

Jason glared at him. "You're the one who wanted him brought in."

"I did, and I'm not criticizing you." He'd wait until they were alone to talk to Jason about his assigned task and why it had taken a backseat, instead of getting him in trouble with the lieutenant. "We need to talk to him, we need to search his place. I have my doubts. That's all."

"I share them," Wilcynski said unexpectedly. "I was watching while you two subdued him. That didn't look like acting to me."

"Let's go talk to him," Sean said.

Two hours later, they conceded defeat for the day and had their prisoner transferred to the jail.

Sean had tried to talk to him. They brought in Louise Acosta from the D.A.'s office, under the theory he might settle down with a woman, especially one so motherly. He told her to fuck herself.

Her placid response was, "Don't have the equipment." When she came out of the interview room, she shook her head. "Sorry."

Daniel had made the drive from Cape Trouble. He got no further than anyone else, and came out shaking his head. "I wish I could tell you, but I can't. My gut feeling is no because he's kind of scrawny, but we all know that anyone being assaulted magnifies the size of the attacker. A badge probably doesn't make me immune."

He did tell them that Ed Fisk had called to let him know that he and his wife were going into hiding.

"In fact, they threw some things in suitcases last night and left not much behind the ambulance. Figured the guy wasn't likely to be watching the house or in a position to follow them. He wouldn't tell me where they are." Daniel's mouth had a quirk. "Said anyone could be listening."

"You're not paranoid when someone actually is after you," Sean couldn't resist saying.

Hoping Fisk had made a smart choice about where to hide, Sean went back to pursuing a possible lead as to what had happened to Braden's possessions after his death. Staff had changed at the group home. They guessed maybe stuff might have been put in the attic, if he wanted to take a look. He did.

Amongst trashed furniture, stored items like fans that wouldn't be needed until summer and a stash of record albums, he found a stack of cardboard boxes. Some did hold what he suspected were possessions left behind by boys who'd been moved, returned to their families, gone to juvie or prison. Some included school notebooks with a name scrawled inside. He didn't find Braden's name anywhere.

One more dead end.

\*\*\*\*\*

Stuck at The Sandpiper for yet another day, Emily made a decision. When this was all over, she would sell the business. She just wasn't very interested anymore. She'd clung to the belief that someday, when her mourning passed, she would want to go back to active participation. Her dream had once been to have her own retail business. If she and Tom had settled somewhere more populous, she might have opened a quilt shop. Here, local crafts were an obvious substitute. Her days of selling her own work at farmers' markets had given her contacts and even friendships among other local artisans. Back then, Cape Trouble was barely beginning to see the benefits of catering to tourists. She hadn't had as much competition as she did now. She'd been so excited about promoting the handwork of Oregon coast artists and craftspeople, with an emphasis on the textiles she had always loved.

Frowning, she tried to decide whether she had become too much of a loner to want to spend her days surrounded by other people. That would imply she really was broken. And it was true that she'd become accustomed to not talking to another soul for days at a time, but…she thought that wasn't her entire reason for being ready to let go of the store.

She didn't need what income she drew from it, for one thing.

While it was true she could never be the same person, the woman who'd loved chatting with acquaintances and strangers alike, maybe she should substitute the word 'changed' for 'broken'.

Truthfully, she was content with focusing on her own quilting. There were so many galleries and gift shops up and down the coast, if The Sandpiper ended up closing altogether or changing focus, none of the artisans whose work she carried would have trouble finding other outlets. For herself, she could quit bothering with the small pieces made to please the tourist trade and concentrate on the traditional quilts she loved, and the art quilts that had increasingly intrigued her. The thought was liberating.

She also discovered how restless she felt. She understood why she had to stay at the store all day, waiting on customers or sitting behind the computer in the office, whatever she'd rather be doing. But she felt as useless as a guest at Sean's every evening. She wanted access to her sewing machine, her quilting frame, her cutting tools.

Back in her own home, surrounded by memories of her husband and child, would she feel the same about Sean? She needed to find out.

She wanted to go home.

Her resolve was temporarily forgotten at her first sight of Sean when he picked her up. "What happened?" she cried.

He gingerly touched his swollen, discolored nose. "Wrestling match."

During the drive home, he told her about the capture of the young vet with PTSD, not hiding the pity and sympathy he seemed to feel for the guy despite the damage he'd done. Her respect for him deepened.

Emily waited until they were eating dinner to make her suggestion.

"You know the pane of glass in the window was replaced at my house."

Without appearing very interested, Sean made an acknowledging sound. He was occupied putting together another taco from the ingredients in serving dishes on the table. She watched as he added a dollop of sour cream. A few bruises didn't seem to have hurt his appetite.

"I know you don't want to leave me alone right now."

His head came up. "You're right. That's not an option."

Emily took a deep breath. "What I'm wondering is, could we stay at my house instead of yours?"

She'd swear he didn't even blink. His eyes bored into hers. "Why?"

"Because I can work there."

"You've been doing hand quilting here."

"Yes, but I can't piece new quilts. I can't work on the one in the frame. My fabrics are there. My sewing machine." When he didn't immediately say anything, she buttressed her argument. "Even if it has a weakness, I do have a home security system, which is more than you have. And it's not as though he doesn't know I'm living here if he's watching."

Sean set the taco down on his plate. "You want to go home so you can get more work done."

"Yes!"

"That's the only reason."

She opened her mouth, hesitated, and closed it. She didn't want to lie to him.

"It's home," she finally said.

"If we move there, I won't be home."

"You've barely settled in here. It's not the same."

"We're sleeping together, Emily. I'm guessing you haven't replaced your bed since your husband died. How are you going to feel having me putting my head on his pillow?"

Oh, God. How would she feel? Why hadn't she thought of that?

She was the one to go utterly still now.

If she had a guest room…but she didn't.

"I…I'm okay with it," she heard herself say, even as her lungs squeezed closed. Was she really? She'd have to be, wouldn't she, if there was to be any possibility of a future with Sean.

The intensity of his stare didn't waver. "I'm not so sure I am."

"I could…buy a new bed. We could probably get it delivered tomorrow."

"It's not just the bed." He scraped a hand over his face, leaving it more expressive, less robot-like, but no happier. "You figuring after we make an arrest, you and I will go back to our own houses? Maybe date? Or is that even on your horizon?"

"Of course it is!" she cried, her chair legs scraping as she pushed back. "I don't know what's going to happen to us! Do you?"

"I was hoping I did. I don't want his and her houses, Emily. I like seeing you the minute I open my eyes in the morning. Coming home to you. Talking about our days. Going to bed together. Making love."

She couldn't look away from his vividly blue eyes. "I do too," she whispered.

"I've been thinking neither of our houses is really big enough for a family," he said, voice husky. "Not given how much space you need for your quilting."

A family? He was thinking a family? Her heart felt as if it was being torn right down the middle. Replace Cody? She couldn't. She wouldn't. But...if she'd been pregnant when he died, if they'd already had other children, she would have loved them. She had so successfully suppressed this yearning for a baby, a wiggly, smart, active toddler, for a family, she had never suspected she held it inside her.

Until now.

She had sat speechless too long. Sean's lashes veiled his eyes. "Good to know where I stand."

"No!" Her eyes burned. She never cried anymore. Never. Until Sean had come along. "You don't understand."

"What don't I understand?" His expression was still shuttered, but his tone gentle.

"I can't leave my house."

His "What?" was almost soundless.

"I'd be leaving them." Her hands had begun to shake. She clasped them together out of his sight, beneath the table. "My memories…"

Sean's stare became incredulous. "That's it? The whole house is an altar to their memory? You meant it when you told me you'd never be ready to move on, didn't you?"

"No." Her vision had blurred. "I was wrong. You've made me see that. I—" *Just say it.* "I'm in love with you. But...why can't we live there?"

"You, me and your dead husband and son. Sounds real cozy. Is there room for three in your bed, Emily?"

"It's not like that," she said hopelessly. Because…it was?
No!

Really? How was she going to feel if she had a baby? Would she strip Cody's room bare and redecorate for the new child? Or insist that son or daughter live in a room haunted by Cody's presence?

Sean shook his head. "Let's clean the kitchen, then pack. I have some camping stuff out in the garage. I'll bring a pad and sleeping bag."

Then he stood up, carried his plate to the kitchen, and scraped the taco he had so carefully constructed into the trash.

Unable to move, Emily wondered if it was possible to bleed out, when the wound wasn't physical.

# CHAPTER FOURTEEN

Mind clouded by tiredness the next morning, Sean sat at his desk, brooding over what to do about the homeless veteran. They couldn't hold him indefinitely, not without charging him with assault on an officer. Once they did that, the guy was screwed, and Sean didn't see it as justified. But, damn it, they weren't any closer to identifying him. His fingerprints weren't in the system, telling them only that he'd never been arrested. They had also been submitted to every branch of the service, but who knew when or if they'd be favored with an answer.

He stood abruptly. "I'm going to talk to him again." After a stop in the restroom to slap cold water on his face.

The closest detective gave Sean a startled look, but a couple of desks away, Jason pushed his chair back. "You want me to have a go? He knows I'm ex-military, too."

Sean wondered if he'd ever been that eager. Given that he currently felt like a zombie, he couldn't imagine.

He shook his head. "I think it's safe to say he hates you. You brought him in. Stick to what you're doing."

Jason was still trying to trace Braden and his mother's movements. The rental application had turned out to be useless. According to Jason, the manager had been more than embarrassed. His ass would be fired if the owner ever found out he was letting renters move in without providing background info. Jason had since widened his search, so far without results. There was no saying she and Braden had even lived in the state before coming here.

Fifteen minutes later, Sean was at the jail, sitting down in a small interview room across the table from the guy, now wearing institutional orange.

He looked...diminished. Scared. He sat with shoulders rounded, head bent. As Sean watched, he rocked in his seat.

"You know Larry," Sean said.

The rocking stopped.

"We're all okay with Larry's lifestyle. No one wants to pen him up. We check to be sure he has enough to eat, and that's about it. Tell us your name. Once we confirm your identity, if you're not the man we're looking for, we'll release you. I know the shots you fired at me were only warnings. The head butt was an accident." Sort of. "Detective Payne has agreed not to charge you with assaulting an officer for the punches you got in on him, either."

The guy looked up. "I didn't hit him. He lies. You all lie."

"No. I'm an honest man."

His face worked. "Why do you care who I am?"

Despite the posture, he didn't look quite so crazy today. He was actually taking in what Sean told him. Asking a straight question.

Sean gave him a straight answer. "Because we're investigating a series of murders. We think the killer is a veteran, fairly new to this area. We know enough about who he is to eliminate you if we can confirm your identity."

His eyeballs twitched and kept twitching for a moment, as if he had a stigmatism. The effect was unnerving. "I can't go home," he said in panic.

"No one said you have to." Sean made sure his voice was even, soothing. "Burris County is good place to live. You're welcome around here as long as you stay out of trouble—" He half-smiled. "Not shooting at law enforcement officers would be a good start."

"You'll let me go."

"I will."

The guy's Adam's apple bobbed. He apparently came to a decision. "My name is Jeff. Jeffrey."

Sean waited.

"Dunn. That's my last name."

"You got out of the service recently?"

Alarm flared on his face. "You trying to claim I'm AWOL?"

Sean shook his head. "I'm not suggesting that. I don't care. What I need to know is where you grew up. How old you are. Whether you have parents."

The eyeball twitching thing happened again and his voice rose. "So you can call them to come get me?"

"No." Sean stayed outwardly relaxed, hoping he projected sincerity. If Jeff Dunn's story panned out, he might call the parents later, just to let them know their son was okay and working through some things. He didn't tell him that. Instead, he said, "I made a promise to you."

Jeff ducked his head and rocked in place a few times. The tendons and veins stood out in his neck and hands and forearms. "Medford," he mumbled. "That's where my parents are."

He finally named them. Brian and Eleanor Dunn.

After having Jeff taken back to his cell, Sean returned to the bullpen, mildly surprised that he was alone now. Within minutes, he found the high school yearbook online and, from a photo, confirmed that Jeffrey Dunn was who he'd said he was. Further search told Sean that Brian Dunn owned an auto parts and supplies store and his wife was a receptionist in a chiropractor's office. Jeff had a sister, two years older, who had married right out of high school and still lived in Medford, an agricultural town in a dry part of the state not far from the California border.

Unfortunately, the next step was clearing his decision with Lieutenant Wilcynski. Neither had said anything since about the confrontation in the hospital, but Sean had to work to suppress the anger still at a simmer.

Wilcynski was in. Sean had begun to wonder if he lived here. His office door stood open, and he glanced up when Sean appeared. Once he heard what Sean had learned, he gave a sharp nod. "Cut him loose." There was a distinct pause. "Good work."

Sean returned the nod, but his smile as he walked away was distinctly humorless.

At the jail, he waited until Jeff changed back into his camo getup and signed for his few other possessions, then offered him a lift, expecting to be given the bird.

Instead, Jeff accepted. Sean's couple of conversational forays during the drive brought no response, which was okay. He didn't feel chatty himself.

"Here's okay," Jeff said abruptly, as the Cape Trouble city limits neared.

Sean put on his turn signal and pulled over.

Getting out on the shoulder of the highway, Jeff paused. "You're okay," he said abruptly. "The other one is still a liar."

Then he slammed the door, leaped the ditch, and vanished into the forest.

Sean felt something akin to amusement. Would Jeff stop and talk to him the next time they spotted each other? Or would he shoot first and remember Sean was okay later?

Time to pick up Emily from her store. He felt certain she wouldn't be any friendlier than Jeff Dunn had been.

The frozen silence between them was killing Sean.

He had slept on the floor last night and would tonight.

Emily had told him with quiet dignity that they could stay in his house. Hurt and pissed, he had insisted they pack up then and there and move to her house. By damn he wasn't going to sleep in the bed she'd shared with her husband, far less make love to her in it.

What he did was open all three bedroom doors to be sure he heard any faint sound of an intruder coming in through a window, then bedded down in the hall right outside her room. She tried to cry quietly, but he heard her anyway.

Had he gone to her, taken her in his arms and told her he'd been a jackass and was sorry? Hell, no. That would have meant burying the hurt, or maybe only his pride. He didn't know.

He hadn't gotten much sleep, that was for sure.

Having the investigation once again at a standstill didn't help, either. Sean had never lived in tornado country, but he'd read about the sickly color of the sky, the ominous heaviness of the air, that served as warning. Too aware that Emily was still a killer's quarry, that's what this felt like.

Even so, it wasn't the investigation that kept Sean awake later, after another stilted evening.

Right before he'd turned out the hall light, he had noticed something he should have seen before. On the wide, white-painted wood molding that framed the door to what he knew was the linen closet, a line had been drawn in what looked like ink. There were some tiny squiggles next to it. Crawling over the air mattress and crouching in front of it to get a better look, he felt like he'd taken a shot to his chest.

Beside the thin, horizontal line was the letter C and a date. February, four years ago.

At his house, there were a whole bunch of lines on a narrow strip of wall that would never be painted over, at least until his parents were gone and the house had to be sold. Once a year, Mom had made each of her kids stand tall, back to the wall, while she used a ruler to draw a new line. Then she'd carefully label it with their initials and the date. He remembered stepping back, his eyes moving from the last line to the new one, being awed at how much he had grown. Sometimes he slid his finger down the wall in search of his initials. Had he really ever been that short?

Because Emily's son had died, no more lines had been drawn above this single one, or ever would. Stricken, he wondered how often she stopped on her way down the hall to look at that one narrow line and remember what it represented. How many other places in the house carried the same emotional load?

And he'd refused to understand why she couldn't imagine leaving this house.

*I'm an idiot.*

He rolled over, punched his pillow and stared straight into her dark bedroom.

Yeah, but could he live with the ghosts of her dead husband and child?

He stifled a groan and returned to lying on his back, this time with his hands clasped beneath his head.

It wasn't as if he'd asked her to marry him. This was just...a tryout.

Uh huh. Sure.

Short-term or long-term, he had to accept the existence of the pair of elephants in the room. So to speak. If she'd had a kid from another man, he didn't think he'd have a problem with it. Likewise, if Emily was divorced, she'd have memories, experiences that would never be erased.

But instinct told him this was different. He struggled with the why for a minute before he understood. It wasn't the memories he minded. It was the knowledge that she would forever hold Tom and Cody in her heart. Love uninterrupted. She might love him, too, love their kids, but none of that would change what she'd felt for her first husband and baby.

He'd never know if she loved him best. That was the kicker. And Sean knew even thinking that way was stupid, too. Love shouldn't be ranked first, second, third.

But still, sleep eluded him.

\*\*\*\*\*

The sound of Sean's phone ringing worked like a shot of adrenaline on Emily. Just like that, she was sitting up in bed, her heart racing. She was starting to really hate these middle of the night phone calls. They never brought good news.

She also hated that this was the third night in a row he'd slept in the hall instead of with her.

As low as he kept his voice, she still heard his "What?" Pause. "How the hell...?"

Somebody else was dead. Chilled, Emily yanked the covers up around herself..

"On my way," he said finally, then raised his voice slightly. "Emily?"

"I'm awake. Who was that?"

"Rebecca Walker. The guy got into her house tonight. She's injured, but the Fisk girl is okay. Unfortunately, he got away. She thought she shot him, but there's no blood. Either she missed, or he was wearing a vest."

"A vest?"

"Kevlar," he said grimly.

Emily shuddered. "He'll never stop, will he?" She wanted to pull the covers higher, right over her head, and pretend none of this was happening.

"Not until we stop him." His dark shape materialized only a few feet from her bed. "I'm sorry. We need to go to the hospital again."

"Will your lieutenant be mad that I'm there?" she asked reluctantly, because the idea of staying behind freaked her out. The killer surely wouldn't go after another target tonight, but... *Call me a coward*, she thought.

"Don't care," Sean said, his tone uncompromising. "Up and at 'em."

She grabbed from her drawers almost at random and dressed in the bathroom. She came out to find that Sean had pulled on the same clothes he'd worn earlier. They were noticeably wrinkled. Stubble darkened his jaw. The bridge of his nose still had a dark bump, and the bruising that crept beneath his eyes was turning yellow. It didn't appear he'd bothered to comb his hair, leaving it even more disheveled than usual. Yet somehow he was still sexy – maybe even sexier battered. The just-out-of-bed look didn't hurt, either.

The same did not hold true for her. She'd been horrified at the sight of herself in the mirror, her face almost gaunt, her eyes shadowed and sunken. One appalled look had been more than enough.

Emily realized immediately that they were going to North Fork and the larger hospital there, not the small one in Cape Trouble. Of course that made sense. This drive would be twenty minutes instead of five, though.

Halfway, Emily realized she must have at least been dozing, if not asleep, when the phone rang. Because her brain suddenly kicked into gear, and she understood why he'd said, How the hell...?

Her heartbeat quickened. "I don't understand. How did he know where Kimberly was?"

The steering wheel creaked as his fingers flexed. "That's a really important question. One I have a very bad feeling about."

"What do you mean?"

He only shook his head and refused to say more.

As usual, he shielded her with his body as he hustled her through the sliding glass doors into the emergency room. He displayed his badge to the receptionist and asked for Rebecca Walker. A minute later, a nurse appeared to usher them back.

The cubicles were all dark except for one. They walked in to find another nurse carefully cutting off a blood-soaked nightshirt while an older, male doctor watched. Kimberly Fisk huddled in a corner of the room. Pixy-cut blonde hair wild, she wore flannel pajama bottoms, a T-shirt and fuzzy pink slippers. She clutched a parka on her lap.

The moment she saw Sean, she jumped to her feet, outrage flaring. "You said he wouldn't find me! I trusted you!"

"How he found you is something we'll be talking about." Then he stepped to Rebecca's side. "Not looking so good," he said, voice considerably gentler.

She grimaced at him. "Just what a girl wants to hear."

Kimberly saw all the blood and dropped back in the chair again as if her legs had given out.

"Son of a bitch shot me," Rebecca muttered.

The doctor frowned at Sean. "Detective, you can get answers from her later. Right now, I need you to back off."

Eyes lingering on Rebecca's bloody shoulder, he nodded and returned to Emily's side.

"Is your boss coming again?" she asked in an undertone.

"Yeah, I thought so." With a frown, he glanced at the wall clock. "He may have gone to the scene first."

The 'scene' being Rebecca's cabin in the woods. Thinking about how violated she felt, Emily wondered if Rebecca's home would ever feel as peaceful to her again.

Eventually, Kimberly, Sean and Emily were herded out of the cubicle and curtains were drawn. A different nurse found chairs for them, which Emily and Kimberly took advantage of. Sean paced. Emily reassured Kimberly, but both fell silent after a bit.

An orderly appeared, and Rebecca was wheeled out in the same bed, her eyes glassy, but her head turning until she saw Sean. He hurried to her, walking beside the bed as it moved down the hall. Emily couldn't quite hear what they said, but after Rebecca and the cluster of people around her disappeared into an elevator, he came back.

"The bullet is still in her. They have to operate."

"Is she going to be okay?"

"Doesn't sound like it hit anything vital."

"You're not wearing one of those vests, are you?" Emily asked fiercely.

"Daytimes. Uh, sometimes." He rubbed a hand over his face. "I'll start sleeping in it, too."

"Thank you," she whispered.

"What about me?" Kimberly asked. "What happens to me now?"

"We'll figure out where you can stay," he said. "For now, the doctor suggested a small conference room." He nodded down the hall. "The waiting room is too open."

That silenced Emily and Kimberly both.

The chairs in the small room were marginally more comfortable than the hard plastic ones in the hall. Sean seemed unable to settle into one. Leaving the door open, he kept pacing. Or maybe, she thought, he was just trying to keep himself awake. She kept dozing off and then, as she would start to list sideways or fall forward, jerking awake.

Sean was barely outside the room when his phone rang. She saw that Kimberly was soundly asleep, her head bent at an awkward angle. Emily struggled to stay alert until she knew what was happening

Of course, he walked away, keeping his voice low.

When he returned, his expression was so bleak, her heart seemed to stop. She jumped up and went to him.

"What is it?" she asked, pitching her voice low.

He took her arm and steered her part way down the hall until they were equidistant from the small room and the nurse's station.

His voice was pure gravel. "Byron Saunders is the cop who shot and killed Braden in that courtroom." A muscle jerked in his cheek. "He was on patrol tonight. When he didn't respond to radio traffic, other deputies went looking for him. They found his car. He was still behind the wheel. Throat sliced."

Emily grappled with that knowledge. With the horror. "Right there? I mean, he wasn't put back in the car...afterwards?"

"No." His face was so grim, it had turned to stone. But his eyes were a shocking contrast, the anger and pain so vivid, it hurt to see.

"He let somebody walk right up and—" She couldn't finish.

"Yes."

"Do you think...he could have told the man who killed him where to find Kimberly?"

Sean groaned and wheeled away from her as if he didn't want her to see his face. "Byron shouldn't have known where she was," he said, with a savagery she'd never heard from him before. "Nobody should have known except the members of the task force."

"And me," she said timidly, then bit her lip. "And Rebecca."

"And Kimberly," he finished for her. "You don't have to tell me."

Emily laid a hand on his back and rubbed it. "I'm sorry. Was he a friend of yours?"

He shook his head and turned back to her, his face ravaged. "No. But he was one of us. He refused to go into hiding. Thought as a cop he ought to be able to take care of himself." His throat worked.

Emily stood, feeling helpless. But suddenly Sean reached out for her, pulling her tight to him, and pressed his face against her head. She wrapped her arms securely around him, offering and accepting comfort. Even under the awful circumstances, the feel of his tall, solid body stirred a response in her. She had ached for him these past nights. Right now, he seemed to need her, which gave her hope.

Eventually he sighed and let her go. His eyes were red-rimmed, although she could tell he hadn't let himself shed a tear.

His hand rasped over his jaw. "Jason is right." He shook his head. "The guy is a fucking ghost."

"You'll find him."

"How?" He showed his teeth. "How?"

She had no answer.

\*\*\*\*\*

Rebecca came through the surgery with no complications. Her father had arrived by then, as had Wilcynski. The three of them listened as the surgeon explained what he'd done. Her left scapula had stopped the bullet, which also shattered it. He had done what he could to put her shoulder blade back together. At a minimum, she'd have her shoulder immobilized in a sling for three to four weeks.

"We need to ask her a couple of quick questions as soon as she's conscious," Sean said.

"I'll alert Recovery to call you back once she's awake." He frowned at Sean. "So long as you do keep it quick." He handed over the piece of torn metal he'd extracted in a small plastic zip-top bag.

They all stared at it. "No wonder there was so goddamn much blood," Wilcynski said. A pulse throbbed in his temple.

"That's not a bullet," Rebecca's father said incredulously.

"Jacketed hollow point." Sean had trouble sounding anything close to normal. Civilized. "Designed to expand on impact."

"To do as much damage as possible," the lieutenant elaborated. Rage roughened his voice, too.

Kevin Walker looked like he wanted to kill, a feeling with which Sean sympathized. "I'll be taking her home with me to recover," her father said. "Will this bastard come after her?"

"She didn't see him well enough to identify him, so he'd have no reason. Tonight, she got in his way. All the same, take what precautions you can."

After Mr. Walker sank into a chair in the same room as Emily and Kimberly Fisk, head in his hands, Sean and Wilcynski walked and talked for a few minutes.

"I can stay if you want to see both scenes," the lieutenant said. He hadn't commented on Emily's presence, nor had Sean seen any change in his expression when he saw her.

"Was there anything new?"

"Aside from the fact that he used a gun at Rebecca's, no." He ground his teeth. "I looked up Saunder's record. He was a hell of good cop. Dishonorable discharge." He spat the last two words. DD had been written in blood on the interior of the side window. The perp had wanted to be sure the blood wasn't washed away in rain or drizzle.

Sean felt a momentary pull. He always wanted to see the crime scenes first hand. But this time, instinct told him he'd have a better chance finding answers elsewhere. "Then no," Sean said. "Not if you're willing to supervise the evidence team."

"I can." He grunted. "We both know it'll be a miracle if they find a damn thing that isn't easily explained."

Yeah, no kidding, Sean thought. "I'm not much of a churchgoer," he said. "Could be that's why I don't see many miracles."

The lieutenant surprised him by quirking an eyebrow. "You've seen a couple recently. The fact that Ms. Drake escaped a killer who'd already gotten into her house, and twice, qualifies, I think."

"Yeah." Tiredness weighed on Sean, but he couldn't surrender to it. "And it's got to piss him off. He missed at the Fisk house the other night, but it wasn't Ed Fisk who outsmarted him. Emily is different. She thwarted him singlehandedly."

"Not entirely. You got there fast."

"But she was already out of the house, waking the whole neighborhood."

Wilcynski shrugged an acknowledgment. "It'll be harder to protect her from a bullet," he said after a minute.

"That's already been on my mind."

Wilcynski nodded. "Call once you talk to Deputy Walker and find out if the Fisk girl blabbed. I'll let you know if we learn anything."

"Will do."

Sean watched him until he pushed through the swinging doors to the waiting room, then turned to rejoin Emily and the others. He needed to talk to her, but even if he could get her alone, this wasn't the time or the place, and he wasn't settled enough in his mind.

\*\*\*\*\*

Emily glanced at the dashboard clock as Sean turned onto their street. 6:22. It had felt surreal walking out of the hospital to daylight. It had been dark when they arrived, and her body thought it should still be dark. Somehow, time had warped while they were inside. She'd dozed enough that the waking periods felt more like dreams.

The drive had passed in silence. She knew Sean was brooding over how the killer had known where Kimberly was. In his brief talk with Rebecca, she'd insisted she had told no one at all. Kimberly said the same.

"I'm not stupid!" she'd cried.

"You didn't hint. To anybody."

"No! I turned my phone off, like you said."

She didn't waver. Her phone was back at Rebecca's, but if he wanted to go get it, he could look at her call logs and texts. "There aren't any," she insisted. "Not since you picked me up."

Sean had still looked doubtful, but Emily believed her. Kimberly looked terrified. Why would she lie about something they could check so easily?

Emily felt a dizzying fear that there was no escape. Why hide, if he could find them despite every precaution? It was as if he was watching all of them, at all times. She caught herself giving surreptitious looks around, even while they were tucked away in that small room back in the ER. During the drive, she'd kept an eye on the rearview mirror.

Sean saw her and said, "He doesn't have magical powers. I'll tell you one thing, I'll be going over this vehicle inch by inch to be sure it's not carrying a tracking device. Ditto for my assigned car."

Emily shuddered. "He'd know everywhere you've been."

"Yeah. It would explain some things." His fingers tightened and loosened a few times on the steering wheel. "Another possibility is that someone has a big mouth."

"You mean Kimberly?"

His mouth tightened and he didn't answer.

Emily had a bad feeling she knew what he was thinking. She had no doubt he intended to grill the various detectives on his task force next. After he got some sleep, she hoped.

"You must be even more tired than I am," she said, the sound of her voice startling her.

"I need to get a few hours," he admitted gruffly.

"Can we go to your house?"

He gave her a sidelong, startled look. "Why?"

"If you don't mind, I think I'd like to sleep with you."

Sean didn't say anything, but a moment later he parked in his own driveway, not hers.

When she reached for the door handle, he snapped, "Wait until I get around there."

He had her bend low and all but run to his front porch. It was not a graceful way to travel. What she'd done was scuttle, she decided. Sort of like a cockroach afraid someone was going to step on it.

He had the door unlocked and them inside in seconds. She felt some of the tension leave his body once he locked.

"We'll nap here," he said, "but I'm thinking it would be better to stay at your house tonight. The security system does offer some protection."

Some protection. Her tiny burst of annoyance was probably a reaction to all the tension.

"I might not have wasted the money if you'd described it that way in the first place," Emily grumbled.

He grimaced. "It did let you down."

She stripped to panties and T-shirt. He placed his gun on the bedside stand within what would be easy reach for him, then undressed, too, leaving on his gray, stretch boxers.

They met in bed.

As if the last two nights hadn't happened and it were a given, he slid an arm beneath her neck and gathered her close. Head resting on his shoulder in the spot that seemed made for her, she saw that exhaustion had aged him ten years. The way he looked at her out of bloodshot eyes was as intense as ever, though.

"We need to talk." His voice slurred. "Later." Then, as if that was all he could manage, his eyes closed and his muscles went slack.

What? That was all he had to say? Emily stiffened. For all her own exhaustion, sleep didn't come quickly, not when apprehension had her stomach roiling.

# CHAPTER FIFTEEN

Sean remembered last night's events even before he opened his eyes. He turned his head enough to see the clock. Ten-thirty. Almost four hours of sleep would hold him until tonight.

He reached for the phone, then thought better of it. Emily was still out of it. He'd have to wake her up soon, but he might as well let her sleep as long as possible.

She didn't stir as he slid from bed. He stood looking down at her, his chest hurting. Curled up like a sleeping child, she looked smaller, or maybe she'd been losing weight. Her braid was half undone. A long, midnight dark lock of hair lay across her cheek, emphasizing the jut of her cheekbone and the clean line of her jaw.

Wilcynski was right, he thought. Her survival thus far was a miracle. She'd displayed amazing presence of mind and courage. Her reward was being treated like a captive. She'd been lucky to be able to decide what she wanted out of the snack machine at the hospital last night. Otherwise, she followed orders, accepted confinement. Yet she'd been both valiant and patient.

The only damned thing she had asked was that he take her home, and he'd been a jerk about it.

Sean shook his head and went to take a shower. Under cover of the running water he called for an update on Rebecca's condition. He was told she was resting comfortably.

He emerged from the bathroom to find the bed empty and heard the shower running in the other bathroom.

Breakfast was as quick as he could manage while providing a half decent meal. Conversation was brief to non-existent. Sean would sneak a look at her, only to find her apparently concentrating entirely on crumbling her toast. Damn. What he wanted to do was scoop her onto his lap, ask her to forgive him, tell her if she'd have him, he could live without ever knowing how he rated on the husband scale.

Bottom line: he was here, Tom was dead. With time, Sean thought, he was bound to come out the winner. He winced, knowing he was a jerk even to be thinking that.

But this wasn't the time for that talk, any more than last night had been. His first priority had to be finding a serial killer before he could regroup and go after anyone again, and in particular Emily.

Which meant tucking her away somewhere safe, and setting out to ask some hard questions.

"I'll have to drop you at the store," he started to say, but saw that she was shaking her head.

"It's Sunday. We're closed on Sunday and Monday."

He swore.

"Maybe you could leave me with Daniel and Sophie…"

Sean shook his head. "I may need him."

"Or…what if I sat with Rebecca Walker? The hospital should be safe."

Given his current suspicions, Emily would be remarkably vulnerable at the hospital. Sean made a snap decision. "No. You're coming with me."

Emily tried one more time. "But—"

He shook his head again. His expression must have been forbidding, because she closed her mouth without finishing her latest suggestion.

Wilcynski wouldn't like it, but to hell with him.

As it happened, Sean had been having some hard thoughts about Lieutenant B.J. Wilcynski as well as Detective Jason Payne. Daniel, he trusted. He wouldn't so far as to say he trusted Rey Mendoza, but he wouldn't have been involved in the investigation beyond the one murder in his jurisdiction if Sean hadn't invited him. Plus, he was clearly Hispanic. Hard to imagine him ever having been called Aaron Voight. Nonetheless, Sean had every intention of doing a background check on him today.

Along with ones on Lieutenant Wilcynski and Detective Payne. Both of whom were new to the department and the area.

Wilcynski had arrived less than a month before the first murder. It seemed unlikely he could be Braden Wilson's big "brother", given that he had to be in his late thirties. But maybe they'd jumped to conclusions. What if he was Braden's father? Or the stepfather, if

Braden had lied for some reason about him dying? Wilcynski hadn't done anything, except for occasionally being abrasive, to give Sean cause to suspect him. But he'd been tapped into the investigation every step of the way. He was one of the few people who'd known where Kimberly Fisk was hidden. That Jeanette Kelley was going into hiding. That Ed Fisk had refused to do the same.

What if Sheriff Mackay hadn't looked too hard into Wilcynski's references? He might have jumped at someone with the experience Wilcynski claimed without wondering if he was too good to be true.

Payne had been here a few months longer. If he was Braden Wilson's big "brother" – and, appearing to still be in his twenties, he was close enough to the right age – you'd think he'd have started his killing spree sooner. But maybe not. He might have wanted to establish himself so well, he wouldn't ping on anyone's radar. He could have planned from the beginning to maneuver himself into being part of the investigation.

Which was exactly what he'd done. Remembering his surprise when Jason had appeared at Frank Lowe's house, Sean shook his head in faint incredulity. It had never occurred to him to check with the dispatcher to find out whether the conversation Jason mentioned had ever occurred. Why would he have been awake and chatting with the dispatcher in the middle of the night anyway?

*This sounded more interesting than the couple of homicide investigations I've been involved in*, he'd said, elaborately casual. *Thought I could learn something.*

And, damn, Sean couldn't believe he was even thinking this. Suspecting other cops, ones who'd been working this case as hard as he had. He was suffering from paranoia, he told himself. Schizophrenia didn't run in his family, as far as he knew, but that didn't mean he hadn't been hit with the first symptoms.

But paranoia or not, he intended to take a hard look into the backgrounds of both men. If Wilcynski found out, Sean would probably find himself stripped of his badge and service weapon.

So be it.

He left Emily inside when he went out to inspect his Outback. He'd driven it the day he transported Kimberly Fisk. Among the rest of the junk in his garage, he had a creeper. It took him a few minutes to find the damn thing, but once he did, it enabled him to roll under the chassis of his Subaru and search for anything that shouldn't be there. By the time he finished, he was pretty confident the vehicle was clean.

That wasn't good news, given the alternative explanations for how Kimberly had been found in what should have been a safe house.

Emily was ready when he went back in for her. She let him hustle her out to his SUV, and obediently crouched on the floor instead of sitting up where she could be a target while he backed out and made it to the highway leading to North Fork.

Then she crawled up into the seat and fastened her seatbelt without complaining.

It occurred to him that she hadn't said anything about the talk he'd promised her. Maybe she'd rather not have it. He was the guy keeping her alive. She might not think it was smart right now to tell him she still loved her husband too much to think about getting deeply involved with anyone else.

Sean reminded himself that she had offered to replace her bed. She had admitted to wanting to live again. She'd made love with blistering passion. She'd told him there wasn't any reason for him to be jealous.

He cleared his throat. Out of the corner of his eye, he saw her head turn and knew she was looking at him.

"I know I said we'd talk," he began awkwardly.

"You have more important things to think about," Emily said.

Sean frowned at that. "Not more important. I just can't afford to be distracted." All the while his gaze roved from the road ahead to the rearview mirror, the driver-side mirror, the forest to each side of the road, opening to occasional glimpses of Mist River, tumbling over a rocky bed. He watched for movement, anything out of place. So far, so good.

"I know that." She touched his hand on the steering wheel, the merest brush of her fingertips.

It felt amazingly good. Out of proportion good.

He cleared his throat. "Thank you."

What if he asked if there was any chance she was thinking about marriage and kids?

Not smart. Either way she answered would provide a punch of emotion he couldn't afford.

*Rearview mirror. Scan the woods to each side. Evaluate the stretch ahead.*

Keep her safe. There would be time.

Neither of them said anything more.

Before he pulled into the concrete parking garage that linked sheriff's department and the county jail, he had Emily unfasten her seat belt and kneel on the floor again. Given the source of his current unease, the shadowy depths had him more tense than he'd been on the open road. Fortunately, the garage was half empty and he was able to park not twenty feet from the entry door. The bulk of his vehicle gave added protection until they were inside.

He passed the sheriff's office every day on his way to his own desk. Normally Mackay wouldn't be in on a Sunday, but this wasn't a usual Sunday, not when a deputy had been brutally slain last night. And, yes, the lights were on, he saw.

He steered Emily in and wasn't surprised to find Mackay's assistant in the office today, too. "The boss in?"

She was obviously curious about who Emily was, but only said, "He is." She picked up the phone on her desk, spoke briefly into it then said, "Go on in."

Sean hesitated. "Wait out here," he told Emily. "Don't go anywhere with anyone, not even if the building is burning down. Got it?"

The PA stared at him like he was nuts. He didn't care. Emily's eyes widened, too, but she took a seat and said, "Yes."

Sean knocked lightly and entered the inner sanctum, an office no fancier than the two lieutenants'. Mackay's only perks were a small bathroom of his own and what appeared to be a closet.

The big, scarred man sat back in his massive leather chair. "Detective Holbeck. Have a seat."

Sean nodded, sat down and, pinned by Mackay's unwavering gaze, wondered if this had been such a good idea. He could make an excuse—

No. What was it his mother used to say? In for a penny, in for a pound.

"I need to ask you something. I'm hoping you'll keep to yourself that I ever asked."

The sheriff's eyebrows rose. "I guess that'll depend on the question. But go ahead."

"I'm wondering how solid your knowledge is of Lieutenant Wilcynski's background," he said bluntly.

Mackay contemplated him for a long time, his thoughts unreadable. Then he said, "Wilcynski told me about the night's events."

"Did he tell you we can't figure out how the guy knew where to find Kimberly Fisk?"

"He did. Could you have been followed when you took the girl to Deputy Walker's house?"

"No. That was a concern, and I kept an eye out. No one stuck with us. Last night, I started wondering about the possibility of a tracking device. This morning, I searched for one on or under my car and found nothing."

Mackay took that in. "I almost wish you had."

"Me, too."

"No wonder you're looking close to home."

Sean fought not to twitch under that unrelenting stare. "I can't afford not to."

Mackay let out a breath. "I don't blame you. You can take Lieutenant Wilcynski off your list. You met Detective Rostov."

Sean nodded. Coming from southern California, Rostov had arrived in Cape Trouble in search of a witness to a cop killing. Unfortunately, he hadn't been the only one looking for Naomi Kendrick. Both Cape Trouble P.D. and the sheriff's department had become involved in the effort to keep her alive long enough to testify against a U.S. Congressman. Sean knew Daniel Colburn had stayed in touch with Rostov, and maybe Mackay had, too.

"Adam had worked with the lieutenant on a couple of multi-jurisdictional investigations and thought highly of him. When Wilcynski needed a change, Adam is the one who suggested Burris County. And, before you ask, I did verify his work and personal history. He graduated from high school and college both in southern California."

Sean drew a mental line through one name on his list. "Thank you. That's all I needed to know."

"Are you having trouble working with him?"

"No. I need to consider anyone whose history could be bogus, that's all."

"When he was up here, Adam Rostov had…concerns about Detective Payne," the sheriff said unexpectedly. "Obviously, they didn't pan out."

"I'm probably chasing my tail," Sean admitted, "but I have to eliminate the possibility of an insider."

When he stood, so did Mackay, looking a little more limber than some days, but as grimly unhappy as Sean felt. "Saunders trusted whoever got to him. That says insider to me, too. I'll call personnel and have them to email me Payne's file. If I see any red flags, I'll call. Keep me apprised."

Sean dipped his head. He didn't have to ask whether Mackay would tell Wilcynski about his query; he knew he wouldn't. He didn't know if he was relieved or made even more worried to have Mackay take his suspicion so seriously.

Ushering Emily toward the bullpen, Sean tried to figure out where he could stash her that she'd be out of the way, but he could keep an eye on her. Wilcynski wouldn't be happy that he hadn't found an alternative to bringing her along today. Probably he should have, but the break-in at Rebecca Walker's isolated cabin was the last straw as far as Sean was concerned. Emily wasn't safe anywhere.

He paused where he could see that the lieutenant's office door was closed and the glass pane showed darkness within. He'd be working today, but might be with Saunder's wife. Sean felt sure he'd show up eventually. From this angle, the only other detective here was Alan Worley, who was currently working the rape of a young woman tourist who'd let herself get separated from a group of friends sharing a rental house.

Worley looked up and saw Sean in the doorway. "I heard about Saunders. He must have let that vicious bastard walk right up to him." The words were clipped, his underlying rage not hidden.

"He might have done that if, say, a car appeared to be broken down and someone waved him to a stop."

"Yeah. Jesus."

"Was he a friend of yours?"

"Yeah." Worley cleared his throat. "He introduced me to my wife."

"I'm sorry."

He gave a short nod. "Catch this scum."

Good plan.

*****

Sean asked her to wait outside the room where the detectives apparently worked. She could see into it, including a slice of Sean at one of the desks facing her. His computer monitor blocked part of her view. There weren't more than eight desks in there, which she supposed made sense. Given that the two most populous cities in the county had their own police forces, there couldn't be that much need for in-depth investigations.

The hall they'd come down from the parking garage ended at a T. Looking one direction down the cross-hall, she could see what appeared to be the main entry to the sheriff's department with a receptionist behind a wooden counter and what was probably the waiting area. Looking the opposite way, that same hall ended not far from where she sat at a heavy metal door marked as an exit to the back of the building. Only one interior door opened off of it. Visualizing the layout of the building, Emily realized that meant the detective bullpen was at this back corner.

Right. Because creating an internal blueprint was so useful. But she had to think about something, and there wasn't much in the way of distractions. She assumed the sheriff's department would be considerably busier if this hadn't been Sunday. Uniformed deputies did pass every once in a while, glancing at her without much curiosity but, in a couple cases, an obviously sexual assessment.

Inevitably, floor plan forgotten, she began to brood. Despite her fears, she was desperate to know what Sean intended to say when they had that 'talk'. She wished she was sure what she should say.

What if Sean really couldn't bring himself to move into her house? Could she even blame him? How would she feel, if it was the other way around and she suspected he was still in love with his dead wife? She honestly didn't know.

The truth was, she did still love Tom. She always would. What she'd begun to realize was that both Tom and her feelings for him had…faded. An old picture turned to sepia. People always said time healed, but she'd refused to believe them. It turned out they were right, in a way. She was also discovering that the emotions Sean inspired in her were more powerful than anything she'd felt for Tom. More volatile. It was partly Sean himself, of course. He was capable of remarkable tenderness, but he wasn't a gentle man. She had no doubt he was fully capable of violence when he believed it was justified. She ought to be appalled that she was drawn to that side of him, too, but how could she not be? If she'd met him in some other way, if she wasn't being hunted by a ruthless killer, it might have been different. As it was, she had absolute faith that right now, everything violent and protective in Sean's nature was channeled toward one goal: keeping her safe.

What was striking about him was that she'd seen no sign of a temper. When he got mad, if anything he became quieter, more closed in. His self-control seemed absolute.

Except when they made love. Remembering was enough to have Emily squeezing her thighs together to try to contain a rush of heat. Knowing she could shake him, when nothing else could, disarmed her.

His job scared her, but his air of competence and control was so reassuring, she had begun to believe he wouldn't die and leave her the way Tom had.

A thought so irrational had her puffing out an impatient breath. For a minute, all she did was watch him through the open door, seeing that intense concentration as he talked on the phone.

So she was irrational. Emotions were irrational. She'd never admitted to anyone at all that her refusal to so much as think of getting involved with a man again was because of her terror of losing someone else she loved the way she had Tom and Cody.

Of course, divorce was a whole lot more likely these days than being widowed again.

That possibility didn't scare her, because she seemed to have an unreasoning faith that, once Sean made a commitment, he'd keep it.

He'd definitely been hinting that he was ready to make one with her, hadn't he, with his talk about wanting to come home to her every day, and about where they'd live?

But that brought Emily full circle. She had a horrible, sinking sensation. Could Sean understand that it wasn't Tom she would feel she was abandoning if she moved?

It was Cody. Her baby. A little boy who had clung to her before leaving that day, who had begged Mommy to come, too. What if he had found his way home and a part of him lingered, comforted by her presence, but suddenly one day Mommy was gone and strangers were in the house instead?

Emily discovered she had closed her eyes and was trying to hug herself.

*I can't think about this. Not right now.*

She became miserably aware of how uncomfortable the chair was. She was a kid left sitting in the hall, waiting to be called into the principal's office. What could she do but fidget and worry?

If only she'd thought to stick a book into her purse instead of a handgun. One she wasn't licensed to own. And especially wasn't licensed to carry concealed in her bag. And, oh, boy, she'd carried into a police station. Had Sean thought of that, or had he forgotten she had the thing?

She made a face. Under the circumstances, she was pretty sure no one would arrest her for having it.

Restlessness overcame her again. She'd never been very good at doing absolutely nothing. And right now, if she let herself think at all, she'd either scare herself about the ever-present danger, or try to make a decision about Sean she wasn't ready to make.

The alternative was being deathly bored.

Not deathly, she corrected herself immediately. Bad choice of words. But...she should have asked Sean how long he intended them to be here. Surely not all afternoon. Why not ask him now? At least she'd know then.

She made a face. Right. All she'd do was sound like a kid whining, *I'm bored. Aren't you done yet?*

Finally she stood and went down the hall to the reception counter. The woman behind it smiled. "May I help you?"

"I'm stuck waiting." Emily gestured toward the cluster of chairs. "I don't suppose there's anywhere I can get a newspaper or something else to read."

The woman contemplated her. "Well, if you promise to bring it back, I have a *People* magazine I can lend you. I haven't finished it yet, though."

"I swear," Emily said fervently.

The receptionist laughed, bent beneath the counter and straightened with a magazine. As desperate as she was, Emily would have gratefully received *Field & Stream*. She turned her head to see Sean standing in the doorway of the bullpen, looking annoyed. She lifted the magazine in explanation and started back to her assigned spot. He nodded and disappeared.

Emily plunked herself back down and soon became immersed in the world of celebrities.

*****

Sean started by calling Rey Mendoza. Turned out he knew Byron Saunders had been killed. No surprise there. Every cop in Oregon and probably far beyond had probably heard by now. The funeral would be well-attended, with representatives from jurisdictions in half a dozen neighboring states.

The break-in at Rebecca's house was news to Mendoza, though. "What the fuck…?" he breathed.

Sean went on to tell him that she and Kimberly Fisk both swore up and down that they hadn't told anyone where she was. Sean knew for damn sure he hadn't been followed when he took her there.

Rey, too, raised the possibility of a tracking device. When Sean told him he'd gone over his Outback with a fine tooth comb, there was a resounding silence.

Mendoza finally said, "Either somebody has a big mouth, talks in his sleep, or—" He cut himself off.

Or.

Sean leaned back in his chair. "You know the saying. If two people know a secret, that's one too many. For all Kimberly swears now, it wouldn't shock me if she told a bunch of people. Every one of them sworn to secrecy. She may be the talk of the college campus by now. I know she didn't take our warnings seriously."

"Bet she does now."

"Oh, yeah." He remembered her distraught face.

Mendoza cleared his throat. "Can't say I know any of your co-workers very well. I've heard more about Chief Colburn."

"You didn't grow up here on the coast, did you?" Sean asked as casually as he could make it.

Blast it, where was Emily? Sean stood and went to the door, spotting her twenty feet away talking to the receptionist. He had a feeling he was scowling at her. When she saw him, waggled a magazine so he could see it and started back down the hall, he nodded and returned to his desk.

He more or less heard what Mendoza was telling him despite the brief distraction.

"No, we moved a lot. My parents are first generation immigrants. We traveled so they could work the harvests. Dad had a knack with engines, though, and eventually he got a job with a fruit growers supply company in Eugene repairing farm machinery. He and Mom are still there." He paused. "My sister and I are the first two members of our family ever to go to college."

Under other circumstances, Sean might have asked why in a presumably Catholic family, there'd been only two kids. Instead, he said, "Where'd you go?"

"Southern Oregon U in Ashland. My sister is the smart one. She got almost a full ride to Willamette and is a nurse practitioner now. Works mostly with migrants."

"Good for her," Sean said.

"Did I tell you what you need to know?" Rey asked politely.

Sean grimaced. "I guess I'm not as subtle as I think I am."

"You had to ask. You should be asking."

"I do, but…crap."

"Anything you want me to look into?"

Anyone was what he meant.

Sean thanked him and said he'd let him know.

He went online and quickly verified what Rey had told him, then began a search for Jason Payne. All he found was found a single reference to him as an officer with the Corvallis, Oregon, police department.

Otherwise…nothing.

Frowning, he checked email and saw one from Sheriff Mackay – complete with attachment.

\*\*\*\*\*

Unfortunately, entertaining as *People* magazine was, there were an awful lot of pictures and not many articles of great depth. Emily mentally critiqued the dresses actresses wore on various red carpets. She pondered the recipes provided by celebrity chefs at the back even though none of them really grabbed her. She flipped through the magazine a second time, then a third.

A *Time* magazine or *Newsweek* would have kept her occupied for longer. *The Economist,* even if it happened to be focused on African politics or ecological issues in China.

She stood, catching Sean's eye. When she nodded toward the reception desk and held up the magazine, he nodded.

The receptionist thanked her for returning the magazine. "There might be something back in the break room," she said doubtfully, "but people here are usually too anxious to be interested in reading a magazine article while they wait."

Emily could see that. Currently, a young man with multiple piercings and a blue mohawk slouched despondently in the waiting area. Two chairs away from him, a matronly woman quivered with anxiety. His mother? As far from them as it was possible to get, a young woman and an older man had their heads together in an intense, low-voiced conversation.

Emily sighed and returned to her seat. Sean had been watching for her and after a nod he returned his gaze to his monitor. Something about the way he hunched in front of it made her think whatever he was reading wasn't good news.

Her heartbeat jumped and she looked up and down the connecting halls. Lights were on in a few of the offices, and she heard distant voices, but the only two people she could actually see were Sean and the receptionist. She suddenly felt isolated, even invisible.

Silly. Sean would look up any minute to check on her. And she didn't want him to worry about whether she was bored. The last thing he needed was a distraction.

Unfortunately, she was starting to think she would need a visit to the restroom soon. Would Sean want to walk her there?

She craned her neck to see if one was close by.

\*\*\*\*\*

Damn, Sean thought, opening the attachment that Mackay's short email said was Jason Payne's personnel file. Letting a co-worker see this kind of information was an invitation for a lawsuit against the county. Something in it had caught the sheriff's eye.

Mackay had highlighted two fields in bright yellow.

Jason Payne's honorable discharge from the United States Army was dated eighteen months ago. He had started as infantry, but ended up an M.P. That military police experience explained his hiring at the Corvallis Police Department and the promotion to detective when he came on here, even though he'd only stayed on the job in Corvallis fifteen months. No wonder he seemed green.

The second field highlighted contained Jason's reason for wishing employment in Burris County: family.

Sean frowned as his gaze lingered on that. He looked at contact info. The two names listed with phone numbers were male. Phone numbers weren't local. Both were described as "friend". Military buddies?

So…where was the family?

Something drew Sean's eyes to the very top of the employment application, to where it asked for name. Jason was listed as his middle name. In the field for first name, he had written only an initial: A.

An icy sensation spread through Sean's body.

A.J. Payne.

# CHAPTER SIXTEEN

Eyes never wavering from Emily, Sean stood, came around his desk and went straight to her. "Need anything?" he asked.

She almost shivered at the sight of his face close up. She couldn't bring herself to ask what he'd learned. Beneath that blank expression, she sensed dark, swirling emotion. Hurricane strength.

She cleared her throat. "I could use a trip to the restroom."

He nodded. "This way."

When they reached it, he leaned a shoulder against the wall right beside the door. "I'll wait."

Sure enough, she came out to find he hadn't moved. His face seemed to be carved out of stone, and when their eyes met she could tell he wasn't ready to talk.

She thanked him and returned to her chair. With a curt nod, he left her to go back to his desk.

The halls grew a little busier for a short while, allowing Emily to people-watch. The arrival of Lieutenant Wilcynski gave her a moment of anxiety, but he stopped and made civil conversation for a minute. She explained that her store was closed today and neither she or Sean could think of a secure alternative.

"I understand," he said with a nod, "but if I were you I'd be going stir-crazy."

"I'm kicking myself for not bringing something to read," she admitted.

He chuckled. "You know, I've always got a couple of books stashed in my desk. Hold on a minute."

As good as his word, he returned with two paperbacks, one a thriller, one science fiction. She skimmed the backs, chose the science fiction and thanked him with an enthusiasm that seemed to amuse him.

Maybe he wasn't so bad after all, she decided.

The quiet descended again. Looking at her watch, she realized the small burst of activity had been during the lunch hour. For no good reason, she suddenly felt terribly isolated. There were plenty of people in the building. But the nice woman at the reception desk had apparently been replaced by a uniformed officer who had his back to her.

Anxiety shivered through her, but she quelled it by turning her head so she could see Sean. He was on the phone now instead of poring over his computer.

After some deep breathing, she went back to her book.

\*\*\*\*\*

Goddamn.

Sean sat back in his chair, trying to think. He didn't want to believe A.J. Payne could be Braden Wilson's stepbrother...but if he was, he'd been involved in the investigation every step of the way. In fact, he'd handled chunks of it. Starting with canvassing neighbors around Frank Lowe's house. Nobody had seen a thing, he said. But what if one of them had?

But then Sean went utterly still, the ice spreading until he was held in its grip.

He had assigned Jason the job of researching Corinna Wilson's history. Supposedly she and Braden had lived in an apartment in North Fork for only a few months before she died. Under pressure, according to Jason, the manager had produced her application and been embarrassed because he'd let her move in even though she hadn't given a former address or references.

The ice cracked enough to let Sean open a website for the apartment complex, grab his phone and dial.

"You're lucky you caught me. I'm the manager, and I don't usually work on Sundays," a man named Brad Sweeney said. "I sure haven't talked to anyone from the sheriff's department recently." He paused. "What was that name again?"

"Corinna Wilson, teenage son Braden Wilson." He gave the theoretical dates of their residency.

"Don't sound familiar, but I guess Wilson is pretty common." A clatter of fingers tapping on a keyboard came through the phone. "No Corinna or Braden Wilson," Brad Sweeney said at last, no doubt in his voice. "Unless they used another name..."

"You're sure you didn't talk to a Detective Payne."

"I said I didn't." He sounded mildly offended. "My assistant manager would have left me a note about something like that. It's been six months or so since we've had a police inquiry, and that was North Fork P.D. This is a decent place. We don't have a lot of problem with crime."

Sean thanked him and ended the call.

At an oblique angle through the door, he saw Emily, apparently absorbed in the book Lieutenant Wilcynski had loaned her. She'd hadn't uttered a word of complaint even though she'd been stuck on a hard chair in the hall for three plus hours now.

*God. Payne.*

A fellow cop.

Visions of the obscenely posed bodies, the gaping throat wounds, the rivers of blood, ran through his head.

*Dishonorable discharge.*

Rage melted the ice. He rose to his feet. He'd give the bad news to Wilcynski, then get Emily the hell out of here. As much as he wanted to arrest the scum himself, he didn't trust himself to handle it professionally. Not when he remembered Emily's terror, the feel of her shaking body plastered to his.

Only once before had Sean wanted to kill, and then he'd been a teenager. Fortunately, he'd never been allowed within striking distance of the creep who'd beaten Matt to death.

Sean tempted himself with a plan. He could set up a meet with Jason in an out-of-the-way place. He knew the guy wouldn't go quietly. If he resisted arrest…shit happened.

Sean looked down to see that his hands shook. He balled them into fists. *I'm a cop. I protect and serve. I believe in justice.*

Sean closed his eyes and conducted an intense internal battle that, mercifully, was brief. Assassination had no place in his value system.

Letting out a ragged breath, he opened his eyes and drank in the sight of Emily, waiting for him. In that instant, he knew he'd have no trouble at all living with her memories of her lost husband and child. What kind of fool had he been? They were part of what made her the complex, compassionate, sometimes sad woman she was.

The woman he loved.

One last glance at her, and he rose to his feet. It was only a few steps to the doorway into Wilcynski's office. Worley was still here, a few desks away, a uniformed deputy half-sitting on his desk talking to him.

Sean didn't want anyone else to hear what he had to say, not yet.

\*\*\*\*\*

Another detective – at least, Emily assumed he was one, since he wore a badge and gun but was dressed in chinos and a long-sleeve polo shirt instead of a uniform – came in through the exterior door to her left. She caught a glimpse of daylight. Maybe there was more parking back there. It would be a lot closer to the detective bullpen. Sean might have used the garage only because he didn't want her exposed.

Sandy-haired, with eyes of an unusually light shade of brown, the guy smiled as he walked toward her. "You must be Emily Drake. One of the guys mentioned you were stuck waiting here."

The few passing deputies had all stared. She made a face. "At least I have a good book now."

He raised his eyebrows. "You know, the break room is right there." He nodded to the single door between them and the exit. She'd seen several of the uniformed cops go in and out of it earlier. "Get yourself a cup of coffee if you want. Or there are snack and pop machines."

She'd been trying to ignore the hollow feeling in her stomach. "Really?"

"Would I lie?"

Hesitating, Emily turned her head to see that Sean wasn't at his desk. She hadn't noticed him standing up, but he couldn't be far away. He was probably talking to the lieutenant. She might be able to buy a can of pop and a bag of chips by the time he returned to his desk.

"Thanks," she said, setting down the book and picking up her purse as she rose to her feet. "I might do that." It would only take a minute.

But then she went still, remembering the steel in Sean's voice.

*Don't go anywhere with anyone, not even if the building is burning down. Got it?*

No, he wouldn't be happy when he got back to his desk if she wasn't where she was supposed to be.

At her hesitation, the friendly detective said, "You want me to go grab you something instead? Or I can walk you that far, if you want."

"Thank you," she said again, politely, "but I can hold out until Sean is ready to go to lunch."

His eyes narrowed slightly. Was he insulted by her implied distrust? Emily didn't care.

She stole another look into the detective bullpen. Sean still hadn't returned to his desk. She could hear voices coming from the room, but couldn't see anyone from here.

The man beside her followed her gaze, then looked toward the entrance. Emily did the same, surprised to see that the counter was temporarily deserted.

"Emily Drake," the detective said softly.

Made uneasy by something in his voice and eyes, she slid one foot back.

He moved so fast his hands blurred. One clamped over her mouth, spinning her so her back was to him. She struggled until a sting of pain inches from her spine had her freezing. Her purse dropped from her nerveless hand, landing with a clunk onto a chair.

"Pick up your purse. Do it," he snarled in a near-soundless whisper next to her ear. "And if you make the slightest sound, I will gut you here and now."

*****

Lieutenant Wilcynski stared at Sean. "Jesus." It sounded prayerful. "I'd better let Mackay know." He shook his head. "We could be wrong."

"If so, why did he lie?"

"I've dealt before with cops who have gone bad." Wilcynski shook his head. "But never anything like this. His whole career is a setup."

"It looks that way." Sean's jaw tightened. "I need to get Emily out of here. I can't make this arrest. I'm not feeling real dispassionate."

The lieutenant nodded, his dark eyes keen. "I'm glad you can see that. All right. I'll give Mackay a heads-up, then call Payne, find out where he is. I'll make an excuse to get him in here."

"Thanks." Sean hesitated. "I hope I'm wrong."

"But you're not," Wilcynski said grimly. "Go on. This isn't a good place for Ms. Drake."

"No, it's not." Sean backed out of the office. At his desk he reached to close down his computer, at the same time glancing through the doorway to the hall.

She wasn't there.

Sean shoved his chair aside and ran into the hall. He stopped dead at the sight of the paperback book she'd been reading, now lying on the floor beneath a chair with pages splayed open.

Frantically, he turned. No sign of the desk sergeant. She'd been to the bathroom not that long ago. Even for that, she'd waited for his escort. She wasn't stupid enough to go off on her own, was she? But she'd taken her purse.

His heart slammed against the wall of his chest like a jackhammer. The roar in his ears had to be his pulse.

He'd taken his eyes off her. He'd fucking left her alone.
*Just like I did Matt.*

*****

Emily whimpered behind the brutally hard grip. She tried sagging to become a dead weight, but the tip of the knife dug deeper into her flesh. The heavy outer door closed quietly behind them. He shoved her down the two steps from the concrete pad, going toward an unmarked police car parked not fifteen feet from this back entrance.

Shuddering, she realized he must have known she was there. Hoped to have a chance to catch her alone. *I was stupid. If I hadn't stood up. If I'd called for Sean...*

Oh, God. Sean. He wouldn't be able to live with her death. Not after his brother. I don't want to die.

She stumbled. The hand over her face wrenched her upwards so savagely, pain lanced through her neck. It felt like whiplash.

If he succeeded in getting her into that car, she was dead.

Panic made it hard to think. He slammed her against the fender of the car, her purse forming an uncomfortable lump beneath her belly. The sharp pain in her back disappeared, but the man used the weight of his body to hold her in place.

Her mind cleared enough to tell her what he was doing. Keys. He had to get car keys out of his pocket, and that required a free hand.

Emily stared over the top of the car, desperately searching the limited parking for another person. Anyone at all.

No motion caught her eye. There were only a couple other cars back here, and nobody sat in any of them talking on a phone. Beyond the lot was an alley, and on the other side of that, an ugly, tall, grey brick wall with no windows. Warehouse.

They might be alone right now, but he wouldn't want to kill her here in the parking lot. Someone could come along any moment. If she could just delay him…

He wrenched her sideways, toward the back of the car.

New horror filled her as she imagined the trunk lid coming down, sealing her into darkness.

Most trunk lids had emergency releases.

Which meant, oh God, he'd have to knock her out.

She began to fight, mindlessly and not all that effectively, but she couldn't have stopped herself.

He cursed, and suddenly the blade of the knife bit into her throat.

"Don't think you're going to get away, bitch."

The knife disappeared momentarily and the trunk sprang open.

*Sean. Please, where are you?*

But she knew. For her, time had elongated, stretched by terror. In real time, no more than two or three minutes had passed. He was still conferring with his boss.

*He'll come looking. Soon. He will.*

If he checked the restroom and break room before he got too worried, he wouldn't be in time.

If she could drop her purse, kick it under the car, her abductor might not want to take the time to crawl under to retrieve it. She knew he'd made her bring it because Sean would have known instantly that she'd never leave it.

A hard arm came around her belly and her feet left the ground. Emily saw that she was going head-first into the trunk.

Still operating on instinct, she twisted in mid-air so she could grab a part of the trunk lid. Kicking out wildly, she swung the purse at him, connecting with his midriff. If bounced off, the strap momentarily tangling with the butt of his holstered gun.

Gun. Oh, God, oh, God, she had a gun.

He was cursing, his expression vicious. Their battle was silent, and Emily knew his greater strength doomed her. And the knife. He'd shoved it through his belt. Could she somehow get her hand on it? But he saw where he was looking and hunched to keep it out of reach.

Suddenly, almost coldly, she knew what she had to do.

If she fell into the trunk, she'd have a very few seconds, a sliver of time, to reach into her purse and pull out the Colt. Maybe she wouldn't even have to pull it out.

Thank God it wasn't the kind of handbag that zipped.

*Reach in, finger on the trigger, shoot.*

*No, no, safety first.*

It was her only chance.

She let go of her determined grip on the trunk lid.

\*\*\*\*\*

This terror was worse than anything Sean had ever felt. It was like looking into hell. He heard himself calling Emily's name, his voice raw. He yanked open the door to the break room. Empty.

Running footsteps behind him had him drawing his gun and spinning around.

It was Wilcynski, alarm on his face. Behind him was Worley, looking worried.

Sean jerked his head at Worley. "You. Parking garage."

The detective must have been briefed, because without any questions he took off at a run.

"Quickest way out is right there," Wilcynski said. His weapon was in his hand.

"I know." Making eye contact with Wilcynski, Sean already had his hand on the doorknob. "On three." After seeing the nod, he turned the knob and began counting.

*****

Emily crashed onto the floor of the trunk hard enough to daze her even if her head hadn't bounced of a sharp-cornered metal box to one side. Her hip had slammed against something hard. Odd-shaped. In a weird, disconnected way, she knew it was the spare tire.

But her hand had already delved into her bag, closed on the butt of the gun. Her thumb found the tiny lever on the side. The trunk lid was already coming down.

*Finger on the trigger, shoot.*

Hand shaking, she pointed the gun in the general direction of the portion of the man's torso she could still see and pulled the trigger.

Pain speared her and she fell back.

*****

"Three." Sean yanked the door open.

Wilcynski went through it, Glock extended. He yelled, "Hands in the air!" even as he jumped off the concrete pad to one side, allowing Sean to follow him.

That son of a bitch Payne wasn't twenty feet away. He was in the act of closing the trunk of his unmarked car. At the sound of Wilcynski's voice, he spun, reaching for his weapon.

A gun fired.

Sean automatically dropped to a crouch and saw out of the corner of his eye that Wilcynski had done the same. His finger tightened on the trigger.

But, stunned, he saw Payne staggering. He'd succeeded in turning to face the threat, but was having trouble keeping his feet under him. Red blossomed on his white shirt. He wove, crashed sideways against the back fender…and, in seemingly slow motion, toppled.

He came to rest with one cheek on the asphalt, his eyes still open. One hand was under him, the other laid helplessly to one side.

Scanning the parking lot, Sean and Wilcynski both ran, guns still extended in classic, two-handed grips. "Did you shoot?" Sean demanded to know, at the same time as the lieutenant said, "That wasn't me. Was it you?"

Oh, Christ. Sean forgot any threat from another shooter.

Emily lay curled on her side at the back of the trunk, her eyes dazed. Dark bruises were forming on her jaw and blood trickled from her throat. She stared uncomprehending at the two men.

Her shoulder bag lay in front of her.

Wilcynski pressed the barrel of his Glock against Jason Payne's temple. "You will turn over," he said from between bared teeth. "Slowly. Make a wrong move and I'll shoot. Don't think I won't."

God. All Sean wanted to do was lift Emily out of trunk of that car and hold her. Instead, he kept his aim on Payne, who hadn't moved, while surreptitiously watching for any other movement. Goddamnit, who was the shooter?

Seeing other cops pouring out of the building, he let go of that worry, crouched and rolled Payne over, not gently.

Blood soaked his shirt. The hidden hand was pressed to the wound. With Wilcynski covering him, Sean unholstered Payne's police-issue Glock and set it beneath the bumper of the car, then did the same with the wicked, black-handled knife.

Then he flipped Payne back over, holstered his own gun and cuffed the creep.

Finally, finally, he could reach for Emily.

*****

*I'm alive.*

The surprise kept her immobile for a long time. That, and the pain.

Sean finally bent, half in the trunk, his face ravaged. "I've never been so scared in my life," he said, voice raw.

"I shot him, didn't I?"

He blinked, as if surprised. "Did you?"

"Yes." Her lips felt numb. "Is...is he dead?"

"No." His voice was impossibly gentle. "I don't see the gun."

"It's still in my purse." Why did everything seem dreamlike? "I guess I'll need a new purse."

He laughed. He actually laughed. She watched as he picked her purse up very carefully and gingerly removed the gun he had given her. Then he poked a finger through the hole she'd blown in the leather. "You're right. You might want a new one."

She frowned at him. "That hurt."

He cradled her cheek with one hand. "Where do you hurt?"

"Everywhere." She bit her lip. "I mean shooting that thing. It's so little, but I think I went flying back in the trunk when I pulled the trigger."

"That's the drawback with small semi-automatics. The recoil sucks." Sean shook himself. "Did he hurt you?"

Emily had to think about it. "He stuck me with the knife a few times. And I fought him. I bet I have bruises."

He began swearing, but also, finally, lifted her into his arms, swung her out of the trunk and held her close.

Emily realized they were at the center of a crowd now. Uniformed and plainclothes cops were everywhere, and an approaching siren was abruptly cut off. Out of the corner of her eye, she saw flashing lights on an ambulance.

"You're going to the hospital," Sean told her.

"No." She grabbed him. "Please. Can't you take me?"

"Emily." The strain in his voice was echoed on his face. "You're bleeding."

"I am?"

He was setting her down. On a gurney, she realized, seeing the dark blue uniforms of a pair of EMTs.

"Wait!" she cried. "What about him?" She turned her head, trying to see her abductor. Was he really a detective?

"He's going, too. Different emergency vehicle. Emily, I'll be there by the time they wheel you in."

Still reluctant, she made herself release her tight-fisted grip on his shirt. "Promise?"

"Cross my heart." Trying to smile, he did just that.

*****

Sean didn't say much during the short drive home. Maybe it was because he had too much to say and didn't know where to start.

The doctor had seen no reason to admit Emily. The worst of the small, penetrating wounds – his words, not Sean's – had required three stitches. Other cuts were cleaned up and closed with butterfly bandages. Otherwise, his last advice had been, "Ice. Use lots of ice."

As Sean had helped Emily into the passenger seat of his SUV, he had asked how she felt.

"I sting, burn and ache." Her expression suggested she was doing an internal check. "My feet and legs are okay." She sounded surprised.

If his laugh offended her, he couldn't help it. The ebullience he felt had to come out somehow. He felt like a helium balloon bobbing on a string. *She's safe! She saved herself! She brought down a serial killer.*

He had a tape playing in a loop in his head. Or a scratched record. His grandfather loved his old Glenn Miller and Frank Sinatra records and played them endlessly despite multiple scratches that required interventions.

*She's safe! She saved herself!*

God help him, he suspected it might take days to shut this down. Days during which he'd ask himself whether he would have been in time. He thought so. But he had cut it too close.

The word 'cut' had him wincing.

Sean didn't much like the rest of what he was thinking, either. Given a minute more, maybe as little as thirty more seconds, Jason Payne would have slammed the trunk closed and driven away. And, no, they wouldn't have found him or Emily in time.

Sean still had no trouble seeing the pits of hell.

He turned into her driveway. For a minute, neither of them moved.

"Will he live?" she asked, not looking at him.

"Yeah." He took her hand. "He came through the surgery. He'll live to go to trial."

"Can you get him for all three murders?"

"It'll depend on what we find at his place. Whether there are any traces of blood on his knife. It's possible he'll only be charged with abducting you."

She was quiet for a moment. "It might have been better if I'd killed him."

Sean shook his head. "No, because then you would have to live with what you'd done."

He knew what she was thinking. Payne would go to trial, all right, but if it was only for kidnapping, the four men he'd murdered wouldn't received justice. Even worse in Sean's eyes, Payne could be freed in only a few years and once more be a threat.

But she didn't say anything, so he opened his door. By the time he came around to Emily's side, she was already getting out, her movements stiff.

"Let me carry you."

"No, I think walking will help loosen me up." She grimaced. "I hope there's enough ice in the house."

"The doctor gave us several packs."

"Oh, joy," she mumbled.

He took the key from her and unlocked. He should help her to bed. Examine her bruises and break out those ice packs.

But they were barely inside, the door closed behind them, when he groaned and wrapped his arms around her.

"Don't ever do that to me again," he said roughly.

Her purse dropped to the floor, but with less of a clunk since the handgun she'd used to shoot Jason Payne had been taken as evidence. Her arms came around him, too, and the tug at his shirt collar told him she was gripping fabric. She burrowed into him, and, God, all he wanted was to lie her down and claim her in the most primitive of ways.

"Emily." His voice came out hoarse.

"Please." She tipped her head back, her eyes huge and unfathomable. "Please."

So he kissed her, drowned in her, and forgot all her hurt places.

They did make it to the bed, so at least he didn't have to feel guilty later for adding to her collection of bruises.

*****

Emily had napped – or, more accurately, lapsed into unconsciousness – after the most astonishing lovemaking of her entire life. A couple of hours later, a pounding headache had awakened her.

Now, she was still ensconced in bed, but sitting up, wearing flannel pajama pants and a sweatshirt, every pillow in the house behind her. A pain pill had done wonders. Sean sat on the edge of the bed beside her, and every so often moved an ice pack from one lump or bruise to another. She had just finished a bowl of soup.

"You know," he said, "if we had a sofa, we could be cuddling on it."

"Is this a suggestion we go back to your house?"

He shook his head, his blue eyes unwavering. "No. It's a suggestion that we shuffle things around a little here to make room for my sofa and, hey, a decent-sized TV."

Momentarily, time seemed to stand still. Neither of them moved or so much as took a breath.

Emily searched his face. "You mean…?"

"Yeah." He cleared his throat. "I mean. I was stupid. Of course we can live in your house. For one thing, it's better than mine. You've got the porch, and I haven't even started refinishing floors or…" He rolled his shoulders. "Plus, your house is full of memories. Of course you don't want to leave those behind."

"It's mostly Cody, you know."

"Yeah." He tried to smile. "I figured that out. But it doesn't matter anyway. They were part of your life. They helped make you who you are. The woman I love."

The resonance in his voice when he said that seemed to fill her with his power. "Are you sure?" she begged. "This isn't because you were scared for me?"

"Emily, I knew the first time I set eyes on you. The fact that you kept dodging me frustrated me no end." He grimaced. "I told myself I'd overcome your resistance. I have to admit, it shook me when I heard old Rumbaugh call you Mrs. Drake."

"After which you followed me to Misty Beach and persuaded me to run with you. No," she corrected herself, "to start out with me."

The curve of his mouth was matched by the smile in his very blue eyes. "We both knew I was sticking with you, didn't we?"

Of course he wasn't talking just about the several mile run. In retrospect, Emily suspected she'd known as much then, too.

Would he have worn her down if all this hadn't happened? If she hadn't had to turn to him to keep her alive? She shuddered at the fear she might have stayed behind her walls and missed the amazing opportunity to be loved by Sean.

"I knew," she admitted.

"I love you," he said again.

She reached out for his hand, which immediately turned over and engulfed hers in a gentle grip. "I love you, too," she said, past a lump in her throat.

"What if I put my house on the market tomorrow?" he said, his gaze watchful.

She should be wary. This had all happened so fast. Which was probably a really good reason he hadn't said anything about marriage. But for some reason she wasn't worried at all, not about this decision. Her heart settled. She had absolute faith in this man.

"The sooner the better," she agreed.

THREE YEARS LATER…

At the very back of the top shelf of the cupboard, Emily found a red plastic sippy cup. Once upon a time, she must have known it was here. She had a feeling she had put it up here, where she wouldn't see it unless she climbed on a ladder.

Her heart gave an old, familiar squeeze. *Cody.*

After a moment, she dropped it into the box she was packing.

She didn't think back often anymore. She had a family again. That didn't mean she ever forgot her first child. She never would.

For a moment, she held him close, almost able to feel his small, sturdy body, the faintest brush of the dandelion fluff of his hair against her cheek. Then she breathed again, and let him go.

Thank God she didn't have to worry about Jason Payne getting out of prison. The police had found blood from four murder victims on the wet suit he'd worn during the assaults and in the tiny crack between blade and guard of his wicked, black-handled knife. He'd kept a print-out of the emails he'd received from Braden, too, as well as some newspaper clippings. Names of people he believed had wronged Braden were highlighted in yellow. Four were dead. It took Rebecca Walker months to recover enough to return to work. Emily had a tiny scar on her throat from his knife. It was barely visible, but her finger knew right where it was.

When she testified at his trial, she had looked straight at him. He had been convicted and given a life sentence. She still had an occasional nightmare, but that was all.

Emily climbed down from the ladder, sealed a cardboard box with packing tape and reached for a black marker. She planned to write "Kitchen – Pans". But at the strange, ripping sound coming from deeper in the house, she paused, her head turning. She would have been alarmed if Molly had been home, but Sean had dropped their two-year-old daughter off at day care a couple of hours ago. So it had to be him making that noise. But what on earth was he doing?

Still clutching the marker, she stepped into the hall and immediately saw him. He seemed to be positioning a tall board. As she watched, he used his hip to hold it in place and quickly tapped in a nail.

"Sean?"

He smiled. "Hey. How's it going?"

When he held out an arm, she walked right into his embrace. "It's going fine." She kissed his stubbly cheek. "But what what are you doing?"

"Replacing this piece of molding."

"But there wasn't anything wrong…" Suddenly understanding, she felt the breath rush out of her.

He was replacing one side of the molding that went around the door to the linen closet. That particular white painted board was the one where they'd recently drawn a line measuring Molly's height on her second birthday. It had been nearly an inch below Cody's height on the same birthday.

Emily had known that, if they didn't paint over those marks, the new homeowners would. The thought had been indescribably painful, but something she had known was coming when she and Sean made the decision to buy a larger house to accommodate the second child she was carrying. Somehow, it had never occurred to her that they could take the whole board with them.

Through blurred eyes, she saw it leaning against the wall a few feet away.

Sean saw the tears and bent to rest his forehead against hers. "It's a piece of our past," he murmured. "It belongs with us."

Emily found herself smiling even as she cried. "I love you. The day you moved in next door was the luckiest day of my life."

"Mine, too." His big hand covered the slight bulge in her belly and gently caressed her before he removed it to pat her butt. "Back to work, sweetheart. We only have another hour before the whirling dervish will be home."

She laughed, as he'd meant, gave him a convulsive hug, and returned to the kitchen to finish emptying cupboards in preparation for tomorrow's big move. The porch swing was going with them, and now so was a piece of their home that linked Cody and Molly, that said Cody had lived and been loved and would always be a part of their family. Suddenly excited, she could hardly wait.

## A Note from the Author

Thank you so much for purchasing my book. This is my third independently published effort, so if you enjoyed the book, I hope you will take a moment to help me get the word out to others by posting a review on Amazon or Goodreads - or "like" my Author Page on Facebook to see future updates.

I also love to hear from readers, so please contact me on Facebook or via my website at www.JaniceKayJohnson.com.

## About The Author

Janice Kay Johnson is the author of more than ninety books for children and adults, including the Cape Trouble novels of romantic suspense. Her first four published romance novels were coauthored with her mother Norma Tadlock Johnson, also a writer who has since published mysteries and children's books on her own. These were "sweet" romance novels, the author hastens to add; she isn't sure they'd have felt comfortable coauthoring passionate love scenes!

Janice graduated from Whitman College with a B.A. in history and then received a master's degree in library science from the University of Washington. She was a branch librarian for a public library system until she began selling her own writing.

She has written six novels for young adults and one picture book for the read-aloud crowd. ROSAMUND was the outgrowth of all those hours spent reading to her own daughters, and of her passion for growing old roses. Two more of her favorite books were the historical novels, WINTER OF THE RAVEN and THE ISLAND SNATCHERS, written for Tor/Forge and now available in e-book format for the first time. The research was pure indulgence for someone who set out intending to be a historian.

Janice raised her two daughters in a small, rural town north of Seattle, Washington. She spent many years as an active volunteer and board member for Purrfect Pals, a no-kill cat shelter, and foster kittens often enlivened a household that typically includes a few more cats than she wants to admit to.

Janice loves writing books about both love and family — about the way generations connect and the power our earliest experiences have on us throughout life. Her Superromance novels are frequent finalists for Romance Writers of America RITA awards, and she won the 2008 RITA for Best Contemporary Series Romance for SNOWBOUND.

Visit her website at www.JaniceKayJohnson.com.

## Also Available from Janice Kay Johnson

Cape Trouble, a tiny Oregon Coast town, was named for the dangerous off-shore reefs. But some of its citizens seek refuge from their own troubles…which have a way of following them.

SHROUD OF FOG (Cape Trouble, Book 1)

*The secrets of the past haunt the present…*

Sophie Thomsen's life had a Before and an After – marked by the terrifying morning when she found her mother dead in the foggy sand dunes, an apparent suicide. Now, twenty years later, Sophie returns to Cape Trouble, only to find her aunt brutally murdered. Although she swore never to set foot again on Misty Beach, Sophie takes over her aunt's crusade to save the falling-down Misty Beach Resort and its wild sand dunes and beach from development. But Sophie's memories threaten a killer…who doesn't dare let her remember too much.

Having come to Cape Trouble to heal his own wounds, Police Chief Daniel Colburn investigates the present day murder, but begins to suspect Sophie's mother was another murder victim, not a suicide. Everything he learns increases his fear for the woman he is coming to love.

Sophie's fate may be to die in a shroud of fog, just like her mother before her, unless she can trust Daniel to help her uncover her past in time.

SEE HOW SHE RUNS (Cape Trouble, Book 2)

*When it's never safe to stop running…*

One night, in her upscale California restaurant, Naomi Kendrick overheard powerful men plotting a political assassination. To save her life, she made a bargain with the devil…and then ran.

Inevitably, she is found. More than one enemy descends on Cape Trouble to learn her secrets…and silence Naomi once and for all.

Detective Adam Rostov suspects she stabbed his partner to death in her restaurant kitchen. Pursuing her to Cape Trouble, he arrives just in time to rescue her from an assault. He conceals his real purpose in Cape Trouble to stay close to her. Because if he can't keep her alive, he'll never find out if she's innocent or guilty.

Naomi's instincts scream, *Run*, but too late, because Adam isn't about to let her go. Not when he has begun to believe she is a victim and not a killer. Not when she is irresistible bait to draw a contract killer, a corrupt U.S. Congressman, and a crooked federal agent. And not when, despite all common sense, he's falling in love with the mysterious chef.

Once Naomi discovers Adam too has been hunting her, she must decide. Run and keep running, or trust him to keep her safe? Of course, once he knows her darkest secret, he may no longer want to protect her…

What people are saying about the romantic suspense novels of Janice Kay Johnson:

• "If you are in the mood for a wonderful romantic suspense story that will have you so engrossed in it that you lose track of the time, than look no further."
-  Night Owl Reviews (on Shroud of Fog)

• "SHROUD OF FOG will immerse the reader in a world of suspense and intrigue. Elements of romance throughout this captivating read will capture your heart. I kept guessing as to whom the killer was up until the very end. Janice Kay Johnson has penned a deeply satisfying story that is appealing to mystery lovers as well as romance aficionados. If you are looking for a tale that has plenty of plot twists and amazing characters that will remain with you, then you should rush out and get a copy of SHROUD OF FOG!"

-   Romance Junkies

•   "[G]uaranteed to have you looking over your shoulder more than once in this explosive, fast-paced thriller."

-   Linda Silverstein, ROMANTIC TIMES (on Dangerous Waters)

•   "Studded with tension and skillfully riveting, [it] will capture you from the first page and won't let go until the end."

-   Kay Gragg, AFFAIRE DE COEUR (on Dangerous Waters)

•   "I've never read Ms. Johnson's work before and all I can say is I will be finding everything else she's ever written. This story is so masterful it takes you inside this small town and really makes you think you are there."

-   Sara HJ, HARLEQUIN JUNKIES (on Everywhere She Goes)

Turn the page for a sneak peek at the first chapter of SHROUD OF FOG - and find both books available online now.

# SHROUD OF FOG - EXCERPT

## CHAPTER ONE

Why on earth wasn't Aunt Doreen answering her phone?

Disgruntled, Sophie Thomsen sipped her coffee from the travel mug as she waited at the red light. The tinge of worry, she could probably blame on the eerie effects of coastal fog. For most of her life, Sophie had hated fog. This morning it was thick enough that she felt peculiarly alone even though she was driving down the main street of Cape Trouble. The tourists passing on the crosswalk in front of her appeared and disappeared, ghost-like and colorless in their anoraks and heavy sweaters.

The morning fog might or might not burn off. You never knew on the Oregon Coast, and especially at Cape Trouble, infamous for hidden, dangerous rocks offshore and the peculiar mist that rose from the river that flowed into the Pacific Ocean and formed the southern edge of town. Sophie had spent enough time here on the coast to guess that yes, the sun would be out in another hour or two, the sweaters would be shed, the kites and beach towels would emerge, and some brave souls who didn't mind standing in waders by the hour in icy water would be spotted casting their lines in Mist River – named, of course, for its mysterious propensity for cloaking itself in drifting tendrils of gray.

She and her aunt had made vague plans to meet this morning at the storage facility, but hadn't set a time. There wasn't any real reason to feel anxiety. One thing you could say for the friendly town of Cape Trouble – sarcasm fully intended – was that if there'd been a car accident or an aide car had been summoned anywhere within a ten mile radius, everyone including Sophie would already have heard every gory detail.

Probably Doreen had simply gone ahead and was happily working inside the storage unit, sure Sophie would show up eventually. Aunt Doreen was very capable of being scatterbrained.

Lucky she'd already given Sophie the code to get in and even a key to the lock.

The light changed, the green less visible than the red through the fog. Sophie looked carefully to be sure the last pedestrian had stepped onto the sidewalk. She drove more slowly than usual along Schooner Street, lined with small seafood restaurants, coffee houses, boutiques and gift shops, their lighted windows made indistinct through the gray shroud of fog.

Although it had been twenty years since she'd spent more than a few days at a time here, she knew the town well. Like other picturesque Oregon coast towns, Cape Trouble had been commercialized, but the changes were mostly cosmetic. The Victorian era homes were nowhere near as grand as those in Astoria far to the north, but charming enough to be a draw along with the lighthouse, the broad sandy beach, the never-ending waves, the much-photographed sea stacks and the whale watching tours that departed from a pier that thrust out into the river.

Sophie's family had spent summers here when she was a child. Before. That's how she thought of it. Before and After. Before the great divide that had riven her life and left her a different person on the other side of it. Sophie would gladly never have visited Cape Trouble again, or even the Oregon Coast, but unfortunately the one person in the world she truly loved lived here, so she'd resigned herself to those occasional visits.

What she didn't understand, Sophie thought with the unsettled sensation she'd had ever since arriving last night, was why she'd let herself be talked into spending the entire month of June here to help with the auction intended to raise money for a cause she didn't personally support.

Not that she could tell Doreen so. It would mean talking about things she didn't talk about. Not with anyone.

Two stoplights and one turn later, she broke out of town, heading away from the ocean, the fog thinning as she drove. She passed first the Safeway and hardware stores, the laundromat and a pharmacy as well as neighborhoods of more ordinary houses where the locals actually lived before reaching the least attractive part of town, never seen by most visitors. Two garages, an auto body shop, some kind of metal fabricating business, plumbing supply, lumberyard, two seedy bars, a wooded stretch and – finally, two turns later – the sprawling storage facility made up of long buildings encased in metal siding, covered with metal roofs, and enclosed in a high chain-link fence.

The metal siding and roof presumably explained Aunt Doreen's failure to answer her cell phone.

With a sigh, Sophie rolled down her window, punched in the eight digit code preceded by a * and ending with the # key, then waited while the huge gate rolled jerkily to one side.

Sophie glanced again at the notebook page on which she'd jotted the information. The auction committee had unit…4079. The buildings weren't clearly labeled, so she turned down the first aisle and discovered herself passing 1001 on one side and 2045 on the other. Which didn't altogether make sense. Well, the first row on her right – the 1000s - proceeded in numeric order, but the ones on her right were given to odd fits and starts.

She wasn't the first here this morning. A moving truck was being loaded at one space, a plump woman, a boy of perhaps twelve or thirteen and a man with a pot belly currently wrestling a sofa up the ramp. The man was shouting at the woman and boy, who weren't lifting their end up as high as he'd like. The woman began screaming back just as Sophie carefully maneuvered through the narrow lane between truck and the storage spaces on the other side. She flinched at the language.

Around the corner, another woman seemed to be poking rather desultorily inside a space that was packed, literally, concrete floor to ceiling and bare-stud wall to wall with…well, household possessions, Sophie guessed, glimpsing the white side of some appliance as well the plush back of a chair, the top of an end table plus lots of cardboard boxes and some bright plastic tubs. If the poor woman was hoping to put her hands on one thing, Sophie didn't envy her.

That was unit 3006. On the other side of the next aisle was…3093. The 4000s had to be here somewhere, didn't they? And surely she'd spot Aunt Doreen's aging white Corolla.

Sophie passed other tenants either putting more possessions into their rented spaces or taking them out. The place really was huge. There were occasional doors that likely opened to short hallways where tenants could access small spaces – maybe five by ten feet or ten by ten – but most units seemed be at least fifteen by twenty or more. And there were parking spaces for RVs, boats on trailers, cars covered by canvas, a horse trailer and… She stared. Good Lord, was that a carnival carousel? She'd swear it was.

A last jog, and she found herself facing a shorter row of buildings that formed an L to the rest of the facility. And yes, she was finally among the 4000s.

It wasn't until she reached the end and turned again that she discovered a couple of units were caps to the rows, and 4079 was one of those. Aunt Doreen's car was not parked in front. And she couldn't miss the lock clipped over the hasp of the closed metal door designed to roll up.

Well, damn.

Sophie parked and tried her aunt's number again. Four rings and she was back at voice mail. She had already left several messages. Wonderful. Well, she had the key and she was here, so why not open up and see for herself the stuff the auction committee had procured? Not to mention how well organized the amateur enthusiasts were.

But when she got out and tried fitting the key her aunt had given her last night into the lock, it didn't fit. Not even close. Sophie frowned. The brand name on the key didn't match the one on the lock, but she hadn't expected it would. She knew her aunt had had copies made of the original keys so practically every member of the auction committee had one – something Sophie thought hadn't been smart. So she supposed it was possible the keysmith hadn't done a good job. But…so bad the key wouldn't even go in the hole?

Had someone replaced the lock in the past few days? Without telling Doreen, who was the auction chair? That didn't make sense unless the committee had decided to expel Doreen but hadn't gotten around to telling her. And that seemed unlikely, given that Sophie's aunt was the moving force behind the whole enormous effort.

Sophie drove back to the office she'd passed at the entrance and went in. A middle-aged woman behind the counter said, "You looking to rent a storage space?"

"No, I was expecting to meet my aunt – Doreen Stedmann – here at the space she rented…"

"Oh, you're Doreen's niece Sophie." The woman beamed. "I'm Marge Hedgecoth. Why, Doreen talks about you all the time! Says you're some kind of fancy event planner."

"Well…"

"She was so excited that you were coming." She frowned. "I haven't seen her yet this morning, although I don't open until ten, you know."

Yes, Sophie had noticed the sign on the door. Tenants had access to their units from six a.m. until midnight with special arrangements required for other times, but office hours were more limited.

"She's probably just late," Sophie said, then explained that the key she'd been given didn't fit into the lock. "I'm wondering if I might have written down the wrong number for the space."

Marge verified that, indeed, the auction committee for the Save the Misty Beach campaign had rented number 4079, beginning in March when the first of the donations had begun pouring in.

"Well, Doreen gave me a key, which is unusual, but she wanted to be sure anyone who needed to drop something off could get in. So let me get my cart and I'll follow you out there."

She flipped the sign on the door to a picture of a clock that indicated she would be back in ten minutes and and climbed into a golf cart parked by the back door. Sophie was able this time to drive directly – more or less – to her aunt's unit, which faced the chain link fence at the back of the property and the woods beyond. As Sophie parked again and got out, it occurred to her that it was really rather lonely back here, blocked by the bulk of the building from being seen by any other units except the one other that faced the same direction.

The golf cart arrived. A small, wiry woman with short, graying hair and skin that was beginning to look leathery, Marge got out and confidently poked her key at the lock.

"What in tarnation…?" she muttered.

Sophie saw immediately that she wasn't having any better luck.

After a minute her hand dropped. The two women looked at each other in something approaching consternation. "Hmph," she said. "I suppose they're entitled to change the lock."

"But Aunt Doreen gave me this key only last night. Could she have forgotten…?"

"Did you call her?"

"She's not answering." Sophie couldn't put her finger on why she was so uneasy, but she was. "I went by her house first, and she wasn't home. Her car wasn't there, either."

"I've a mind to cut that lock right off," Marge declared.

Sophie stared at the metal door. "I'll happily pay for a replacement lock."

"Well, then, you just hold on and I'll be back in two shakes."

The morning was chilly enough Sophie began to pace. Wisps of fog lingered. If she went one way, she could see down the aisle at the far side of the property, which was currently empty. The other way, she could see the same people working in their units that she'd earlier passed. A few covered vehicles were parked back here, too. She ended up at the chain-link fence, staring into a forest that looked surprisingly primeval, considering how long this area had been settled and that it had likely been clear-cut at one time.

There wasn't much forestry on this side of the coastal range anymore, though; winter storms and ocean winds kept trees small compared to farther inland and therefore unprofitable. These were hemlock, spruce and cedar, she thought, although she couldn't have told a hemlock from a spruce from a fir, if the truth be told. The evergreens were underlaid with shrubbery, some native, some not. Oregon grape, she thought, the ubiquitous salmonberry, huckleberries, the ferns that loved the damp climate, and other bits of foliage and even a few late spring flowers she didn't recognize.

Movement, caught by the corner of her eye, made her jump until she saw that a squirrel was scampering up the trunk of a tree. It paused on a branch to gaze at her with suspicion before darting out of sight.

She was smiling when Marge returned with a pair of lethal-looking bolt cutters.

Sophie hit re-dial on her phone and, at the sound of her aunt's voice saying, "I'm too busy to take this call," shook her head at Marge, who marched over to the door and applied the bolt cutters.

Marge appeared entirely too scrawny to cut through a quarter-inch or more of steel, but with a snap, the lock fell open. "There you go," she said with satisfaction.

Sophie took the lock off, set it on the concrete to one side, turned the hasp and heaved the door up. With a squeal and clatter, it rolled on its tracks.

Beside her, Marge gasped.

The interior was shadowy and astonishingly full, but Sophie was instantly riveted by the mess. Boxes were open, items spilling out. Smashed ceramic and shattered glass sprinkled the concrete floor. A framed picture lay face down, glittering glass around it and a hole stomped through the back. Somebody had broken in, was all she could think. Rifled the contents without caring what was destroyed. What a disaster.

Dear God, Sophie thought in shock, had Aunt Doreen seen this? Might she have gone to the police?

The committee or her aunt had obviously bought multiple shelving units, the kind that could be easily assembled and then taken apart to be moved, because a number of them lined the walls. Most were still packed with boxes of assorted shapes. Peering in, Sophie saw framed pictures carelessly stacked to one side. Tall or awkward things filled the middle. Was that a cat climber? A huge basket that had been covered with cellophane spilled gourmet foodstuffs across the floor.

Along with her dismay at the implications of the mess, it was the clutter and the dim lighting that explained why her eyes didn't immediately focus on the figure crumpled at the back. Even when she saw…what she saw…she rather stupidly gaped at the drying pool of a dark substance that had crept far enough from the – body? – to soak the corner of a cardboard box and possibly damage the contents.

It was only then, reluctantly, that her eyes focused on that ruined head, and she saw the face.

"Oh, dear God," she whispered, at the same moment as Marge whirled, raced to the fence and lost her breakfast through it.

*****

The gate to the storage facility stood open when Daniel Colburn drove up in his squad car. Marge Hedgecoth stood just inside, waiting beside her golf cart. She didn't look so good.

Rolling down his window, he asked, "You okay, Marge?"

She summoned a smile that didn't help much. "I've been better."

Daniel nodded. "Around back, you said?"

"Far corner." She waved. "4079."

"Once I see what's what, I'll need to talk to you."

"Yes, Chief. I'll be in the office."

"Good," he said. "In the meantime, I want you to shut down the gate. No calls, either," he told her sternly. "Don't let anyone in, or anyone out. Ask folks to wait until I can talk to them."

She agreed. He figured he could trust her. He'd gotten to know Marge since he took on the job as police chief of Cape Trouble ten months ago. During his tenure, the fence around the facility had been cut a couple of times, a car stolen once, a lock cut off a unit and the contents ransacked another time. There'd been some vandalism. Marge was a tough lady.

He eyed the people he could see industriously doing whatever you did in a storage space, but drove directly to the far corner where Marge had told him the victim's niece waited.

He noted the isolation of this particular unit and automatically scanned eaves and fence line for a camera. He knew there were several sprinkled throughout the facility and that Marge kept an eye on monitors during the day in her office. He'd arrested the idiot who drove away in the very collectible, shiny red, 1962 MG roadster by watching video footage that showed the guy clear as day. But – didn't it figure? – Daniel didn't see one back here.

The car parked to one side of the gaping door was a sleek, four-door blue Prius. A woman sat behind the wheel. She got out when he parked and walked to meet him.

His immediate reaction shook him a little. Crap. He liked to look at a sexy woman as well as the next guy, but this was piss poor timing. He couldn't let himself forget that this woman was involved in some way with a death and therefore a potential investigation. And the feeling of a fist in the gut meant he was doing more than looking.

She wasn't even beautiful, not exactly. Medium height but leggy, maybe a little short-waisted which might be making her breasts look bigger than they actually were. Wavy dark-blonde hair – yeah, he did like blondes – bundled carelessly up on the back of her head with tendrils already escaping. A pretty oval face without noticeable cheekbones but somehow…delicate. As they got closer, he saw how fine-textured her skin was.

Uh huh, and how waxy pale. His nose had already caught the scent of puke. Not surprising. Rookie cops invariably puked at their first murder scenes or after seeing the gruesome result of a major vehicular accident.

"Chief Daniel Colburn," he said, holding out his hand. "I'm afraid Marge didn't mention your name."

Her eyes were green. Hazel probably, but mostly green.

"Sophie Thomsen," she told him. "That's, um, my aunt in there." She nodded sideways without looking into the storage unit. "Well, sort of my aunt."

"Sort of?"

"She's my stepmother's sister. Doreen Stedmann."

Oh, hell. "I know Doreen."

Ms. Thomsen nodded unhappily. "Everyone in town does."

"Please stay here while I take a look."

She didn't appear to be sorry to stay behind.

Daniel knew all about the auction, which was being held as part of the effort to raise the funds to buy a sizeable piece of land the other side of Mist River from town. Forty or fifty acres, he understood, of prime river- and ocean-front land that included forest, dunes, an old lodge and a string of cabins, now all but falling down. The long-time owner had passed away and his heir wanted to unload the property, which had resort chains salivating. Locals were determined to keep their pretty town pristine and save it from the evil giant condo developments that were sure to take over if that land was chopped into pieces and made available. The heir was apparently giving them a little time to raise the money. Daniel didn't see much hope, but you never know.

Doreen Stedmann was a local character, an eccentric woman known as an activist but lacking real solid follow-through, gossips said. She started a lot of projects but finished few. From the bulging contents of the storage space, she'd been doing surprisingly well on this one.

Until somebody had gone berserk in here, that is. And until she'd died or decided to kill herself amongst the auction items, if that was what had happened. He hadn't had the impression from Marge's frantic call that there'd been an accident. She hadn't asked for an aide car. She hadn't even asked for police in a generic sense. She'd wanted him, Chief Colburn.

He stepped carefully around the clutter and the broken bits, trying not to touch anything, ready to begin revival efforts if there was any chance at all. But he could tell from twenty feet away that it was too late, and had been for a couple hours, at least. What's more, Doreen hadn't killed herself. Somebody had taken care of that for her. She was definitely dead, and the sight wasn't pretty. No wonder the sort-of niece appeared about ready to keel over.

He stood for a long time, doing nothing but studying the scene. Taking in her position, the sizable dent in her head, the cord tied around her neck as a finishing touch. The hefty, cut crystal vase that had been tossed to one side and the blood and tissue that marred its sharp cut edges.

No obvious sign of a struggle. The auction stuff closest to her was still neatly piled. The cat climber might have been rocked; it sat unevenly now, one corner of the base on top of something he couldn't see.

Why that cord around the neck? Symbolic, or had the killer been unsure the blow to the head did the job?

"Damn it," he muttered, and carefully retraced his steps. Once in the open air, he made some calls, then turned to the niece who stood with her back to him, staring into the trees on the other side of the fence. He followed her gaze, scanning for an opening cut in the chain link, but didn't see one. The ferns and salal and salmonberries appeared untrampled. Moisture from the mist glistened on leaves. From here, he couldn't see the back gate required as an emergency entrance. He'd be wanting to verify that it was still locked as soon as he had a minute.

"Why don't we sit in my vehicle," he suggested. "I've got the medical examiner coming and some crime scene folks I'm borrowing from the county."

She shivered and turned. "Yes. All right."

"Marge didn't mention cutting the lock off," he said thoughtfully. "When she called, she said only that you and she had found a dead woman. I was half-expecting a heart attack victim or suicide."

Ms. Thomsen explained about the keys not fitting this lock, and how she'd felt uneasy when she couldn't reach her aunt by phone after they'd made arrangements to get together this morning.

"I intended to change the lock anyway," she admitted. "I gather that any number of people have keys right now, and that's asking for trouble."

That was one way of putting it, Daniel would concede. Murder probably wasn't quite what she'd had in mind, though. Unless, of course, after murdering her aunt she'd just happened to have a new lock in hand because she'd intended to replace the old one anyway.

A patient interview later, he thought he knew everything she'd done from the time she drove into town last night, but her reserve was so deep, he had to wonder what she wasn't telling him. Either Sophie Thomsen was holding back on him, or she was one complicated woman. He was leaning toward the second explanation, because the one thing that rang clear was her affection for her shirt-tail aunt.

When he temporarily ran out of questions, she asked, "Was...was she strangled?"

"The cause of death will likely have to wait for the autopsy," he said gently. "That head wound looks to me like it would have been fatal."

A shudder wracked her, the most profound sign of distress she'd yet displayed. "I wonder if she saw it coming."

"Likely not. It was on the back of her head."

"I hope not," Ms. Thomsen burst out. "I hope she had no idea."

He hoped for the same. That way, Doreen's death, while brutal, was also a good one. One minute, she was involved in life, productive, maybe happy, the next, wham, one blinding moment of pain and she was gone. No lingering, knowing her fate, no misery. There were certainly worse ways to go.

Which did not mean he felt any more merciful toward the man or woman who'd killed this decent woman for no justifiable reason.

"It had to be quick," he said. "You don't have to worry about her suffering."

Some of the tension left Ms. Thomsen's shoulders. "Thank you for telling me that."

He nodded.

She breathed audibly for a minute. He was about to make his excuses when she said, "Does the gate record when people come and go? Or does everyone have the same code?"

Interesting that she was thinking so analytically. Almost like a cop.

"No, each tenant has a unique code." He already knew that much, from previous investigations. "So the answer is yes, we'll be able to pinpoint arrivals and departures based on what code they used." Maybe. The gate moved with ponderous slowness. He'd observed before that two or even three cars could pass through once it opened. If the guy was patient, he could have ridden someone else's tail coming and going and left no record of his presence at all. "You're wondering where your aunt's car is."

"Well...yes."

He'd been mulling that over himself, and now said, "I had a thought about that." He jumped out of his squad car and walked over to the row of vehicles that were being parked here presumably because of the security. He ignored the RV on the end and the camper next to it, as well as the aging but well-cared-for Cadillac that inexplicably lacked a cover. Nope, it was the vehicle on the end that was hidden under a canvas tarpaulin. He lifted one side only enough to confirm his suspicion, then let it drop.

Ms. Thomsen had gotten out, too, he saw, and stood watching him.

"White Corolla, rusting bumper?"

Looking numb, she nodded.

"The question is, how did *he* get out of here?"

"Or her."

He looked at the niece.

"From what I can gather, most of the people working on the auction are women. Doreen has mentioned only a couple of men."

She blanched at speaking her aunt's name, but hadn't let herself cry yet. He'd begun to suspect she wasn't the one who'd puked.

Marge had looked considerably more rattled than this woman when he arrived.

Ignoring the approaching sirens, he asked, "Why do you assume the killer is an auction volunteer?"

She frowned. "Are you suggesting it was someone who just happened to wander by?"

"I didn't say that."

Her eyes widened in alarm. "There were a whole bunch of people already inside the gates when I got here. What if they leave?"

"Marge won't let 'em." He turned when a white van rolled around the corner and stopped behind his city car. "The troops are here, Ms. Thomsen. You said you're staying at the Harrison cottage? Why don't you go back there, and I'll be by to update you later. Say, mid-afternoon."

She gave a half nod, then changed her mind. "Will you ask everyone to be really careful when they're working in there? I'd hate to see anything else get broken."

He stared at her, struck by her coldness. "Why would you care at this point?"

She transferred her stare to him, startling him with the pure ferocity in her eyes. "Because Aunt Doreen cared. She cared a whole lot. And I'm thinking the only thing I can do for her now is finish something that mattered to her. Make it my memorial to her. That, Chief Colburn, is why I care."

After a minute, he said, "Got it."

She nodded and walked to her Prius. For maybe thirty seconds his brainwaves altered, letting him see only *her*. The confidence of her stride, the delicacy of her bone structure, the sway of her hips in snug jeans, the way she carried herself with shoulders squared and head high. Then he blinked and called, "Wait!"

He lifted a hand at the two men and one woman who'd gotten out of the van, but jogged to Ms. Thomsen.

"Is there any chance you – or someone – have a list of what should be in there?"

"Yes, in theory."

He raised his eyebrows at that.

She grimaced. "That's one of the reasons I'm here. It became apparent to me, talking to Doreen, that while the group was doing a heck of a job begging donations, they weren't doing nearly so well organizing the stuff once they had it. Apparently somebody had volunteered to enter donations as they came in and work on a catalog, but she's been full of excuses and not really doing it."

"And who would that be?"

"Rhonda…Rhoda…something." She lifted her hands. "I have a list of volunteers with contact info back at the cottage. I haven't met any of them yet, except for a few I already knew from visits to Doreen."

"All right," he said. "See what kind of inventory you do have, too." He stared at the daunting contents of the storage locker. "Do me a favor, though. Please don't call any of the other volunteers or accept any calls. In fact, don't talk to anyone, okay? I'll want to give each of them the news myself."

Still remarkably composed, she nodded. "I wonder what happened to the lock."

"I think the fact that the lock was replaced suggests the killing of your aunt was thoroughly premeditated. He – or she – came prepared. The replaced lock was likely intended to slow down the discovery of the body. Any volunteers who came out here would be puzzled and possibly annoyed because their keys didn't work, but most of them wouldn't have demanded Marge cut the lock off." Which, the more he thought about it, made Ms. Thomsen an unlikely killer. Why would she put the damn lock on, then immediately insist Marge cut it off?

"No. No, I suppose not." She hugged herself. "No." She stole a look toward the cluster of people now waiting for him outside the space and the grim sight past them, then hurried the rest of the way to her Prius.

A moment later, she drove around the corner of the building without looking back.